EARLY MORNING MURDER

I kept my eye on the side of the road, waiting for the koi pond to come into view. As soon as it did I saw a problem. What appeared to be a huge black fifty-gallon garbage bag bulging with trash was lying at the edge of the pond. I supposed it could have fallen off a collection truck, or perhaps a gardener's truck. Dolores was going to be upset over the mess.

When I got closer the shape of the large bundle became clearer. It was far worse than a bag filled with trash. I stopped in my tracks and took my cell phone out of my pocket.

Cautiously, I walked down the driveway. The nearer I got, the surer I was that what had looked like a garbage bag from a distance was actually the lifeless body of a man dressed in black, with the tail of a bright red and orange koi fish slapping against his shoulder.

It took only a few more steps for me to see that the man was Willis Nickens.

Killing in a Koi Pond

A *Murder, She Wrote* Mystery

A Novel by Jessica Fletcher &

Terrie Farley Moran

Based on the Universal television series created by
Peter S. Fischer, Richard Levinson & William Link

BERKLEY PRIME CRIME
New York

BERKLEY PRIME CRIME
Published by Berkley
An imprint of Penguin Random House LLC
penguinrandomhouse.com

ISBN: 9780593333617

Berkley Prime Crime hardcover edition / June 2021
Berkley Prime Crime mass-market edition / October 2021

Printed in the United States of America
1   3   5   7   9   10   8   6   4   2

In memory of my father,
Thomas M. Farley,
who never met a book he didn't want to read

Chapter One

As I carefully made my way down the steps from the business class car at the rear of the Amtrak train, Dolores Nickens stood on the station platform waving both arms, her gold bracelets flashing in the bright South Carolina sun. The instant I stepped onto the platform she grabbed me in a crushing hug. I'm sure she pressed out a few of the wrinkles my tan linen suit had collected on the long ride south from Washington, DC.

"Jessica Fletcher! It's been far too long." She held me at arm's length and eyed me critically from the top of my head to the soles of my beige pumps. "My goodness, you never age!"

When Dolores started to lean in again, I took two quick steps backward to save myself from another colossal squeeze and said, "I can't tell you how sorry I am to have missed your wedding. By the time I received my invitation, my nephew Grady had already asked me to babysit while he and Donna went on an anniversary cruise, although their son, Frank, objects strenuously to the term 'babysitting.' He claims to be quite grown up."

"Ah, the young ones—if only they knew how fast the years go." Dolores tucked her hand into the crook of my arm.

"He's like the proverbial weed, already as tall as my shoulder. Anyway, no matter what his parents call it, he and I have agreed that my official title is 'the adult in the house' whenever Grady and Donna are away."

Dolores laughed. "That's so like you. Always quick with a diplomatic solution. Do you remember sophomore year when I roomed with Lila Huggins, that redhead who always *just knew* she would be a famous artist one day? When she announced she'd decided to paint a jungle mural complete with lush green trees and assorted wild animals on every wall in our tiny room, you, my dear Jess, saved the day and probably prevented me from lifelong recurring nightmares of cheetahs and panthers and what all."

"I merely told her that since she was going to be so famous in a few short years, she surely didn't want to waste her time and effort painting murals since they aren't portable. How could she leave her masterpieces behind once we graduated? I suggested that she paint her vision of the jungle on those superlarge canvases that were stored in the basement of the arts building. When fame hit she could have them shipped to galleries anywhere in the world."

"And three months later she changed her major from fine arts to psychology. Today she is a well-known Hollywood shrink, appearing on television talk shows all the time. Who knew?" Dolores chuckled.

A porter carried my luggage off the train and, without missing a beat in her nonstop reminiscences, Dolores led us to the parking lot.

She stopped in front of a snazzy red convertible and swept her arm across the hood. "Voilà! A Porsche 911 Carrera Cabriolet. What do you think?"

I hadn't seen many like it. "Very fancy."

"A gift from Willis. I can't wait for you to meet my new husband. Do you remember all the bad boys I dated in college, not to mention the two charming but wicked men I ultimately married?" Dolores raised her eyes skyward and sighed at memories of the past. "Willis is so different. He may seem a little gruff at first, but once you get to know him he is a sweetie pie. It may have taken me longer than most, but I have found the perfect husband."

She popped the trunk, which, surprisingly, was in the front of the car. It barely held my carry-on, so the porter loaded the rest of my luggage in the backseat. I slipped a few bills into his hand and he tipped his cap jauntily. "Enjoy your visit, ladies."

"Elegant, isn't it?" Dolores said as she unlocked the car doors.

"Oh my, it certainly is." I burrowed into the passenger seat. "And so comfortable. Sometimes these fancy cars look a lot better than they feel."

"Willis constantly says there is nothing too good for his doll. That's me. I'm his doll. Seat belt on?"

I gave my seat belt a reassuring tug. "On and secure."

Dolores glided the car out of the parking space and headed toward the exit. "I always say there is nothing like a decent man and a flashy car to keep a lady smiling. So, what do you think, Jess?"

"I think you seem bubbly, energized. Happier than I have seen you in years. You are a totally different woman than you were at our last reunion. When was that, four years ago?"

"Just about. Right after husband number two emptied our bank accounts and ran off with mistress number ninety-eight or ninety-nine, whichever she was. Not a problem I will ever face again. Like any man, Willis has his quirks, but philandering isn't one of them. I can work around the silly quirks he does have. . . . Most of the time he treats me like a queen."

Most of the time? I didn't like the sound of that. I wondered what went on in the spaces in between.

Dolores chattered along. "Instead of taking Main Street to Route 321, I am going to wander off our path just a smidge and drive along Taylor Street. I can't wait to show you all the marvelous things Columbia has to offer. The art museum is exceptionally noteworthy— the children's room is really a treat. Then there's the Mills House and Gardens. And of course we must tour the State House. So much history. It wouldn't hurt us a bit to do some shopping in the lovely boutiques that are popping up all over downtown."

I was already tired from my long train ride, and Dolores's enthusiasm began to drain what little energy I had left.

"We can do all our girl talk and catching up while we wander around the city," she continued, "but all that is for another day. Here is our first and only stop. Look."

Look? Oh my, I couldn't miss it. Looming ahead of us: a gleaming silver fire hydrant standing taller than most of the surrounding buildings.

I gaped. "What on earth?"

"Welcome to Busted Plug Plaza," Dolores crowed. "I bet this is a first even for the well-traveled mystery writer J. B. Fletcher."

"It certainly is. I'm at a loss for words."

Dolores turned off the engine. "Dazzling, isn't it? Local artist and sculptor Blue Sky designed it. Jump out and I'll take a quick snap of you in front of the world's tallest fire hydrant. A picture will be all the evidence you need to prove to those Mainers in Cabot Cove that we Carolinians have a thing or two they can't match."

The size of the hydrant was hard to take in and I stopped a few feet in front of it. Dolores waved her hand, signaling me to move backward. "You have plenty of room. Plenty. I promise, even if you stand right underneath the lowest outlet cap with the thick chains hanging down, it would still be way above your head."

Dolores held her cell phone high. "Oh, too much sun. I'm going to move left. Can you turn to your right? Great. Stay there. Don't move."

For the moment I felt awkward, as I always do when asked to pose for a picture, but then I relaxed and smiled gamely. In a minute Dolores pronounced us done and hustled me back into the Porsche.

"Now, no more touring for you, young lady. I'll hit

Main Street, which will lead us right onto Route 321 and out into the countryside."

"I must say, the last thing I expected was a gigantic hydrant. Who did you say designed it?" I asked.

"Blue Sky. Oh, he has another name, but around here he is Blue Sky, famous local artist. And the hydrant is forty feet high and weighs over six hundred thousand pounds. Can you imagine the work that went into designing and building it?"

I admitted I couldn't fathom it.

Dolores continued. "But now the treasure I want to show off is my home. Wait until you see Manning Hall. Built in the late 1890s, it is a replica of the old plantation that preceded it but was burned to the ground during the Civil War. The Ribault family owned it for generations but they fell on hard times, and luckily, Willis's star was in the ascendant. I never dreamed I would live in such a house. Why, it's almost a castle."

I leaned back on the headrest and smiled. Dolores had been through a lot of ups and downs in her life. More downs than ups, to be honest, so I was doubly delighted to see her so happy.

"And I have a grandchild." Dolores's voice softened. "Oh, Jess, wait until you meet her. Abigail is nine years old. Everyone calls her Abby. Such a sweet girl. And smart! She loves to wear her hair in braids, just as I did at her age. So we have that in common. Of course, she never got to meet her real grandmother. Willis's first wife died nearly twenty years ago, so I think she might have been longing for a granny.

That's what she calls me—Granny Dolores. It's such a thrilling experience."

"And what about her parents?" I wondered out loud. "How is your relationship with them?"

Her excitement dropped a few levels. "Oh, that is a very sad situation. Abby's mother was Willis's only child, his daughter, Emily. She died from an aggressive brain tumor a few years ago. Very sudden. Very swift."

A worried note crept into her voice. "Emily's widower, Clancy Travers, has sole custody of Abby, of course, but he doesn't have Willis's resources . . ." She hesitated and then went on. "I sometimes think Willis's generosity is the only thing that keeps Clancy bringing Abby around to visit. It's . . . it's almost as if Willis is *buying* access to his only granddaughter."

"Well, however the access is granted, don't you think it's important for the child to have a relationship with her grandfather? Not to have one would be the real sadness," I said.

"I guess you're right." Dolores stopped to let a car pass before she made a left turn. "In any event, I can't wait for you to meet my new family. Would you mind opening the glove box and taking out the black and silver clicker?"

As I retrieved the clicker, Dolores made a sharp turn and stopped in front of an iron gate anchored by two decorative stone columns, replicas of ancient Roman pillars.

"Give the red button a push," Dolores said.

I did, and the two doors of the gate slid quietly apart.

The driveway curved immediately to the left. After a few yards, we turned to the right and Dolores idled the engine. "Manning Hall. Isn't it something?"

A quarter of a mile or so in front of us, a broad three-story brick house surrounded by a sandstone veranda rose majestically in a clearing bordered by trees flowering with pink and purple bonnets.

"It is indeed. And the trees! What are they?"

"Crepe myrtle. They are very common in South Carolina. I'm glad they bloomed a little early this year so you could see them. And we have a lovely sitting garden with lots of benches, and each section of plants is set off by those large white river rocks that sunshine seems to brighten over time. I know you enjoy a nice garden."

I smiled. "Yes, I do like to putter in my garden at home. Of course, in Maine we don't have as much gardening time as you do down here."

"That's true, I'm sure." Dolores switched back to talking about Manning Hall. "Willis said that the moment he saw the house, he knew he wanted it to be our home. So he made an offer on the house and asked me to marry him all on the same day. That's the kind of man he is. Some would say brash, but I think he's a hardworking go-getter. That's how he has managed to be so successful in business and in life."

Dolores accelerated slowly and again came to a full stop. "Let's get out here. I want to show you my one contribution to the landscape."

As I opened the car door, I heard small splashes.

Dolores hurried around the front of the car to show me a square pond edged by broad timber beams and surrounded by low-lying bushes. "This is my koi pond. All the gardens on the property are so formal and still. I wanted something happy, lively."

We stood side by side and watched dozens of multi-colored fish swim around, sometimes circling one another, sometimes going off on their own. One chubby orange-striped koi stopped midpond and seemed to stare at us for a few seconds before continuing on its way.

"Why, this is lovely, Dolores. What made you think of it?"

"When Willis bought the property, the driveway was way over there." She waved her arm vaguely to the left. "He thought that a driveway coming from this angle would be, I don't know, more attractive and would enhance the value of the property. I always wanted some sort of fishpond, and since they were digging up this whole area anyway . . . I met with the landscape architect and he advised a koi pond. Willis agreed, and here are my sweet beauties. Just watching them gives me such a peaceful feeling."

The fish were mesmerizing. I had to agree that watching them was extremely relaxing.

After a few moments Dolores said, "We'll have plenty of time for quiet contemplation by the koi pond over the next few days. And as you can see, the sitting garden is right along here, leading from the pond to Manning Hall. But now let's get you up to the house and settled in your room."

That sounded perfect to me.

We drove the short distance to Manning Hall, and before Dolores finished parking the car, the wood-

and-glass French doors of the house opened and a slim young woman wearing light blue jeans and an oversized pink T-shirt bounced down the front steps to greet us.

Dolores popped the trunk. "Marla Mae, this is my dear friend Jessica Fletcher, who'll be staying with us for a while. Would you please see to her luggage?"

Marla Mae gave me a big, toothy grin. "Welcome to Manning Hall, Miss Jessica. So nice to see Miss Dolores entertaining a longtime friend." Then she hoisted my suitcase and travel bag and started up the steps to the house.

I went to reach for the travel bag, but Dolores put her hand on my arm. "It's fine. It's her job."

We entered an extremely formal foyer. The inlaid marble floor gleamed and the walls were covered with lush brocade. To our left was a wide staircase.

Marla Mae said, "Mr. Willis is in his office. Do you want me to tell him you're home?"

"That won't be necessary. Please take the luggage up to the bedroom at the far end of the hall. Jessica and I will surprise him." Dolores took my arm and led me to a door on the right side of the foyer, a few feet past the bottom of the staircase. She gave a light tap and opened the door. At the same moment we heard a crash behind us. I turned to see my suitcase bounding down the stairs.

A balding gray-haired man who I assumed was Willis bolted up from the chair behind his oak desk, and bellowed, "What is going on out there?"

He strode right past Dolores and me and rushed

into the foyer. Marla Mae ran down the stairs, trying to grab the suitcase before it landed at the bottom, which it ultimately did with a loud thud.

"Stupid, stupid girl. You can't even do a simple chore like carrying luggage up the stairs. You're done. Fired. Get out now." Willis was red-faced, and his yelling got louder with each word.

I'd stepped around him and got to the bottom of the stairs at the same time Marla Mae did. We both reached for the suitcase. When I saw the pleading in her eyes I stepped back and let her rescue it. I think we both hoped that would calm Willis down. It didn't.

He turned to Dolores. "I want her gone. Now."

"I know you do, dear, but we have guests this evening and I need her to serve dinner." Dolores sounded like a mother placating a small child in desperate need of a nap.

Willis grimaced, then nodded. "I'll give you tonight, but"—he pointed to Marla Mae—"that clumsy girl is gone at the end of the week. Is that clear?"

"Very clear, darling. Now let me introduce you to one of my oldest friends. Jessica Fletcher, this is my husband, Willis Nickens."

I could understand why he was so successful in business. Willis Nickens had the ability to change his entire personality in a flash. He broke into a wide smile, took my hand between both of his, and said, "Dolores has told me so much about you, her old college friend who is now a famous mystery writer."

"Oh, I don't know if I would say *famous*." When anyone used that word in reference to me, it always made me ill at ease. I tried to change the subject. "You have a lovely home, and from what I have seen the landscaping is magnificent."

"Thank you. We are delighted to have you as our guest here at Manning Hall. And believe me when I tell you being famous never hurt anyone. Dolores will show you to your room. I'll see you for cocktails before dinner." He dismissed us both, reentered his office, and shut the door firmly behind him.

Dolores sighed. "I'm sorry that you saw Willis at his worst, Jess. He demands perfection and really goes off the rails when someone fails to meet his expectations. Marla Mae broke a crystal vase last week and now this . . ."

I put my arm around her shoulder. "Dolores, the important thing is that you and I will have a few days to spend together. Anything going on around us will be only so much background noise."

I had no idea how wrong I was.

Chapter Two

While she was showing me to my room on the second floor, Dolores told me about the other guests.

"We'll have three people, neighbors of ours, joining us for dinner tonight. In addition, Norman Crayfield, Willis's business partner, is here for a day or so, and his room is on this floor. Willis's son-in-law, Clancy, and my little princess are on the third floor. Abby loves it up there because the old nursery has lots of books and games the previous owner left behind. They are hopelessly old-fashioned but new to her." Dolores opened a door. "This is your room. I hope you will be comfortable here."

Sunshine poured through two large windows and danced among the bright yellow daffodils and blue forget-me-nots scattered about the chintz comforter covering a four-poster bed. "Oh, it's lovely. I'm sure I'll relax quite easily here." I ran my hand along one of the bedposts. "This looks like natural cherrywood."

"You have a sharp eye, Jess. It certainly is. And that door leads to your bathroom."

"This is certainly far grander than any rooms we ever lived in when we were at Harrison College, isn't it?" I laughed.

"Absolutely. Do you remember when in junior year our building had no hot water for what seemed like months? And we had to run across campus to Rider Hall to 'borrow' a shower!"

I nodded. "I remember it well. I don't suppose I'll have that problem here."

"And you will have as much privacy as you wish. It is one of the things I love about this house. There is so much room that family, guests, and the household staff can all go about their day without tripping over one another.

"Cocktails will be in the living room at six, with dinner to follow at seven. Come down whenever," Dolores said, then blew me a kiss and left.

I found my suitcase on a luggage rack handily placed between the closet and the bureau. I'd started to unpack when I heard a gentle knock. I opened the door and Marla Mae held out a tray.

"Lucinda—she's the housekeeper and cook—thought you might like something to eat after your long trip." She placed the tray on the desk that stood between the windows and removed a cloche to reveal a tempting plate of grapes, berries, and cookies next to a steaming pot of tea.

"Oh my, this is wonderful. I hadn't really thought

about it, but I am more than ready for a strong cup of tea and a snack. Please thank Lucinda for me."

Marla Mae tucked a dark curl behind her ear. "Sure will. She made those benne wafers fresh this morning. Real Low Country treats, they are. Oh, and she said I should ask if you would like me to help you unpack."

"Thank you, but I can manage."

"I suppose you think it's safest never to let me touch your cases again." Marla Mae looked forlorn.

"Oh, don't be silly. Accidents happen all the time."

"I wish Mr. Willis was as understanding as you are. I need this job. Got bills to pay."

"Well, I don't know if it will help, but when I get the chance I'll have a word with Dolores."

Marla Mae perked up. "That's mighty kind. Thank you, ma'am. Will there be anything else?"

I shook my head and she retreated out the door. I pulled a light blue wing chair away from the wall and turned it to the window so I could enjoy the view of the crepe myrtle trees while I sipped my tea. I did wonder how much influence Dolores would actually have on Willis's decision to fire Marla Mae. And how much influence she had on any of his decision-making. I got the impression he was a strong-willed man.

The tea was a full-flavored Earl Grey. I hoped a cup or two would give me the oomph I needed to finish unpacking and to shower and change. I had never heard of benne wafers, and I couldn't resist trying one. It was light and oh so crisp. The sesame seed flavor was strong but not overpowering. Altogether delicious. After a few sips of tea and nibbles of the cookies, I felt so relaxed in the comfy chair that I decided it would be a good idea to "rest my eyes" for a few minutes.

It was well past five o'clock when I woke. Panic-stricken, I ran for the shower. I thanked my lucky stars that I'd brought my favorite little black dress with me. The stretchy lyocell fabric traveled miraculously well. Fold, unfold, hang, and fold again. No matter how badly I treated it, the dress managed to look as though it had just returned from the dry cleaner. I dropped it over my head, adjusted the jeweled neckline, and smoothed the fit-and-flare skirt, and after applying a touch of lipstick, I was ready to go.

Hurrying down the staircase, I checked my watch. Ten after six. Not bad for someone who had been dead asleep less than an hour ago. The murmur of conversation floated through the foyer. I followed the sound of voices past what appeared to be a library and into a fastidiously designed living room. At least half a dozen Edwardian-style chairs covered with beige and tan prints and several rose-colored floral settees were scattered about the room. Two extra-long sofas covered in hunter green damask were facing each other on either side of a white brick fireplace. An elaborate chandelier hanging from the center of the ceiling was a larger version of the wall sconces affixed above the oil paintings that lined the walls. The enormous portraits of stern-looking gentlemen who'd been dead for more than a hundred years added a somber air to the room.

I had always admired Dolores's confident flair when it came to wardrobe choices, and tonight was no different. She was resplendent in a pair of black and gold harem pants and a black off-the-shoulder knit top. Her ubiquitous gold bracelets completed the outfit.

"Here is our guest of honor." She took me by the arm. "Jessica, come meet our charming neighbors."

A short, slim man dressed in a white dinner jacket and a black bow tie stood and immediately bowed at the waist. "Ah, J. B. Fletcher. Tom Blomquist here, and I must confess to being a huge fan." He faltered for a second. "I am not sure it is appropriate to 'confess' to a mystery writer. I'm afraid I would wind up a killer in your next book."

I laughed politely as if I had not received a thousand similar comments over the years.

Evidently he didn't expect more of a response, because he charged on. "I got hooked on *The Corpse Danced at Midnight* while I was on a red-eye flight coming home from the West Coast many years ago. I have been reading your delightful, artfully challenging mysteries ever since."

After I thanked him for the compliment, he said, "Ah, let me present my wife, Candy, and believe me when I say she is every bit as sweet as her name."

I did hear him say "sweet," but the Candy sitting on the couch was a pinched, sour-looking woman with drab brown hair pulled back into a severe bun. A voluminous black dress with a gray crochet collar did nothing to brighten her. She scarcely raised her eyes, only sort of nodded and almost smiled. She put her sherry glass on the mahogany end table, started to reach out a hand toward me, thought better of it, and picked up the glass again. I suspected she was the type of person who had trouble deciding between poached and boiled when it came to breakfast eggs.

Dolores beckoned a gray-haired woman sitting stiffly on the sofa on the far side of the fireplace. "Marjory, come meet Jessica."

The woman stood, pulled her hands from the pockets of her midnight blue blazer, and looked down at me. At five feet eight inches I am not used to women who are half a head taller than I am. She moved to the edge of the glass-topped coffee table and reached her hand across. "How do you do? I'm Marjory Ribault."

"How nice to meet you," I replied.

Candy Blomquist cleared her throat and spoke just above a whisper. "Mrs. Fletcher, you really must admire Marjory. It has to be extremely difficult for her to be a guest in what was her own home from the day she was born until very recently."

Marjory glared at Candy, a definite signal that she should stop talking, but Candy took no notice and continued. "Personally, I commend you, Marjory. But, of course, since your dear little cottage is on Manning Hall property, I suppose you are obliged to be social with the landlord."

A bitter laugh exploded into the room. Framed by the doorway, Willis Nickens sported the sort of smile I'd seen on gamblers' faces when they'd won a sure bet. Gleeful, with a side of smirk. Marjory pressed her lips together forcefully. She appeared to be desperately struggling for control.

Willis turned his attention to Candy, who'd shrunk back into her seat, aiming for invisibility. "I invite Marjory to dinner for the aura of old Southern family charm that she provides. As for you, Candy . . . you'd better remember exactly whose house you are in, or you may not be invited back. And wouldn't that be a shame? I am sure Tom wouldn't want that. Would you, Tom?"

With his eyes locked firmly on the floor, Tom Blomquist shook his head.

Our host's dramatic entrance had shocked everyone in the room to silence. Everyone, that is, except Dolores, who seemed to be oblivious to the roiling tension that had arrived with her husband.

"Willis, darlin', I am so very glad you're done working for the day. I worry that you work much too hard. And don't you look handsome in your tuxedo? I love a man who dresses for dinner." Dolores stepped closer, gave him a quick peck on the cheek, and walked to the bar, which was arranged on an ornately carved sideboard. "Would you care for a scotch or something lighter?"

Willis's eyes roamed slowly across the faces of the other three guests. He nodded to himself, plainly satisfied that he'd caused just enough turmoil to put each of them firmly in their place. Then his eyes lit on me, and in a nanosecond his personality changed to that of a gracious host. "What's this? Dolores, how is it that our newest guest is empty-handed? Jessica—or do you prefer J. B.?—would you join me in a scotch? It's Macallan Eighteen. Some men fancy themselves connoisseurs, obsessively demanding Laphroaig or the Balvenie, but for my money you can't beat Macallan Eighteen; or in a pinch, even Macallan Twelve will do. What do you say?"

"I do prefer being called Jessica. As to a drink . . ."

Before I could finish Dolores came back and handed a heavy crystal rocks glass to Willis. "Here you go. Just the way you like it. Three ice cubes and a double shot of Macallan."

"That's my doll," Willis said as he took the glass in both hands. "And what is that in Jessica's glass?"

Dolores handed me a glass similar to Willis's but with a lot more ice swimming in a vaguely familiar amber-colored liquid.

"You didn't." I laughed.

"Oh yes, I did. Knowing you were coming, I made sure to add it to our order from Longstreet Liquors. You are holding a glass of Disaronno amaretto. Does it bring back memories?" Dolores asked. "The night Ellen Bradley's boyfriend dumped her?"

"How could I forget? We sat in a circle on the floor of her dorm room while Ellen alternately fumed and cried. Every time she said his name we all would shout and chugalug amaretto."

Dolores sighed. "I had a headache for days. And now for the life of me, I cannot remember him at all. What *was* his name?"

Her husband, obviously irritated by our moment of nostalgia, interrupted brusquely. "I can tell you for certain his name wasn't Willis."

He unquestionably preferred to be the center of attention. Dolores was immediately contrite. She murmured, "Sorry," and tried to pat his cheek but Willis brushed her hand away.

"It looks like the party has started without me." A deep baritone pulled everyone's attention to the doorway. A rotund man, looking very patriotic in a navy blue pin-striped suit, white shirt, and bright red tie, grinned at us all.

"Norman. Late as usual. If our business relied on your being on time, we would have filed for bankruptcy years ago," Willis sneered.

Norman twirled his old-fashioned handlebar mustache and said, "Every villain has his place in the unending drama of life."

I couldn't help laughing, but I was totally alone. Everyone else stayed stock-still, barely breathing until Willis guffawed and said, "Well, as long as you're true to your role . . . Now, for Pete's sake, man, what are you drinking?"

The tension in the room fizzled like the air in a balloon pierced by the pointy end of a tree branch. The guests began talking among themselves, although they kept their voices so low that I sensed some nervousness still existed. It appeared to be Willis's forte to keep everyone on eggshells, wondering which Willis would be in their midst in the next five minutes, Mr. Genial or Mr. Churlish.

A small girl, pigtails flying, ran into the room. "Grampy! Grampy! Look what I found." She ran directly to Willis, who crouched impossibly low and, with the first genuine smile I'd seen on his face, said, "First a kiss. Then show me your treasure."

Leaning in obediently, the child planted a solid kiss on Willis's cheek. Then she stepped back and held out her hand. "Look at the ears! It's a bunny! Daddy said someone carved it out of wood a long time ago. But I only just found it. Did you know there was a drawer inside the big yellow toy box in the nursery? Did you? I didn't until a few minutes ago. First I found the drawer, and inside I found the bunny."

I heard someone mumble what sounded like "hopper," and when I looked around Marjory Ribault was wringing her hands. Everyone else was fascinated by the change in Willis.

He rocked back on his haunches, and in a few seconds he was sitting on the floor, stretching his legs out until his black patent leather shoes hit the base of a settee. He patted the floor next to him. "Abby, come. Sit down while we figure out a name for this little guy."

"Daddy said I mustn't get my dress dirty before dinner." Abby spread out the gauzy overlay of her pink dress. "See, I'm keeping it clean."

Willis frowned. "Clancy? Where . . . Oh, there you are."

Willis fixed an austere eye on the young man, whom I'd seen come into the room behind the little girl and immediately walk to the bar to fix himself what looked to me like a stiff drink.

Heading off a confrontation, Clancy smiled at his daughter. "Abby, honey, of course you can sit on the floor with Grampy. I just wanted to be sure he saw how pretty you look in the dress he sent you for Easter."

Abby dropped to the floor, and she and Willis plunged into a serious discussion on the pros and cons of various bunny names. Willis was a strong supporter of "Honey Bunny" until Abby shot it down because "everyone knows honey is for bears. Bunnies eat carrots." Willis conceded she had a point and offered "Carrot Bunny" as an alternative, which brought nervous laughter from some of the guests. After a few more, they finally settled on "Fluffy."

Marla Mae, now wearing a black dress and white ruffled apron, announced that dinner was ready. Dolores chimed in, "Feel free to bring your drinks with you," and we followed our host and hostess into the dining room.

Dinner was particularly delicious, and with Willis engrossed in chitchat with his granddaughter, everyone relaxed and enjoyed themselves.

After dessert, a mouthwatering sweet potato pie, the entire group adjourned to the living room, where Dolores refilled glasses while Marla Mae served coffee and tea. Peach-flavored sparkling water appealed to me, and as Dolores filled my glass I heard Clancy Travers say, "Come on now, Abby. It's long past your bedtime."

I wondered if Willis would intervene. He and the Blomquists were sitting at a card table set up in a far corner of the room. Willis was intently shuffling a deck of cards and seemed to take no notice of anything else.

"Daddy," Abby said in that singsong voice children often use when they are trying to sound cute, "can Granny Dolores read me the next chapter of *The Mysterious Benedict Society* before I go to sleep?"

"You can ask," Clancy said, "but don't be upset if Granny Dolores can't leave her guests right now."

Dolores set down the wine decanter and the glass she'd been filling with it. "No one will even miss me.

Abby, I'm as curious as you are to discover how Reynie and his friends solve their secret mission."

"What about our bridge game?" Willis barked. "How do you expect me to play without a partner?"

Willis instantly seized control of the room. No one spoke; no one moved.

Clancy ventured, "Well, I could sit in . . ."

Willis banged his hand on the card table. "You are joking. You play a hand of bridge like it was a game of Go Fish. No strategy whatsoever."

Then he looked at his business partner. "I'm glad you didn't volunteer, Norman. Your business tactics have our company hemorrhaging money. I can't imagine how you could manage to win a rubber."

Norman's smile was less than sincere. "No problem. I'm really more of a seven-card-stud kind of guy."

Marjory had turned her back on the room and was studiously gazing into the fireplace as if the stacked logs were aflame with a comforting glow. That left me as the only option. I decided to volunteer rather than wait to be recruited.

"I wouldn't mind filling in until Dolores is ready to play."

"Of course," Willis said. "I should have realized. A well-traveled world-famous author—I'm sure bridge is practically a requirement in your lifestyle."

Rather than respond that my card-playing days usually involved a hand or two of gin rummy in my kitchen with my old friend Cabot Cove town doctor Seth Hazlitt, I quickly took my place in the vacant chair and became South as partner to Willis's North.

Of course there was no picking a card to choose the

dealer. Willis dealt. The bidding went smoothly, and I was not surprised when Tom Blomquist, who sounded very confident, won the bid. I threw out the first card. Willis harrumphed when he saw my ten of spades. Candy set out the dummy hand and the game began in earnest. Tom seemed to be an astute player, which agitated Willis to no end.

I was the dummy in the next hand, which gave me time to observe that Tom had begun making clumsy mistakes. He seemed a completely different player than he was in the first round. I chalked it up to the hour growing late. Then I noticed the more errors Tom made, the more Cheshire Cat–like Willis became. I suspected there was a definite connection, and was proved correct when, after the final hand, Willis puffed out his chest and announced that he had thoroughly trounced the Blomquists.

Dolores, who had reentered the room a few minutes before, said, "Well, I am pleased to see that Jessica plays a better game than I do. Congratulations to the winners."

There was some polite clapping, and then Marjory and the Blomquists began to take their leave. In the midst of all the hand shaking and polite cheek kissing, Willis Nickens disappeared without a word.

Chapter Three

Dolores handed me a fresh peach sparkling water and led me to a comfy settee at the opposite end of the room from Clancy and Norman, who were sharing a nightcap by the fireplace. She thanked me for taking her place at the bridge table. "Willis is a very demanding player. I hope he wasn't too rough on you."

"On the contrary, he seemed to save his glares and harrumphs for poor Tom, who was a nervous wreck by the time we finished playing."

"That makes perfect sense. When he heard that Tom and Candy won the Oak Hills Duplicate Bridge Championship last year, it rankled Willis to no end. He prefers to be the only winner at everything he touches. So now whenever we have Tom and Candy to dinner, bridge is a requirement, even though I would much rather do something fun like charades.

But beating a 'champion' at his own game, so to speak, makes Willis feel like a king."

Hmmm, I thought. *It's more than that. Willis likes to make other people feel like they are nothing more than court jesters.*

"How did story time go?"

Dolores glowed. "Well, it took more than a few minutes for Abby to unwind. But once she was in her pj's, with her teeth brushed and pigtails untied, we snuggled on her bed and got down to the book. Usually she has lots of questions and comments about the story as we go along. Not tonight. By the time I reached the end of the chapter, she could barely keep her eyes open. When the little wooden rabbit she found earlier today slipped from her hand, I knew she was a goner."

"I remember when Grady was that age. He would fight against going to sleep and then collapse." I took a sip of my sparkling water. "And now Frank is the same way."

"We are lucky to have children in our lives, aren't we?" Dolores smiled. "And speaking of our lives, now that we got the 'Welcome, Jessica' dinner out of the way, I don't think Willis has any more designs on our social time. It will be girls only from here on out. What do you think of a late breakfast tomorrow, and then spending the day at the art museum?"

I stifled a yawn. "I think that sounds like a plan."

"And you, my dear friend, sound like one very tired lady. I think it's time I check the kitchen. Make sure Lucinda and Marla Mae have gotten everything tidied up. You should take yourself up to bed and get a good night's rest. They begin serving breakfast at seven thirty, but you can request something at any time. Lucinda lives in a suite behind the kitchen and is very accommodating if you need anything at all. Sleep well."

Marla Mae had removed the tray and teapot from my room and left a snack on the desk, some grapes and two sesame-flavored wafers, along with a pitcher of water. I resisted temptation until I was in my pajamas; then I pulled a couple of grapes from the bunch, popped one in my mouth, and sat in the comfy chair, mulling over my very long day.

I was delighted to see Dolores so happy in her new life. Although her husband had a strong, self-centered personality that I knew I could never abide, as long as he made her happy, I was determined to be happy for her. I took a bite of a cookie and idly wondered why Willis worked so hard to be abrasive to his other guests, trying to make everyone uncomfortable. And he enjoyed every minute of it. The only conclusion I could reach was that Willis Nickens was what we in Cabot Cove would call an odd duck.

I crawled under the covers, and when my head sank into the pillow I sighed, expecting to fall asleep instantly. But every minute dragged by like an hour. I grew increasingly restless. I rearranged the pillows twice and moved from side to side and back again. At one point I heard an owl hooting off in the distance. *Quiet, mister. You are not helping one bit.*

I flicked on the light and sat up in bed. If I had been

at home, I would have made myself a nice cup of hot cocoa and read for a while, but I hadn't been in this house long enough to know where the kitchen was, and I was afraid to disturb the live-in housekeeper if I bumbled around trying to find it.

Luckily, I did know where to find the library. With or without the cocoa, a good book was sure to help me fall asleep. Perhaps I could find a collection of short stories or a volume of poetry. Something that would have an ending every few pages, making it easy to put down once I started to yawn again. I slid my feet into my slippers and put on my robe.

The second-floor hallway was dead quiet, but when I neared the bottom of the staircase I heard voices coming from Willis's office. I rounded the bannister and peered inside the room. I could see Willis leaning back in his chair, his legs propped up on the desktop, ankles crossed. The light from the desk lamp bounced off his patent leather shoes. He was loud and nasty but clearly enjoying himself. His tone was so obnoxious I hoped he wasn't speaking to Dolores.

I crept closer and saw his son-in-law, Clancy, standing on the visitor's side of the desk with his arms folded across his chest. I couldn't see his face, but his body was so rigid I knew he didn't like whatever he was being told.

"I have my granddaughter's best interest at heart." Willis reversed his crossed ankles. "After Emily died I named you as the trustee for Abby's trust fund because there was no other choice. I could have named a bank or a law firm. But those are businesses, interested in conserving money. I wanted someone whose main concern would be what is in Abby's best interest in every way, not just financially. It's a revocable trust, and legally, I can change it. I have decided Dolores will make an excellent trustee. She genuinely loves Abby, and when I am gone she will inherit so much on her own that Abby's trust fund will seem an insignificant amount."

"Willis, I am her father, and I assure you, since . . . since Emily . . . all of my focus has been on giving Abby the best life possible."

"Sure, it has. The best life *my* money can provide." Willis dropped his feet to the floor and leaned forward, both elbows on the desk. "Listen to me carefully. One of the reasons I married Dolores was that I can see how much she loves my granddaughter. And there is no competition, because she has no grandchildren of her own."

I was astonished that Willis would consider Dolores's lack of grandchildren to be a plus for their marriage. If Dolores ever found out, I suspected she would be extremely hurt.

He continued. "I'm willing to bet that Dolores enjoys being a grandmother more than you enjoy being a father. And that is why I am going to make her Abby's trustee."

Clancy was close to shouting. "That's completely unfair. I have dedicated my life—"

"Lower your voice before you wake up everyone in the house. Consider it a courtesy that I'm telling you before I have my attorney draw up the paperwork. Rest assured that the decision is made." Willis slapped the desk. "And before you elect to fight me on this, remember I have accountants, lots of smart accountants. It won't take them long to trace the money you slip out of the trust and into your own pocket."

"How can you even think—?" Clancy blustered.

"I'm sure that redheaded tart you've been wining and dining would be surprised to learn it is your nine-year-old daughter who is footing the bill."

"Are you having me followed? Are you spying on me? You sick son of a—"

"Hold your tongue, boy. Now get out of my office before I throw you out of my house."

I ran to the library door and slipped inside just as I heard Clancy slam the office door behind him. He clomped up the stairs, muttering to himself.

I could only imagine how uncomfortable breakfast was going to be.

I wondered if Dolores knew anything about Willis's plan. He seemed more than capable of doing as he pleased without consulting with her at all. How would she feel about being trustee for Abby if it caused a problem with Clancy? Suppose Clancy decided to create a rift between Dolores and the child? When all was said and done he was the custodial parent, the only parent.

All those questions were making my head hurt. They could wait until morning. Now was the time to find a peaceful book to read. I was grateful that moonlight was streaming through the French doors. It gave me just enough light to read the titles on the spines of some of the hundreds of books filling the floor-to-ceiling shelves. Poetry! There it was, right in front of me, the poetry section, alphabetically arranged. Maya

Angelou, E. E. Cummings, Emily Dickinson. I reached for *The Poetry of Robert Frost*, a collection with so many reminders of New England that it was sure to transport my mind to Cabot Cove and home. What better way to relax?

I peeked into the foyer. Willis's office door was still shut and there wasn't a sound anywhere in the house. I tiptoed upstairs, clutching the heavy volume of Frost's work, confident that a few minutes reading New England poems would lead me to an excellent night's sleep.

Sunlight brushed the dreams of woods and snowy winter nights from my mind and I woke up with a start. Then I looked around and realized that I was in South Carolina in spring, not home in Maine in winter. I stretched my arms toward the ceiling and thought about how Robert Frost was able to relax me with only a few verses of his poetry. I jumped out of bed, and touched my toes ten times. The clock on the night table read six thirty-five; I had plenty of time for a run before breakfast. I put on my navy blue sweat suit and my Nike Air Zooms, filled my water bottle from the pitcher Marla Mae had left the night before, and tiptoed down the stairs and out of the house without disturbing a soul.

There was not so much as a whisper of a cloud in the sky, and the scent of fresh dew on the grass was invigorating. I stood on the veranda and took a couple of deep breaths. I'd already decided that I would save exploring until I was more familiar with the property.

The smartest run for me this morning would be along the driveway and back.

I walked a few yards and then began a slow jog. Farther along I picked up my pace and decided that as soon as I could see the koi pond, I would sprint to it. A little high-intensity interval training would get my blood pumping. Then I'd take a light jog from there to the gate and back to the house. I kept my eye on the side of the road, waiting for the koi pond to come into view. As soon as it did I saw a problem. What appeared to be a huge black fifty-gallon garbage bag bulging with trash was lying at the edge of the pond. I supposed it could have fallen off a collection truck, or perhaps the gardener's truck. Dolores was going to be upset over the mess.

When I got closer, the shape of the large bundle became clearer. It was far worse than a bag filled with trash. I stopped in my tracks and took my cell phone out of my pocket.

Cautiously, I walked down the driveway. The nearer I got, the surer I was that what had looked like a garbage bag from a distance was actually the lifeless body of a man dressed in black, with the tail of a bright red and orange koi fish slapping against his shoulder.

It took only a few more steps for me to see that the man was Willis Nickens.

Chapter Four

I tapped 911 on my phone, and when the dispatcher answered I said, "My name is Jessica Fletcher. I am calling to report a death at Manning Hall." Then I realized I had no idea what the street address was. "I don't know the address."

The dispatcher was a calm young woman with a soft Southern accent. "Don't worry about it, ma'am. I got your phone location right on my screen. We'll send someone out to you immediately. Are you alone with the deceased?"

"Well, yes and no. I'm on the driveway and the deceased is partly in the koi pond. There are other people in the house but I don't think anyone is awake yet." I was sure I sounded as confused as I felt.

"Did you hit the deceased with your car, ma'am?"

"Oh heavens, no. I don't own a car. I don't even

have a driver's license. I was out for a run and just happened to find Willis."

"Willis, ma'am?"

"Yes. The deceased. Willis Nickens, owner of Manning Hall, where I am a houseguest. I am a friend of Mrs. Nickens."

"I see. Well, we have a deputy en route. He'll be there in a quick minute. In the meantime please don't touch anything."

"Oh, there is an electronic gate. Your deputy will need a clicker to open it," I said. "There may be a clicker in the glove compartment of Mrs. Nickens's car. Shall I try to find it?"

"Don't worry your head at all. We can override that gate lickety-split. The property owner has the gate registered in our emergency system. Are you feeling okay, ma'am? Must be quite a shock, finding a body and all. Is there a place you can sit down?"

I looked around, but the chairs and benches in the sitting garden were too far away. I certainly didn't want to leave Willis alone. "I can manage waiting for the deputy."

There was genuine concern in her voice. "I can stay on the phone for as long as you need me."

"That won't be necessary. I am perfectly fine." While we were talking I was trying to examine the general area, but the dispatcher was a total distraction. I was getting impatient for her to cut me loose.

"Okay, then, ma'am, just give us a call back if I can help in any way." And at last she was gone.

I bent down to take a closer look at the body but

was careful not to touch it. Willis was in a fetal position on his right side. His head was turned into the pond and partly underwater. One of those white river rocks that lined the sitting garden was lying in the water inches from his face. I wondered how it had wound up in the pond.

I stood up to examine the surrounding area. *That's odd,* I thought: Willis was still dressed in the tuxedo he'd worn last night, but instead of his fancy patent leather shoes, he was now wearing slippers. I also spotted the remains of a cigar tucked against the border of the koi pond. It had a long ash, as if it had been half smoked, then dropped, and had burned itself out on the ground.

A dark sedan came up the driveway. As it turned toward me, I saw the words DEPUTY SHERIFF and RICHLAND COUNTY printed across the side and a six-point sheriff's star on the front door. In case I had any doubt, the driver flashed red and blue roof lights quickly but silently. He parked several yards away and got out of the car, talking into what I supposed was a radio on his shoulder. I heard him say, "Copy that."

Each sleeve of his navy blue uniform sported a large yellow patch declaring him to be a member of the Richland County Sheriff's Department. He put on a baseball cap, adjusting the fit as he ambled toward me. "You Jessica Fletcher?"

"I am. And this"—I pointed to the body—"is Willis Nickens, the owner of this property."

"Pleased to meet you, ma'am. Sorry about the circumstances. Deputy Sheriff Luther Lascomb's my name. I'll be handling things until Sheriff Halvorson shows up." He hitched his equipment belt, causing his handcuffs to rattle. Was he trying to show me he was prepared for any trouble I might cause? "Now, would you mind moving over there and standing under that big ole bald cypress for a few minutes? Let me take a look at Mr., um, Nickens."

I did as I was asked but I watched him very closely. Deputy Lascomb leaned over much the way I did when I first saw Willis lying there. He didn't touch anything but didn't seem to be looking for much either. After a while he walked back to me and took out a notepad.

"Hmmm, could have fallen, I guess. We'll see what the coroner says. Now, tell me what you are doing here, Miz Fletcher. How you come to be on Mr. Nickens's property."

I explained I was a houseguest out for a morning run.

He scribbled on his pad, then raised one eyebrow suggestively. "Would you mind telling me exactly how it is you're sleeping here?"

I wasn't going to let that insinuation float for so much as a second. "I barely know Mr. Nickens. I'm here because I went to school with his wife, Dolores."

"Oh. There's a Miz Nickens. And where might she be this morning?"

"Up at the house, I suppose. Possibly still sleeping." I was losing patience with these questions, when it was obvious, at least to me, that Willis Nickens had been murdered. "Deputy Lascomb, did you happen to notice the large white rock in the pond? It belongs in the sitting garden, and I can tell you that it certainly was not in the pond yesterday."

"You sure about that? Folks use these rocks as decorations all over the place. Time was, you hardly saw them at all. Now they are around every fishing hole, lily pond, and even some swimming pools I've seen. So tell me, besides you and Miz Nickens, who else might be around and about."

I was exasperated that he so pointedly ignored my suggestion but decided it was best to answer his questions until I could try again. "Well, I know there is some household help that sleeps in, but I am not sure how many. Mr. Nickens's son-in-law—they call him Clancy, though I can't recall his last name—and his daughter, who is only nine, are also guests."

"Do you know where Mr. Nickens's daughter is? This Clancy fella's wife."

"Tragically she passed away from a brain tumor some time ago."

"Unlucky kid. Lost her mama and now her granddaddy." Lascomb shook his head. "Some families do get hit hard. So, is that the list or is there anyone else?"

"Oh yes. I nearly forgot Norman Crayfield is a houseguest as well. He's Mr. Nickens's business partner."

"Really? That's interesting. Would you happen to know what kind of business the two were in?"

I searched my mind. "Sorry, no. I don't believe it ever came up in conversation. Dolores—that is, Mrs. Nickens—introduced Mr. Crayfield as her husband's business partner and Willis—Mr. Nickens—mentioned their partnership once or twice during the evening."

A second car pulled up and the word "deputy" was

nowhere to be seen, although SHERIFF was prominently displayed. A tall man with broad shoulders and intense gray eyes stepped out of the driver's seat. He wore a brown corduroy jacket over a denim shirt, along with jeans and brown leather boots. He had a tan cowboy hat in one hand and stood by his car waiting for his deputy to report. While they conferred I could tell when Lascomb mentioned me, because while he listened the sheriff gave me an appraising look that read either "suspect" or "nuisance"—it was hard to tell which.

I was hopeful he would pay more attention than Deputy Lascomb to my theory about the white river rock. But that hope faded when he stood in front of me and said, "I am Sheriff Zeke Halvorson. Thank you for being so cooperative with my deputy, Mrs. Fletcher. If we need you, we'll be sure and look for you at the house. For now you might want to go and get some breakfast."

He might as well have said, *Dismissed!*

"But, Sheriff . . ."

He had started to walk away but he stopped and swiveled his head toward me. "Mrs. Fletcher, would you like Deputy Lascomb to escort you to the house?"

"That won't be necessary," I said more sharply than I'd intended. "What I would like is a moment of your time."

His face became a mask of frustration, his Southern manners wrestling with his desire to get rid of me. Then he sighed. "Okay, you have two minutes."

"Well, I didn't want to touch anything, but it is possible that when you remove Willis's head from the water you will find a wound that may have been caused by the white rock that is in the pond but obviously doesn't belong there."

"Mrs. Fletcher, why don't you leave the detective work to us? You are looking for a crime that probably never happened. We have techs and a deputy coroner on the way. You just toddle along. We got work to do."

"But don't you think you should talk to Mrs. Nickens? Shouldn't someone tell her . . . ?"

"Now, there is a job you *can* do. Luther here tells me you are a friend of the wife, er, widow. Perhaps you could tell her the sad news."

He didn't finish his sentence with *and stay out of our way*, but the look he gave me said it loud and clear.

To say I found him exasperating would have been putting it mildly. I jogged away before I said something I might regret, and then began to walk slowly back to the house. Poor Dolores. Just yesterday she had been happier than I had seen her in years. And now . . . this.

I dreaded the role the sheriff had assigned to me; still, I supposed that it was better to hear bad news from a friend than from a stranger. Perhaps I could offer some comfort.

I climbed the few steps to the veranda and was surprised to find Willis's son-in-law standing behind a pillar.

"Good morning, Jessica. It looks like you and I are the only two early birds in the house."

"I came out for a brief jog. May I ask what brings you outdoors so early?"

"My reason is far more devious than yours. Willis

had a putting green installed on the far side of the house." Clancy held up a putter. "Of course, he doesn't allow anyone to use it without his explicit permission. Since I am an early riser and he is not . . ."

I understood completely. "You get your practice in and no one is the wiser."

"Exactly. Now I have a question for you. I've been watching the hubbub down at the koi pond. What happened? Did someone poison the fish? Dolores must be completely distraught."

I paused, not quite sure how to tell him the truth. I had a sense that Dolores should be told first. Yet I couldn't brush Clancy off. He needed only to walk to the pond himself, and I was sure Deputy Lascomb would chase him away, citing a dead body as the reason.

"There's been an accident." Even though I was certain there had not been. "Willis is dead. He died near the pond. I found the body and called nine-one-one."

Was that a mix of joy and relief I saw in Clancy's eyes before he morphed into the grief-stricken son-in-law and said, "Willis? Dead? How awful! How is Dolores holding up?"

I noticed he didn't ask how Willis had died, and I deliberately answered only the question he did ask. "Dolores doesn't yet know. I am about to find her and tell her the terrible news. Perhaps you would be willing to join me?"

Clancy's indecision was palpable until he came up with an answer that he was sure I would find satisfactory but would still get him out of the position of bearer of bad news. "Abby! I can't have her find out from someone else. She will be completely devastated. But"—here he put on his brave face—"she should hear about Willis from me. I am her father."

Yes, you are, I thought, *and by a stroke of luck or something much worse, you will remain her trustee as well.*

Clancy barged into the house and left the front door ajar. I could hear him banging up the stairs. Before he awakened the entire house, I thought I'd better find Dolores. I checked the living room and the dining room but there was no sign that anyone had been there. I looked at my phone. Seven fifteen a.m. Nearly time for breakfast. Definitely time to talk to Dolores. I decided to look for her upstairs.

I was at the top of the stairs in the hallway of the second floor when I realized that I had no idea which of the many doors led to the master bedroom. I walked along the hallway, hoping that Dolores was awake and I would hear her bustling around her room. A door creaked open and Norman Crayfield, wearing jeans and a bright yellow T-shirt that read CRAFTY OLD BUZZARD, stepped into the hall.

"Good morning. You are up early. Have you been out? From my window it looks like a glorious day. I thought I'd take a quick stroll through the gardens before breakfast. Sharpen the appetite, as it were." He noted that I didn't react. "Jessica, is something wrong?"

I nodded. "Yes. Something has happened. It's Willis. I need to find Dolores. Do you happen to know where her bedroom is?"

"Yes, of course." He took me by the elbow, led me down the hall, and stopped. "This is Dolores's door.

Her room is right next to Willis's. I believe the rooms are adjoining, although I have never been inside. Oh, listen to me babbling on and on. I'm so sorry. I get nervous when there is trouble, and from the look of you, there is trouble. I guess I should ask, can I help in any way?"

"No, thank you, but I do appreciate the offer."

"In that case, I will leave you to it." As Norman headed to the staircase, I realized he'd neglected to ask me *what* had happened to Willis. First Clancy, then Norman. It seemed no one cared about Willis at all. Well, that's not true. There was one person, and I was about to give her the terrible news.

Dreading the conversation we were about to have, I stood outside Dolores's bedroom door, lifted my hand, and knocked.

Chapter Five

There wasn't a sound from the other side of the door. I waited a few seconds and knocked again, slightly harder. This time I heard something, a slight rustling of fabric. "Dolores, may I come in?"

"Oh, Jess, of course. The door isn't locked. Come on in."

Dolores was sitting up in bed, leaning on a pile of pillows. I couldn't quite make out what she had in her hands but whatever it was, it had her annoyed. "Look at this mess. When I heard the knock, I thought it was Willis. He is so polite. Even though we have adjoining rooms, he never barges in. And I'm happy that he never sees me wearing a hairnet and eye mask, which I call my 'old lady' look. After all, there are some secrets a woman should keep."

She held up a pink satin eye mask with a set of

eyelashes embroidered on each eye patch and a jumbled blob hanging from the back strap.

"When I heard the knock, I woke, ripped off the hairnet and mask, and somehow managed to get the hairnet caught on the mask's Velcro strap. Looks like I'll have to tear the hairnet and toss it."

I moved closer and stood by the side of her king-sized bed and waited for her to finish. I was in no hurry to break the news.

She tossed the mask toward the foot of the bed and looked at me. "Sweats and sneakers. You aren't going to ask me to join you for a run, are you? You know my rule about exercise. I don't like it, so I don't do it."

When I didn't scoff at her oft-repeated exercise denial, Dolores sensed that I was bothered and she looked at me keenly. "Jess, what is it?"

I sighed, leaned down, and took her hands in mine. "I'm afraid the news isn't good. It's about Willis."

Dolores widened her eyes and grasped my hands tightly, as if preparing herself. "Okay. I am ready."

I spoke as gently as I could. "While I was out jogging this morning I found Willis on the driveway by the koi pond. He had been . . . there for a long while."

"Is he hurt?" The hope in Dolores's eyes was agonizing to see.

"I am afraid it is worse. Much worse."

"No." Dolores lurched backward, pulling her hands from mine, and her eyes welled with tears. "That's not possible. We're still practically newlyweds."

I picked up a box of tissues from her night table

and set it on the bed beside her. "I'm so sorry. I wish it wasn't true but, unfortunately . . . he's gone."

Dolores began sobbing uncontrollably. I sat down on the edge of the bed and she flung herself at me. I hugged her while she wailed. "Why Willis? Why now? I was finally happy. *We* were happy."

She pulled her head back and began mopping her face with some tissues. "Oh, Jess, what am I going to do without him?"

I hated to see Dolores's pain, and remembering how desperately bereft I had felt when my husband, Frank, died, I knew it would continue for many years to come.

Dolores struggled to hold back her tears and began sniffling. "I am ready to hear more. How did it happen? Did he fall and hit his head? Was it a heart attack?"

I shrugged. "I honestly don't know. The sheriff—"

"Sheriff? Why the sheriff? Shouldn't there be a doctor? An ambulance?" She threw back the covers and leaped out of bed, and for a second I was afraid she was going to run to the koi pond in her rose-colored nightgown, but her mind had made a quick turnabout.

"Abby. Willis was the only true connection she had to her mother, and now he's gone, too. I have to go to her." Dolores grabbed a robe from her chaise longue and crouched down to peer under the bed. "Where are my slippers?"

"Dolores, please. Clancy was outside this morning, so he knows about Willis. He went directly upstairs, and I am sure he will take care of talking to Abby."

"Clancy is an inconsiderate, indifferent lout. I can't trust him to tell Abby with the least bit of sensitivity. Don't even get me started on all the things Willis told me about his behavior while poor Emily was sick." Dolores looked even more stricken, if that was possible. "Oh, Jess, what will I do if Clancy decides to take Abby away from me? I can't bear to lose her, too."

"Before you upset yourself any further, I suggest that you get dressed and we can go downstairs and find out exactly what is happening."

Dolores blew her nose rather noisily. "Yes. Of course. Downstairs. I want to see Willis before they take him . . . wherever they take people. And I can talk to Clancy about Abby. I'm glad you're here. I so need a trusted friend right now."

A few minutes later Dolores emerged from her dressing room in a white tee and black slacks, with a black and white cardigan thrown over her shoulders. "This is the closest I could come to widow's weeds."

"You look fine," I assured her.

Dolores pulled a wad of tissues from the box. "Okay, I am ready to face whatever comes"—she took my hand—"with a good friend at my side."

We walked downstairs and checked the dining room, which was so quiet we were surprised to find both Clancy and Norman sitting at the table, plates piled high with food from a delicious-looking buffet set out on the breakfront.

Clancy got up immediately and rushed to Dolores. "I am very sorry about . . . Willis. I know how it feels to lose a spouse. The loneliness, the emptiness."

He sounded a little too melodramatic to me, and

Dolores might have felt the same. She stiffened for a moment but then accepted the hug he offered. I considered that a good first step if the new relationship they would have to forge around Abby was going to have a chance.

Norman Crayfield stayed in his chair, sipping coffee. Then, as if it had dawned on him that he was going to have to work with Dolores, at least in the near term, regarding whatever business interests he had shared with Willis, he got up and went to her side.

"Dolores"—he put a hand on her shoulder—"I am so sorry for your loss, but I can guarantee you that I will take care of our business ventures as diligently as I did when Willis was . . . here. Believe me, you have nothing to worry about financially. Now why don't you sit down? Can I get you a cup of coffee?"

"I appreciate your kindness, Norman, but right now all I want is to make sure Abby is all right, and then I want to walk down to see Willis."

Clancy waved his hands as if warning off a driver headed toward a gaping hole on a highway under construction. "Abby is still asleep, Dolores. I'm sure you don't want to wake her. You take care of . . . whatever you have to . . . and I promise I will not tell Abby . . . anything . . . until you and I can talk to her together."

Dolores burst into tears. "That's so kind of you. I am worried about Abby. She and Willis were close. After Emily . . . Well, I can't stand to see her heart broken again."

I wasn't sure Clancy was being kind. After what I had overheard last night, I thought perhaps he'd behave considerately until he could be confident of his own financial status apropos Willis's estate and Abby's trust. Was he in the money or out?

"Excuse me, Miss Dolores. I am so very sorry for your trouble, but Sheriff Halvorson came to the door. He would like a word. I put him in the library." Marla Mae wore a long black sweater over a bright green shirt and dark green jeans. I wondered if she had put on the dark sweater out of respect for the man who only yesterday had screamed that she was fired and tried to throw her out on the spot.

"I can't. I just can't do this. What does the sheriff want with me?" Dolores began sobbing again.

Her tissues were long since shredded, so I was thankful to find cloth napkins by the buffet. I gave one to Dolores and stuffed a couple more in my pocket, sure that they would be needed.

Marla Mae poured a glass of water and gave it to Dolores. "Just take a sip or two. Make you feel better, I promise."

Dolores took the glass, and after a few sips passed it back to Marla Mae; then she looked at me. "Okay, Jess. I'm ready."

We linked arms and headed to the library. Sheriff Halvorson was standing with his hands behind his back while he perused the bookshelves. He turned when he heard us enter.

"Morning, ladies. Mrs. Nickens, you have a mighty fine library here. Happened to notice this mystery section. And when I saw the name J. B. Fletcher, I took a quick look at the author's photo. You won't be surprised who I saw. Famous mystery author, is she?"

"Well, I wouldn't say . . ." I started just as Dolores said, "Yes, she is. And I have every book she's ever written. You can see there are quite a few."

Sheriff Halvorson set those piercing eyes on me. "Mystery writer, eh? That explains a lot. Now, Mrs. Fletcher, if you will excuse us, Mrs. Nickens and I need to have a brief chat."

"Oh no." Dolores started to cry, and dabbed her eyes with the wrinkled napkin she was holding. "Sheriff, I don't think I can, at least not without Jess. I need a hand to hold."

"I have some questions about the past, say, twenty-four hours, and answering or not answering is really not your choice." He went on. "Don't you want to know what happened to your husband?"

Dolores began to wail. "More than that, I want to see Willis." She turned to me. "You saw him. The sheriff saw him. I'm his wife. Why can't I see him?"

I looked at Sheriff Halvorson, who, it seemed, had a gentler side after all. He indicated a nearby settee and suggested that Dolores and I sit down. He leaned on the back of an armchair and looked at Dolores, who was sobbing into her napkin; then he sent a questioning look to me.

I nodded permission and he moved the chair closer so that it was a few feet in front of Dolores. Then he sat down and waited for her crying to subside.

I put my arm around her and said softly, "Dolores, it's probably not the best idea for you to see Willis just now. Perhaps later . . ."

I handed her a fresh napkin.

She brushed the tear tracks from her cheeks and

whimpered. "If you think so. Maybe it would be best to wait until I . . . adjust to the idea. I'd better go fix my face and then find Clancy. It's time we went to see Abby."

"Not quite yet, Mrs. Nickens." Sheriff Halvorson put up his hand like a traffic cop. "We still need to talk."

Dolores was half standing. She wavered for a second or two, and then, completely deflated, sat back down and asked petulantly, "My husband is dead. What on earth could be so pressing?"

The sheriff gave me a pointed look, and when I didn't move he ordered, "J. B. Fletcher, mystery writer, it is time for you to leave Mrs. Nickens and me alone for a bit."

Dolores started to object, but then heaved a prolonged sigh. "I'll be fine, Jess. Why don't you find Clancy and tell him I will be with him shortly?"

I walked out of the room, purposely leaving the door ajar, but Sheriff Halvorson called after me, "The door, please, Mrs. Fletcher."

Deputy Lascomb was standing near the front door like a sentry. I gave him my broadest smile. "Would you like a cup of coffee, Deputy? There's plenty in the dining room."

"No, thank you. I have to watch the door. No one in or out. How you holding up, ma'am? Stressful day all around."

"Yes, it certainly is. Here I thought Dolores—Mrs. Nickens, that is—and I could have a nice visit, talk about old times, catch up on the present, and now this." I shook my head. "Tell me, is there any news?

Have your technical people arrived? What have they found?"

A "should I or shouldn't I?" look flitted across his face, and apparently "shouldn't" won. He gave me an apologetic smile. "Lots of busyness out there at that pond. Forensics, deputy coroner, all sorts of folks, but as to what they find or don't find, that is way above my pay grade. They'll report to the sheriff, not to me."

"I understand. It's just that Dolores will have to make some arrangements. Do you know how soon Willis might be returned to her?" I hoped the question sounded innocent enough; past experiences told me that death by foul play meant the body would have an extended stay with the local authorities.

"Sorry, ma'am, but anything you want to know has to come from the sheriff." Lascomb nodded toward the library door. "Maybe he is telling your friend some details right now."

Although I was sure that was not the case, I nodded in agreement. "That's probably so. Well, I am going to find some breakfast."

I headed to the dining room interested more in what tidbits of information I could glean from Clancy and Norman than in whatever delicious food was on the breakfront. As I passed the library door, I walked as close as I could without arousing the deputy's suspicion. Unfortunately, not a sound penetrated the solid oak.

It's a good thing Deputy Lascomb declined my offer of coffee, because when I entered the dining room I was surprised to see there was not a person in sight, and the detritus of breakfast had been completely removed. The room was spotless. I thought about sitting and waiting until I heard the library door open, but opted to explore the first floor instead. Perhaps it would have been a good time for me to look for the kitchen, now that it was daylight. I passed Willis's office on my right and the staircase on my left. Just behind the staircase was an alcove, its only furniture a serving table covered with neatly piled table linens and a tray of cutlery. I was sure the unobtrusive spot saved Marla Mae many a trip back to the kitchen for an errant fork or dropped napkin. The alcove led to a hallway, and I heard faint voices from farther along.

Should Dolores need me I didn't want to be too far away, but I decided to follow the voices. I reached a double doorway, both doors wide open, just as a woman, whose voice I didn't recognize, said, "I'm not understanding any of this. How could Mr. Willis fall into the koi pond?"

I said, "If you'll pardon my intrusion, I don't think he fell."

Chapter Six

The two women sitting at the kitchen table sharing scones and coffee stood so quickly that their chairs bobbled and rocked behind them. I recognized Marla Mae, but it was the older woman, with silver hair piled neatly on top of her head, and wearing a light blue bib apron, who spoke.

"Good morning. You must be Mrs. Fletcher. I am Lucinda Green, the housekeeper. I hope you don't think we were gossiping . . ." She trailed off, and then, as if she saw her way out of an awkward situation, said, "Is there something we can do for you, ma'am?"

I glanced at the table and saw my opportunity to talk to the ladies without appearing to pry. "Those scones look delicious. Blueberry?"

Lucinda got my message. "Blueberry. Made fresh this morning. We'd be pleased if you would sit for a bit. Can I offer you a cup of coffee, or perhaps some Irish breakfast tea?"

"Coffee, please. I definitely need caffeine." I absent-mindedly ran a hand through my hair. "What a day it's been, and it's still early morning."

As I sat down, Marla Mae put a mug of coffee at my elbow and Lucinda passed me a plate with two large blueberry scones covered in a light glaze.

"Would you care for some butter?"

I took a bite. "These are so moist, no butter needed, but thank you."

In spite of the stress of the morning, Lucinda radiated delight. The ladies sipped their coffee and gave me ample time to finish an entire scone before Lucinda asked, "What did you mean, ma'am, when you said you didn't think Mr. Willis fell into the pond? Do you think he had a stroke or a heart attack, something like that?"

"Well, those things are always possible, of course, but they're not what I had in mind. I think it's likely someone else was involved, someone who hit or pushed Willis and killed him, accidentally or otherwise. Although I'm not sure if the sheriff has come to the same conclusion yet. I'm concerned because he is speaking to Mrs. Nickens right now. Interviewing her."

Marla Mae's eyes popped wide open. "I thought he was talking to her, like, you know, telling her what happened, not questioning her like she was a suspect on TV."

Lucinda took a prolonged deep breath, shook her head firmly, and said, "That can't be right. No one could ever think Miss Dolores would . . . That's just plain foolishness."

"I wholeheartedly agree." Knowing that Lucinda and I were on the same wavelength, I wanted to stay for a while longer, but there was Dolores to consider. "Marla Mae, would you mind going out to the foyer? And when the sheriff is, um, finished talking to Dolores, please tell her that I am in here polishing off a plate of Lucinda's delicious scones."

"Certainly, ma'am." She drained her coffee cup in one long gulp and left.

The housekeeper was eyeing me shrewdly; I suspected she knew what I was after—information. Now I would find out if she was willing to share any. I took a sip of coffee, then set my mug on the table.

"Lucinda, how long have you worked for Willis and Dolores?"

"I've been with Mr. Willis for nearly ten years. When I first came on as his housekeeper, he lived in a little town house in Columbia. I was truly happy when he decided to marry Miss Dolores. She is such a cheerful lady, and Mr. Willis is such a . . . I guess 'hard worker' says it all. So little time for joy. But Miss Dolores could bring a smile to his lips. Mind you, she often had to work hard to do so, but she didn't seem to mind."

I laughed. "That does sound exactly like Dolores. Tell me about the others who were at dinner last night. Are they frequent guests?"

"Mr. Clancy and Miss Abby do come by, but not often enough to suit Mr. Willis. Miss Abby is the only one who could make Mr. Willis smile like he smiled for Miss Dolores. He'd have her live here full-time if it was his choice."

I'd already gotten that impression from both Dolores and Willis. I tried to hurry Lucinda along, knowing we could be interrupted at any moment once the sheriff was finished with whatever he'd come here to do. "And Norman Crayfield? What about him? As business partners, he and Willis seem wholly unsuited to each other."

"Maybe so, but they must make a lot of money together. Mr. Willis bought this big fancy house when him and Miss Dolores were getting married, and he never so much as blinked at the price. Just paid up. So there's that," Lucinda said.

"And Marjory Ribault—how did she feel about the sale of her former home?"

Lucinda's lips tightened as if to keep some words captive. "I couldn't tell you, ma'am."

Couldn't or wouldn't? I'd clearly hit a nerve, but, pressed for time, I moved on. "And what about the Blomquists? I understand they are neighbors."

"Could call them that, I guess. They own a hotel down the road. Small one for rich people. What do they call them? Like a bouquet of flowers—I forget the word."

"Are you thinking of 'boutique,' as in a boutique hotel?" I suggested.

"That's it. That's the word I was looking for. Anyway, they want Mr. Willis's company to invest in their hotel so they can modernize. I heard Mr. Willis tell Mr. Crayfield that he wasn't willing to put a cent into that derelict hunk of junk. Mr. Crayfield wanted to make the investment but Mr. Willis was a big loud no."

I turned toward some clattering out in the hallway. Marla Mae had her arm firmly wrapped around Dolores's waist, guiding her into the kitchen. Dolores kept sniffling into a napkin she held against her tear-streaked face. Lucinda jumped from her chair and ran water over a cloth. She wrung it out and pulled the chair next to mine away from the table.

"Here you go, Miss Dolores. Sit down, lean your head back, and press this on your eyes. There, now don't that feel better?"

"Thank you, Lucinda, but my heart is so heavy I am not sure I would know how 'better' feels. Jess, my Willis is gone."

I caressed her hand. "I know, Dolores. It will take time—"

"I don't mean dead—I mean *gone*." Dolores straightened up and pulled the cloth from her face. "While that sheriff babbled along in the library, someone came and took Willis's body to some government place. As soon as the sheriff opened the library door, the deputy standing there told him the body had been transported somewhere or another. That's all Willis is to any of them, 'the body,' and if Marla Mae wasn't waiting in the foyer, standing close enough to grab me when I began to swoon, they might have had another body on their hands."

There wasn't much I could say in response. I took a final sip of my coffee, which had cooled considerably, and suggested that Dolores go to her room and rest for a while. I was relieved when she agreed. I followed along as Marla Mae took her upstairs, but I left while Marla Mae got Dolores settled into bed.

I was curious if there was any activity at the koi pond and decided to walk down the driveway to check. I'd gotten only a few feet down the driveway when I heard my name.

"Jessica! Jessica, wait." Marjory Ribault was huffing and puffing as she hurried across the lawn. By the time she reached me, she was winded. She put her hands on her waist and bent forward, gasping for air. After a few moments she stood and touched her chest. "The old ticker, as they say, isn't what it once was." Her pale face confirmed that.

"Take a few more deep breaths," I urged. One thing was certain: I'd already had all the calamities that I could handle in one day.

"Not to worry—I'll be fine. I am going home for a lie-down, but before I do, I have to know, and as a complete outsider you are the only one here I trust to tell me the truth: Is that miserable wretch Willis Nickens really dead?"

I was shocked. "Marjory, really! How can you speak that way? After all, he was a human being, and his body is barely cold. His poor wife is upstairs, distraught with grief."

"Pshaw. If you only knew the torture he's put people through, sometimes for money, more often for his own amusement. I'm telling you, I can't wait to dance on his grave. And I'm not the only one." Marjory turned, and there was a real spring in her step as she sauntered back the way she'd come. I heard her begin to hum a tune, and it was far from a dirge.

Much of the activity at the koi pond had concluded. There was no sign of the Sheriff's Department. An unmarked SUV was parked where Deputy Lascomb's car had been. Two technicians, dressed in white plastic suits and headgear, were studiously examining the site. One was pushing a digital measuring wheel and recording the results on a clipboard. The other tech was taking water samples from the pond.

Nothing to learn here, I thought, and turned back toward the house. I was surprised to see Marla Mae walking down the driveway to meet me.

"Miss Jessica, Lucinda wants to know what's your pleasure about meals. People are sure to be hungry, but we don't want to bother Miss Dolores," she explained.

I looked at my watch. Somehow time had jumped from six thirty in the morning to well past one o'clock in the afternoon. I thought for a moment. "Why don't you set out a tray of sandwiches and pitchers of iced tea and water in the dining room, along with a bowl of fruit and perhaps a salad? If there are any left, a few of Lucinda's delicious scones are sure to be a hit. And please let everyone know when the food is available. Except Mrs. Nickens. I want to check on her, so I will stop in her room myself," I said.

Marla Mae scampered to the kitchen while I headed up to my room to make a quick phone call.

A few more buds had opened on the crepe myrtles outside my window. In spite of all that was going on, their graceful beauty made me smile. I sat in the comfy blue wing chair, pulled out my cell, and hit speed dial for my friend Seth Hazlitt, who I hoped would not have to miss my call because he had a patient sitting in front of him.

He answered on the second ring and started talking before I could say so much as "Hello."

"Ayuh, Jessica, I have been wondering how your conference went. And I suppose you are down south visiting your friend about now."

Wherever I was, no matter how far I traveled, Seth's Yankee dialect always made me long for a decent-sized bowl of clam chowder and home. "Malice Domestic, as always, was an outstanding conference—lots of friends, lots of fun. As I've often told you, there is nothing more revitalizing for a writer than to spend a few days with other writers, and especially with our most enthusiastic readers. I enjoy their company so much, and it really gets my writerly juices flowing."

"I, for one, am glad you are done with that conference. You know I don't like going to big cities, or having you visiting one either," Seth groused.

"Really, Seth. Malice Domestic is held in Bethesda, Maryland, hardly a booming metropolis. Bethesda is a charming little town. Lots of trees and lovely homes. Nothing big city about it."

"But I seem to remember that to get there, you took the train to Washington, DC. Now there's a place bound to be trouble—filled with politicians and tourists. I always feel better when you are in smaller places and away from crowds. Less likely to trip over a dead body."

I wasn't sure how to answer, and when I hesitated, Seth shouted, "Good grief, tell me you didn't . . ."

"Now, Seth, don't get your blood pressure up. And no, I didn't trip, or I might have wound up soaking wet." I tried to sound lighthearted but the situation was too somber for me to pull it off, so I decided to give him the straight truth. "Unfortunately, my friend Dolores's husband did pass away sometime late last night or in the early-morning hours."

"Pass away? Be honest, Jess: Did he die of natural causes, or is this another one of those murders you happen to find everywhere you go?"

"I don't know the answer to that just yet. That's why I'm calling you," I said.

"Calling me? Do you expect me to diagnose cause of death over the telephone? Woman, have you lost your senses?" Seth's voice went up several decibels.

While I hadn't lost my senses, I was definitely losing my patience. "Seth, please, just let me speak. My friend's husband did die under what I consider to be suspicious circumstances. We won't know for certain until there's a coroner's report, or until the tight-lipped sheriff gives us some indication of what he believes happened. And if he does believe Willis was murdered, I am afraid that Dolores will be his prime suspect."

Seth's tone softened. "I am sorry to hear all this. I know you were looking forward to a nice, friendly visit, a little 'remember when' talking with a whole lot of shopping thrown in. How can I help?"

"Well, I couldn't possibly leave Dolores alone with all this going on. So of course I need you to keep an eye on my house for a few days longer, if you wouldn't mind. Also, could you call Doris Ann over at the library and let her know that I won't be able to attend the Friends of the Library meeting, but I will, as promised, serve on the committee to select the new tables and chairs for the reading room?"

"I'll call Doris Ann first thing, if you promise to tell the other committee members that we library patrons want thick cushions on the chairs in the reading room. It takes me a while to get through the daily *Boston Globe*, not to mention the monthly issue of *Salt Water Sportsman*. And those hard wood chairs can be murder on the, uh, posterior."

"Oh, Seth, surely you can afford a subscription to the paper and the magazine so you can read them in the comfort of your home." I raised my eyebrows so high they nearly met my hairline.

"I already pay for them every year in my home-owner's taxes. You know, the tax that's marked 'library.' I'm certainly not going to pay twice."

No, you're not, I thought.

He went on. "You stay safe down there, Jess, and be sure to let me know when you are coming home. We can have a welcome breakfast at Mara's Luncheon-ette."

"I'll give you plenty of notice. Good-bye, Seth." I tapped the off button. I was always amazed how that man could squeeze a penny 'til it squealed, as the saying goes.

I shook the Cabot Cove cobwebs out of my head. Now it was time to check on Dolores.

Chapter Seven

I tapped lightly on Dolores's door, half hoping she was asleep, but she was wide-awake and exceptionally jittery.

Dolores paced back and forth, not quite bouncing off walls, while her words tumbled out at warp speed. "Clancy kept his promise. We brought up a breakfast tray to the playroom, and when Abby woke up, Clancy and I had tea and scones while Abby ate her cereal and fruit.

"For a while we played with that toy rabbit she found yesterday. Clancy actually deferred to me and said, 'Granny Dolores has something to tell you, sweetheart.'"

Dolores might have seen it as Clancy letting her take the lead, but I thought it was pure cowardice on his part.

She went on. "Abby climbed into my lap, expecting

a story, I suppose, and I told her as gently as I could that Grampy had gone to heaven to be with her mother. Abby said if she knew he was going today, she would have given him Fluffy—that's the wooden bunny— to take as a present for Mommy. Isn't she the sweetest little girl?"

Then Dolores's anxiety got the best of her. "Oh, Jess, just because Clancy kept this one promise doesn't mean he will let me stay in Abby's life. I told her I would always be her granny but . . ."

I understood her fear. If anyone had ever tried to take our nephew Grady away from Frank and me after Frank's brother and his wife died all those years ago, we would have moved heaven and earth to stay in Grady's life. I knew Dolores felt the same about Abby, and I thought her fear was quite rational, given what I had seen of Clancy so far. Of course, I had no idea how Willis had bequeathed his assets. I knew only that he had threatened to remove Clancy as Abby's trustee. Was that just an example of what Marjory meant when she talked about Willis's tormenting people for his own amusement, or was it something Willis actually planned to do?

I distracted Dolores from one problem by bringing up another. "I am so sorry that Sheriff Halvorson didn't allow me to stay with you in the library. How was your conversation with him?"

Dolores shrugged. "He has no idea what happened to Willis. No matter how many times I asked him, he couldn't tell me a thing. I mean, he's the sheriff— shouldn't he know what happened?"

I nodded. "I quite understand your concern, Dolores,

but what worries me is not his lack of answers to your questions. We need to think about what he asked *you*."

Dolores folded her arms across her chest. "Nonsense. That's what he asked me—a whole bunch of nonsense. Even went so far as to question our sleeping arrangements. Can you imagine? He wanted to know why we had separate bedrooms and if there was a connecting door and all sorts of other silliness.

"And when he wasn't snooping in our private lives, he was asking about our financial lives. How much money did I bring to the marriage? What kind of arrangements had Willis made for me should anything happen to him? He went on and on. I kept begging him to tell me what happened to Willis and he kept not answering. Let me tell you, it was maddening."

"I'm sure it was, but you must realize, you and Sheriff Halvorson were on different paths." I knew I had to tread carefully, but I needed to make a point to Dolores, a point she wouldn't want to hear. "You want to know what happened to your husband. The sheriff wants to know what happened, how it happened, and perhaps who made it happen."

Dolores stopped pacing and stared at me. "'Made it happen'? The sheriff thinks someone killed Willis?"

"Calm down, Dolores. We don't know that yet, but the sheriff does have to examine every possibility, explore every avenue. Wouldn't you want him to do that for Willis?"

Dolores began walking back and forth again, but her steps were slower, her expression thoughtful. "Yes, I guess I would, but really, Jess, who would harm Willis? Everyone loved him."

I'd met Willis only twenty-four hours earlier, and I could have drawn up a list of people who didn't even like him. Love him? Doubtful. Dolores must still have been looking through newlywed eyes. "That's true, I am sure, but in my experience, law enforcement always takes a good, hard look at family members and close friends."

"Surely not in this case . . . Oh, wait—are you trying to tell me that I am a suspect? That the sheriff thinks *I* killed Willis? Are you insane? Is Sheriff Halvorson insane? No, Jess. Just . . . No."

I tried again. "We don't know anything for certain as yet. I want you to be prepared, because I am sure the sheriff will want to interview you again."

"Enough. That's enough." In all these years, I'd never heard such a sharp edge to Dolores's voice. "Please keep your mystery-writer ideas to yourself. Find Lucinda, if you would, and ask her to send up a bottle of sherry and a bucket of ice. I am going to need a nap."

Dolores turned her back toward me and stood looking out her bedroom window and across the sitting garden. For the second time today I was being dismissed.

The walk-in pantry just off the kitchen was lined with floor-to-ceiling shelves trimmed with old-fashioned flowered shelf paper with scalloped edges. Inside, Lucinda looked up from her task of marking items on a clipboard.

"How can I help you, Mrs. Fletcher? I'm afraid we're all out of blueberry scones," she said with a grin.

"That's fine." I patted my stomach. "I had more than my share, although I do hope you'll make them again before I head north. Dolores sent me down to ask for a bottle of sherry and a bucket of ice."

Lucinda's face clouded over. "Should have been expecting that, I guess. Still, the first and only time she looked for the sherry bottle was after that one big quarrel she and Mr. Willis had. Not sure what it was about, but she stayed in her room for thirty-six hours straight, with both doors locked, if you get my meaning. Only time I ever saw Mr. Willis eat humble pie. I swear, he would have danced naked down Main Street to get back on her good side. I'd still love to know what that fight was about."

"And you never got as much as a hint?"

"No, ma'am. And nothing like that ever happened before or since. 'Course Miss Dolores got a good reason to be drinkin' now. I'll see right to getting her fixed up with a bottle of Tomás García. Maybe some crackers and cheese, too."

I wandered around the house at loose ends. If I could bump into Norman or Clancy and start a conversation I might be able to wheedle some useful information from them. But useful in what way? Given the white river rock I had seen in the koi pond and the half-smoked cigar right where he would have dropped it if he'd been struck from behind, I was sure Willis had been murdered, and not by Dolores. I still didn't know where Sheriff Halvorson stood on all this. If he was convinced Willis was murdered, I was sure he'd be counting Dolores as his number one suspect. And if he thought Willis died accidentally, well, in either scenario a killer would get away with murder unless . . .

Marla Mae was emptying the dishwasher when I barged into the kitchen, sounding more demanding than I'd meant to. "Is there a competent local car service, or do you know if Uber or Lyft has drivers in this community?"

"Got you covered, Mrs. Fletcher. My brother, Elton, drives for Success City Cars, a twenty-four-hour car service, bonded and insured. Says so right there on his business card. Papa teases him with no mercy about that card sounding highfalutin."

"Excellent. Can you call your brother and ask him to drive me to the Sheriff's Department this afternoon? I am going upstairs to change, and will be ready when he gets here."

As I flew out of the kitchen, I heard Marla Mae say, "Sure thing, Mrs. Fletcher."

I ran a comb through my hair and dabbed on some lipstick. My cropped gray and white bouclé jacket over a flattering gray A-line skirt was perfect for the look I was going for—successful mystery writer with lots of high-flying connections. If the sheriff had no regard for a woman out for a jog in sweats and sneakers, we'd see how he would react to a woman in a Brooks Brothers suit. I fastened the clasp on my double strand of pearls and went downstairs.

In the foyer Marla Mae and Lucinda were talking to a tall young man with wire-rimmed eyeglasses whose red and black plaid bow tie jazzed up his white short-sleeved shirt and black slacks. He moved quickly to greet me at the bottom of the staircase, reaching out a hand in a courtly manner to assist me down the final few steps.

"Good day, Mrs. Fletcher. Elton Anderson at your service." His Southern accent enhanced his strong baritone voice. "I want to thank you for allowing me and Success City Cars to take care of your travel needs today."

I made a snap decision. "It's a pleasure to meet you, Elton. I am planning to be here at Manning Hall for the next few days, perhaps even longer. Would it be possible for you to be available to me each day? I'll gladly pay the going daily rate."

"That would be my pleasure, ma'am. And I will be sure you get the multiday discount. Now, may I show you to your car?"

A metallic blue Cadillac Escalade was parked in front of the house. "Oh my, Elton, that is quite a car."

"Not too big for you, is it? I was coming back from an airport run—husband, wife, two kids, and lots of luggage—when Marla Mae called. I can bring a sedan tomorrow if you'd be more comfortable." Elton opened the rear door and once again extended an assisting hand.

"No, this car will be fine. I would, though, prefer to sit in the front seat so we can get to know each other, but only if Success City Cars allows passengers to do so."

"Sure 'nuff." Elton opened the front door on the passenger side. "And I am one of those drivers who like to talk."

The interior was black leather trimmed with silver.

As I clicked my seat belt shut, I complimented Elton on how immaculate the car was.

"Yes, ma'am. We have a top-notch cleaning crew. Still, I make it my business to get to work early for my shift, and soon as I get my assigned car, I give it a good once-over. You never know. One time the cleaning crew missed an empty chips bag stuffed in the glove compartment."

We started down the driveway. When we passed the koi pond, the only remnants I could see from the morning's tragedy were yellow police tape and black smudges along the pool's edge. I assumed the smudges were fingerprint powder.

Elton said, "Sorry to hear about the mister. Accidents like that cause all kinds of grief. Marla Mae did say he was a handful, but I know she never wished him harm."

We stopped at the gate and Elton reached into his pocket, and out came a clicker just like the one Dolores had me use when I arrived.

"I was wondering how you got through the gate. I didn't realize you had a remote control."

"Not mine to have. Marla Mae has a clicker, and she walked down to the gate to let me in. There are always extras on hand for houseguests, so Marla Mae will just use one of those until I return hers. I expect Mr. or Mrs. Nickens would have given you one of your own had you come by car."

I mulled that over for a mile or two, then asked, "You mentioned that your sister found Willis Nickens to be quite a handful. In what way, exactly?"

Elton made a left from one main road to another.

"Oh, you know. There's bosses, and then there's bosses. Some are pleasant and treat you good. Some . . . don't."

Remembering the various principals who supervised me when I was a teacher, I knew exactly what he meant. "And I suppose Willis fell on the 'don't' side of the equation."

"That he did, Mrs. Fletcher. That he did. Marla Mae said he made her so nervous that she would tiptoe around to see where he was before she started her chores. If it was dusting day and he was in the living room, she'd make it her business to start in the dining room. Lucinda took to giving Marla Mae a cup of chamomile tea before she served dinner, just to steady her nerves."

"What was it about him? Can you pinpoint that for me?"

"I guess you could say he was bad-tempered, always loud and bullying. Not just to the staff, even to guests and friends. Just last week Marla Mae walked in on him throwing a manila folder across the room while shouting up a storm. And that time he was all alone. Crazy, huh?"

"Crazy," I agreed, although I did wonder what could have been in the folder to get Willis so riled.

"Sure 'nuff got Marla Mae's nerves atwitter, that I can tell you."

"Oh, I imagine it did." Even as I spoke I realized that Marla Mae had been so intimidated by Willis that it would have been impossible for her to stand up to him, much less hit him with a rock. She might be relieved that he was gone but she would never have had the wherewithal to make him go.

Elton turned into the driveway of the Sheriff's Department headquarters, a neat redbrick building surrounded by a well-manicured lawn and a fine selection of shade trees. He pulled to the curbside near the entrance. "Would you like me to park the car and accompany you, ma'am?"

"You're very kind, but I can manage."

Elton handed me a business card. "I will be in visitor parking. Call me when you are coming out and I'll meet you right here. You do have a cell with you?"

I put the card in my purse. "Oh yes, I've learned to keep my phone handy."

As I opened the car door, Elton gave me a snappy salute. "Good luck."

I would need all the luck I could get. Even if his technicians had found something to support my suspicion that Willis Nickens was murdered, would the sheriff loosen up enough to tell me?

Chapter Eight

The lobby of the Sheriff's Department was bright and cheery, not at all dingy and dour like the hoose-gows in the cowboy movies of my childhood. An older couple sat side by side on blue visitors' chairs in front of a row of wide windows partly covered by venetian blinds. Several deputies were busy tapping on computers and shuffling paperwork behind a sleek counter with a beige faux-marble top.

A female deputy, with wide blond streaks in her pixie hairdo, looked across the counter. "Can I help you?"

"Yes, please. My name is Jessica Fletcher. I met with Sheriff Halvorson earlier today and I would like to continue our discussion."

The deputy, whose name tag said REMINGTON, tapped her keyboard, glanced at her computer screen, and looked puzzled. "You say you were at a meeting with the sheriff? Earlier today? The schedule doesn't indicate . . ."

"It wasn't a formal meeting. I discovered a body, and the sheriff arrived . . ."

I must say she had excellent control of her facial muscles; her mouth barely twitched and her brow stayed steady, but I could see she was thinking, *possible cuckoo.*

"Mrs., uh, Fletcher, we haven't met before, so maybe you could explain a little more. Do you often discover dead bodies and have conversations with the sheriff?" she asked just loudly enough to get the attention of the other two deputies working nearby.

"Actually it has happened before, although not in this jurisdiction, and certainly not with Sheriff Halvorson, at least not until today." I thought that would clear things up, but instead one of the other deputies stood and walked over to the counter.

"Sheriff Halvorson is not available today. If you would like to leave your name and phone number, perhaps someone else can help you at a more convenient time." The deputy slid a pad and pen across the faux-marble countertop.

Frustration mounted on both sides of the counter.

"Really, I must insist. If you tell Sheriff Halvorson that I am here, I am sure he will want to speak with me."

"Listen, Mrs.—"

"Mrs. Fletcher! What on earth are you doing here?" Sheriff Halvorson was loud enough to grab the attention of everyone in the room.

I twirled around and he was right behind me, along with two uniformed deputies and a man dressed in a blue seersucker suit. Then, as if we were at a community social, Sheriff Halvorson introduced me.

"Gentlemen, this is J. B. Fletcher, world-famous mystery author, probably come to give me a few lessons in crime solving." His laugh was tinged with sarcasm.

Sheriff Halvorson's fanfare was intended as blatant ridicule. The deputies smiled uneasily, but the man in the suit stepped forward, hand extended. "How do you do, Ms. Fletcher? I am Arnold Bailey, president of the local merchants' association. Sheriff Zeke here should of told me we have a celebrity in town. I would of asked you to join our weekly meeting. Maybe next week? Our membership would be interested to hear what you have to say. You could give them pointers about how to prevent shoplifting, or the best anti-burglary measures for a shop owner to follow. Something like that."

"Oh, gracious no, I'm afraid I wouldn't be much help. I write mystery fiction, not true crime. My work is based on imagination and lots of research."

Sheriff Halvorson gloated as he stepped in to close the conversation. "Exactly right, Mrs. Fletcher. Law enforcement is best left to the professionals. Now, if you'll excuse us, I promised to show Arnold the patrol area maps."

"Just a minute, Sheriff. I've come to discuss Willis Nickens. Surely you have a moment. After all, the man is dead. Doesn't that deserve some attention?"

All eyes were on him now. Even his deputies waited for his reply. In response to the stricken look on the sheriff's face, I had to force myself not to shout, *Check and mate.*

He tapped a deputy on the shoulder. "Billy, please take Arnold to the map room. I'll be right with you, but first I need a moment with Mrs. Fletcher." He turned on his heel and walked quickly, as if daring me to keep up, which I certainly did. We went down a long hallway, and when he opened a door I expected that it would be to his office, but I was mistaken. One barred window sat high on the wall opposite the door, and a camera was mounted near the ceiling. An interview room. A table and three chairs occupied the center of the room, but he did not invite me to sit down.

"Okay, Mrs. Fletcher, what is so urgent?" The sheriff crossed his arms and tilted his head slightly.

"Well, Dolores—that is, Mrs. Nickens—is anxious to arrange for her husband's funeral, and she hasn't even seen his remains yet."

"Anxious, is she? We're awaiting the coroner's report, and may provide more information to her when we receive it."

I was surprised that he'd said "may provide" instead of "will provide." Didn't Dolores have a right to know what happened to her husband?

"As to viewing," he continued, "we thought we would spare her the chore of identifying the body since you, as a family friend, were able to do so."

"But, Sheriff, Dolores wants to see Willis. I thought perhaps she and I could go to wherever he is being kept and—"

"Okay, okay, I will arrange for you to visit this afternoon."

Remembering that Dolores likely was still locked in her room with a bottle of sherry, I suggested tomor-

row morning might be a better choice and was relieved when Sheriff Halvorson said he was sure it
could be arranged.

"Deputy Lascomb will be in touch. If there is nothing else, Mrs. Fletcher . . ."

"Well, I know it's a long shot, given that it was in
the pond for hours, but I did wonder if your technicians found any traces of DNA or other matter on the
white river rock that inexplicably appeared in the
pond near Willis's body."

"Mrs. Fletcher, rocks don't 'inexplicably' appear or
disappear. This isn't one of your novels. This is *my*
investigation of a suspicious death."

As soon as he said "suspicious" I was sure he
wanted to bite his tongue.

I pressed for the advantage. "So you agree that it's
likely Willis was murdered."

"Don't put words in my mouth. Any death, unless
certified by a physician, is technically suspicious until
I have a coroner's report that tells me otherwise. Now,
I've given you more time than I can spare." He opened
the door, led me back to the lobby, and said a curt
"Good-bye."

Elton was leaning on the bumper of the Escalade
when I walked out the front door.

"You must be a mind reader. I hadn't even taken
my cell out of my purse to call you, yet here you are,"
I said as he opened the passenger-side door and helped
me get seated.

He waited to answer until he'd rounded the front
of the car and slid into his seat. "I thought you were
in there a longish time, so I decided to come and wait

here in case you came out a-runnin' and we needed to make a quick getaway!" He chortled at his own joke.

I laughed along, which helped release the tension from my brief conversation with Sheriff Halvorson. Our ride home was uneventful until we reached the koi pond. I asked Elton to stop the car so I could look closely at the scene, something I supposed I should have done earlier. An oval was chalked on the ground where I'd last seen the cigar butt. *Good. The forensic team will examine it.* The koi were gone. Not one brightly colored fish remained in the pond. Had they been removed for their own safety, out of fear of contamination? Or could they contain evidence? I wondered if the forensic team had a fish expert on staff. There was so much I didn't know.

I got back into the car and invited Elton to come to the house for a cup of tea.

"That's very kind of you, ma'am. Do you happen to know what Miss Lucinda is baking today?"

"No, I don't, but so far I've eaten her blueberry scones, benne wafers, and sweet potato pie, and all were scrumptious. Do you think there is more in her repertoire?"

"Lots more. Her pralines are delish, and you haven't lived until you've tasted her cola cake." Elton licked his lips.

"I have heard that cola cake is popular in the South but I have never actually tried some."

"Soon as Lucinda finds that out, she'll have a cola cake in the oven in no time. You are in for a treat, Mrs. Fletcher."

The house was silent as a tomb. I wanted to check

on Dolores but thought it best to head for the kitchen to see if Lucinda or Marla Mae could give me an update.

Marla Mae stopped polishing silver and wiped her hands on a dish towel when she saw us come into the kitchen. "Hey, Mrs. Fletcher, did Li'l Bro treat you right?"

"Elton is a courteous and safety-conscious driver. Who could ask for more? He and I would both love a cup of tea."

"Did Miss Lucinda bake anything special today?" Elton was hopeful.

"If you stop drooling, Elton"—Marla Mae laughed— "I will get you a healthy slice of Lucinda's cherry banana bread."

Elton fell into the nearest chair and clutched his chest. "Be still my heart. I suppose you have some cream cheese in the fridge?"

Marla Mae winked at me. "Elton never met a fruit bread he didn't want to smother with cream cheese. Waste of good fruit bread, if you ask me."

She put on the kettle, then took cups and plates from a cabinet and set the table for four. "Lucinda went to check on Miss Dolores. I expect she'll be joining us shortly."

That answered one question; Dolores was still in her room. "And what about Mr. Crayfield and Mr. Travers? How are they spending their day?"

"Mr. Clancy took Abby down to the Riverbanks. It's a zoo and a garden in town. Lots of distractions for the child. As to Mr. Crayfield, he could be anywhere.

I saw him in the sitting garden early on, and then he was doodling around that putting green that Mr. Willis liked to keep to himself. No harm now, I suppose." She poured boiling water into a pink-rose porcelain teapot. "I'll let that steep for a few minutes while I cut the cherry banana bread. Oh, now what?"

The harsh noise of a buzzer cut through the kitchen, while elegant chimes sounded in the distance.

I followed Marla Mae. She pulled the front door wide open and there was Tom Blomquist holding an oversized basket of fruit. Candy stood slightly behind him with a bouquet of pink lilies and white roses tucked in the crook of her arm.

"Ah, we thought we'd come to express our condolences to Dolores," Tom said. "Terrible thing to happen. Just terrible."

Marla Mae looked at me uncertainly. We both knew that Dolores was surely indisposed. I decided to play hostess, and perhaps have a few questions answered in the process.

"How kind of you both. Please do come in. Dolores is resting, but I hope you will stay for tea. Marla Mae will be happy to put those gorgeous flowers in a vase."

Marla Mae took the fruit basket and the flowers. I led the Blomquists to the library.

Once we were seated, Tom Blomquist was first to speak. "I was horrified to learn about Willis's accident. Ah, such an energetic man. A mover and a shaker."

"Yes. It's very sad. Tell me, how did you hear about it?"

"Marjory Ribault called me. She even offered to let us in the gate when I said we would definitely make a condolence call," Candy answered for them both. "Marjory told me she'd seen a lot of fuss and flutter around the koi pond. Later, when she went out for her walk, she met you and you said that Willis fell into the pond."

"Yes, it's quite true—I did meet Marjory on the lawn this morning and I did confirm that Willis was dead. She didn't seem at all upset. In fact, quite the contrary—she seemed almost gleeful."

"Ah, but you don't know the whole story," Tom said. "Marjory's father succumbed to particularly hard times and had no choice but to sell this house and the land that had been in his family since before the war. You know, the Civil War. Marjory is the last of a long line. Her father wanted to see she was provided for and not wind up house rich and money poor, like so many others we know."

"Still, I think she'd rather have the house than the money," Candy said, "while I'd opt for the money every time."

Tom glared at her. "Candy, please don't be so crass."

Lucinda came in carrying a tea tray, followed by Marla Mae, who'd made a pleasing arrangement of lilies and roses in a tall crystal vase that reminded me of several Waterford pieces I'd seen on my last visit to Ireland.

"Thank you, ladies." I looked directly at Lucinda. "I told the Blomquists that Dolores is confined to her room and offered them some of your delicious cherry banana bread."

Lucinda replied, "Miss Dolores is getting the rest she sorely needs."

Good. Then I needn't fear Dolores, after imbibing too much sherry, would come down the stairs wondering loudly where everybody was.

Lucinda poured tea and set out a plate covered with slices of cherry banana bread. I hoped Elton had gotten a piece or two before these slices left the kitchen. Which reminded me, I'd done enough traveling for one day. As the ladies were leaving the room I said, "Marla Mae, please tell Elton he won't be needed again today. We'll give him ample notice of a start time tomorrow."

Candy broke a slice of cherry banana bread in half, while Tom opted for a whole slice. I took the opportunity of the interruption to change the subject.

"I understand that you are the proprietors of a charming hotel that is the pride of the neighborhood."

Tom preened. "Jessamine House is a jewel. The main structure survived the Civil War intact, and over the past one hundred and fifty years various owners added rooms, balconies, and fireplaces, and when French doors became popular, one owner added quite a few."

Candy said, "You must come and see it."

"Thank you. I would enjoy that. I suppose an older home that gets the wear and tear of so many travelers is hard to maintain. Not to mention expensive."

Tom and Candy exchanged a fleeting look. "Actually," Tom said, "for a while we had some difficulty finding business partners to help us modernize, but I'm confident that problem is resolved and the investment is forthcoming shortly."

The Blomquists talked enthusiastically about their

hotel for a while longer, before they again asked me to express their condolences to Dolores and took their leave.

I thought it was interesting how quick Candy was to say that Marjory had let them through the gate this afternoon. Since everyone knew Willis was still alive after the Blomquists left the dinner party, Candy seemed to be confirming that they did not have access to the gate. I didn't think that was quite enough to eliminate them from the suspect pool. Could one of them have driven their car out through the gate while the other hid on the grounds to try to get Willis alone? I thought Tom was too timid for such an exploit, but Candy—now, she was a bit of an enigma. Quiet and shy but, based on her comments about Marjory's situation, definitely interested in money. And, as frequent visitors, could they have gotten their hands on a gate clicker, since spares seemed so readily available?

I found Lucinda in the kitchen relaxing with a glass of merlot, and I gladly accepted the glass she offered me. We agreed it was for the best that Dolores had fallen asleep early. She would need her rest. Tomorrow was bound to be another stressful day for us all.

Chapter Nine

I was briefly aware of the birds chirping before I opened my eyes, and I looked at the clock on my nightstand. After seven. I must have been exhausted to sleep so late. Then I remembered all that had happened yesterday and decided it was a miracle I hadn't slept 'til noon.

I had finished my stretches and was about to jump into the shower when I heard a gentle tap on my door. I hoped it was Marla Mae with a carafe of coffee, but I found Dolores standing at my doorsill. I reached out and gave her a welcoming hug, hoping it would cure yesterday's rift.

"Jess, I am so sorry. I didn't mean any of the things I said yesterday. It was . . . Oh, I don't know. My heart is broken and my head is jumbled all at the same time."

"Believe me, I understand what it is to have your

life turned upside down in a single moment." I guided Dolores to the comfy wing chair, and I sat on the edge of the bed.

"I know you do. I well remember when Frank . . ." She reached over and squeezed my hand. "It's only that I don't know how to survive this."

"No one does in the beginning. Somehow, over time, we each find our way. Now, I do have some good news. I went to see Sheriff Halvorson yesterday . . ."

Dolores went totally wide-eyed. "How on earth did you manage that?"

"Never mind. The important thing is that he is arranging for you to go to the Coroner's Office sometime this morning to see Willis. I am expecting a call from Deputy Lascomb to confirm the details."

"How can I ever thank you? It's so important to me to see Willis one last time before he is embalmed and covered with pancake makeup. I'd almost rather a closed coffin. How did you manage . . . Never mind; you're right—it doesn't matter," Dolores said.

"Plenty of time to talk in the car. Right now we have to shower, get dressed, and find a cup of coffee."

"I'll meet you in the dining room." She opened the door, and turned back to me. "Thank you for all your help. I hope we can just forget yesterday."

I swept my hand back and forth in an arc as if there was a blackboard in front of me and I had a huge eraser. "Already done."

Norman Crayfield had a newspaper spread out on the table. The remnants of scrambled eggs were congealed on a plate that he had pushed to the side. He barely nodded when I said, "Good morning." I poured myself a cup of coffee, put a bran muffin on a plate, and left plenty of space between us when I sat at the table.

I was halfway finished with my muffin when Norman folded his newspaper and said, "I suppose you'll be leaving soon."

"Leaving?" Did he mean leaving the dining room, or leaving the house? Had Dolores told him of our plans for the day?

"Sure, going up north. Home. No point in staying around this gloomy place. I'm sure it will only get gloomier in the days to come."

"And yet you are still here."

"Well, of course." He puffed out his chest. "Someone has to guide Dolores through all the financial complexities of Willis's business interests."

"Oh, I see." I nodded in pretend agreement. Why would he expect Dolores to rely on him? I was sure she would have accountants and lawyers of her own choosing who could review Willis's holdings and report their findings to her.

Marla Mae came in. "Good morning, Mrs. Fletcher. Deputy Lascomb called. He can meet you at the Coroner's Office at ten thirty, if that is convenient."

"That's perfect. Dolores and I will be ready in plenty of time. Please let Elton know. Oh, and tell him it could be a very busy day. We have several stops to make."

Norman gave me a withering look. "Hasn't Dolores been through enough? Can't you spare her the ordeal of a visit to the coroner?"

"Stop badgering Jessica, Norman. It was my idea. I want to see Willis one last time." Dolores's voice wafted into the room. "Jess, I'll be right in. I want to check my car. I may need gas. And do we have the address so I can put it in the GPS?"

"Don't worry about the car. Come in and sit down," I said. "Have something to eat. I've arranged for Marla Mae's brother, Elton, to bring a car, and he will be our driver for today. I thought that would be less stressful for you."

"That is genius. I never gave a thought to transportation. Who knows how I will feel . . . later? And I always forget that you don't drive." Dressed in a stunning navy blue suit and prim white blouse, Dolores looked like a society matron on her way to an upscale luncheon. She stopped at the breakfront to pour herself a cup of coffee. "I don't feel like eating, but I do need caffeine."

"Try some grapes. Break off a bunch and I'll share it with you."

Before she got to the table, Norman sprang up to pull out a chair nearer to him than to me. "Sit here, Dolores. I've been so sorry not to have seen much of you since the unfortunate . . . Anyway, I wanted to tell you again how sorry I am."

"Thank you, Norman." Dolores gave him a tight obligatory smile.

"It's important that you know I will stand by you financially until you are comfortable managing your own affairs. Take all the time you need. It's the least I can do for my old partner and friend."

Dolores pressed her lips together, then swiveled in

her seat and said, "Have some grapes, Jessica." She set the plate of fruit between us.

"Norman," I said while reaching for some grapes, "the Blomquists were here yesterday and mentioned they are expecting some funding so they can update Jessamine House. Since they are part of your social circle I can't help wondering if that money will come from your firm."

He grunted and squirmed, discomfort oozing from every pore. "Actually, that was a project Willis and I discussed at length. Willis was extremely supportive but we never finalized dollar amounts or whether we would prefer a percent of ownership or a low-interest-loan repayment. Of course now you will be party to the negotiations, Dolores."

"Please, Norman, no business talk, especially at the breakfast table. As you very well know, that was one of Willis's hard and fast rules: no business at mealtime."

"Of course, of course. So sorry, but"—Norman gave me an acerbic look—"Jessica did ask. I was merely being polite."

He excused himself and left the room.

Dolores slumped back in her chair. "Jess, I dread having to work with that man. He's so infuriating. Whenever he is around I fully understand that old saw 'He sets my teeth on edge.'"

Marla Mae came to the doorway. "Miss Dolores, Elton is in the kitchen having some muffins and coffee. He wanted me to let you know that he will be ready to leave whenever you ladies say."

"Twenty minutes or so. I have one last chore to do.

Oh, and would you please call the Harrold Brothers Funeral Home and let them know I will be stopping by later today . . . to make arrangements?" Dolores said; then, without missing a beat, she looked at me. "Jess, wait here. I will be right back."

I took a final bite of my muffin and had barely swallowed it when Dolores was back. She was waving her cell phone. "Come with me, please. I need you to witness something."

I dropped my napkin on my chair and followed her to Willis's office.

"Jess, I want this room locked up so tight that Houdini himself couldn't escape. Would you check the French doors, please?"

I made sure the doors were secure, and when I turned back around I saw Dolores opening mahogany cabinets and snapping pictures of the tabs of the file folders inside. She kept moving from cabinet to cabinet, tapping her phone feverishly. "Now the windows. Make sure they are locked. And please close the drapes."

At last Dolores stood in front of Willis's desk and surveyed the room. "Okay, we're good."

She closed the heavy oak door, took a key from her pocket, and turned the lock. "There. Now we can go."

Elton was waiting by the car. Today's bow tie was a subdued black and white checkerboard pattern. He offered his condolences to Dolores, and then settled us each in a captain's chair in the second row of the Escalade. He pointed to the area behind our seats to let us know we were well prepared for a long day.

"We have a cooler filled with bottles of water and sweet tea. Miss Lucinda was kind enough to pack some fruit, which I put on ice, and she boxed up some muffins. They are right on top of the cooler. Now, tell me, is the Coroner's Office still our first stop?"

"It is," I said, "and it was very thoughtful of you and Lucinda to provide refreshments."

"Sure 'nuff. I am not one to pass up Lucinda's baked goods, and that's a fact." Elton started the engine, and we were on our way.

"Thanks for coming with me, Jess. Although I know plenty of people in this part of South Carolina—not to mention that once I married Willis, my social circle greatly increased—it occurred to me this morning that I don't have one true friend I can count on who is living nearby."

"I'm glad that my being here gives you some comfort." I tried to lighten the conversation. "I must say I enjoyed our little caper this morning, although I am curious as to why we did it."

Dolores was mystified. "Caper? You make us sound like Thelma and Louise. What are you talking about?"

"Just before we left the house, I was running around locking up the office while you were photographing everything in sight. I followed your orders, boss lady, but I wasn't sure what was on your mind."

"To be honest, Willis wasn't a man who liked to share his financial information, even with me. Take the koi pond. I asked if we could place one along the driveway, and Willis said that it sounded like a terrific idea. When I asked if we could afford it, he just laughed and told me not to worry, that we could afford to buy the house and alter it and the property any way we wanted. Either he was rich as Croesus, or I am now a widow in hock up to her ears."

I was surprised Dolores even considered that Willis might have been living above his means. It never occurred to me that Willis was pretending to be wealthy, not with everyone around him kowtowing to his every wish and whim.

Dolores continued. "I don't want anyone—not Clancy, not Norman, not even some expensive accountant—to go through Willis's papers before I have had a chance to look at them. I can't handle any more shocks."

"Surely that can wait. There will be plenty of time in the weeks ahead . . ."

"No. It can't wait. Evil hubby number one and evil hubby number two each left me penniless. For my own sanity I need to make sure that whatever Willis left, he left in good order. And there's Abby to consider. Her financial future."

Abby! I mentally reviewed the conversation between Willis and Clancy I had overheard a couple of nights ago. I had no idea if Willis really intended to make Dolores the trustee of Abby's trust fund. For all I knew, he was merely tormenting Clancy, as Marjory suggested he was inclined to do.

"Dolores, did you know that Willis had already set up a trust fund for Abby?"

"No, I didn't. That's such a relief. She'll be taken care of. How do you know about the trust and I don't?"

"I overheard a conversation, but never mind that. What's important is that you confirm the terms of the trust and the name of the trustee."

"Wait. Who is her trustee? Clancy, I suppose. Of course it would be. He's her father."

I sighed. "That may be so, but the other night Willis was telling Clancy that he was about to be removed as trustee."

"Removed? Could Willis do that?"

"Well, he seemed absolutely sure he could, and he told Clancy that he wanted to put you in charge of the trust. Clancy vehemently objected and stormed off. I went to the library to pick out a bedtime read, and that was that."

Even as her eyes welled up with tears, Dolores's smile was radiant. "Oh, Jess, do you know what this means? Willis loved me and trusted me enough to know I would take care of Abby with all the love in my heart."

I dug around in my purse and passed her a packet of tissues. "That is pretty much what he said. He was adamant when he told Clancy that you would always have Abby's best interest at heart. He trusted you, and yes, I do believe he must have loved you very much."

Elton turned into a long driveway past a bright blue and white sign announcing we were at the county Coroner's Office. As he pulled into a parking spot, Dolores took out a compact and began fussing with her hair and makeup. "I don't want to embarrass Willis by showing up tearstained and disheveled. He would want me to look good, to show off the lady he married—his doll. That's why I wore this outfit. He always said his doll looked extra classy in navy blue."

When Elton opened the car door he was wearing a dark gray jacket. He helped me out of the car, and then offered his arm to Dolores. "I don't want to intrude, but I do think, ma'am, it might be useful if I came along inside."

Dolores slipped her arm through his and walked resolutely toward the building. I had to admire how she held herself erect when she was about to face one of the worst moments of her life.

Chapter Ten

Deputy Lascomb was waiting in the vestibule. "Sheriff Halvorson sends regards. He hopes this won't be too difficult for you, Mrs. Nickens. I took the liberty of signing us in. An escort will be here in a jiffy. Why don't we have a seat in the lobby while we wait?"

Dolores's "Thank you" was barely a whisper.

Lascomb ushered us to an austere but immaculate waiting area, and after Dolores and I were seated he turned his attention to Elton. "And you, sir? Are you a relative? I know Mr. Nickens had a son-in-law. Would that be you?"

I would guess Elton's age to be somewhere in the twenty to twenty-five range, so I wasn't at all surprised when he giggled nervously. Being a son-in-law would mean he'd have to have a wife somewhere, and he undoubtedly wasn't ready for that. "No, sir, I'm not family to Miss Dolores. I'm brother to Marla Mae."

"Marla Mae? The housemaid?" That seemed to confuse the deputy. "Then why—"

I cut in. "Since I don't have a driver's license, I hired Elton to ferry me around while I'm in town. With all that's happened, it seemed like a wise choice"—I nodded slightly toward Dolores—"to ask him to drive us today."

"Makes perfect sense. I wish more families would think the way you do when they have to deal with, er, something like this." His own words made him uncomfortable. He brushed his hands together lightly, as if he was shaking off cookie crumbs, then walked to the edge of the room and peered down the hallway, but didn't see anyone coming to his rescue.

He was moving back toward us when we all heard a door closing, and then quick footsteps coming nearer. A petite woman with wavy black hair in a stylish blunt cut walked into the room. There was a hint of a sunny disposition behind her somber professional face. Her deep brown eyes moved from Dolores to me and back again. She looked at the folder in her hands, then back at the two of us.

"Mrs. Nickens?"

Dolores looked up and nodded.

"I'm Evelyn Young"—she pointed to the emblem on her gray golf shirt—"deputy coroner. I am so sorry for your loss. My job is to make the process of identification as painless as possible for you and your family."

Lascomb opened his mouth, perhaps to correct her assumption that Elton and I were family, but then he closed it without speaking.

Evelyn pulled a chair closer to Dolores. "I am going

to explain our process to you, and then when you are
ready to see your husband, you let me know. There is
no hurry."

I was sure Dolores found Evelyn's soothing demeanor as comforting as I did, because by the time
Evelyn had completed her explanation, Dolores had
released my hand from her viselike grip.

We sat in silence for a few moments, and then Dolores stood. Elton was by her side in a flash, and she
took his arm. Deputy Lascomb and I fell in behind
them. Evelyn led us to a small room with light blue
walls and one wide window, with white drapery on
the far side of the glass.

Evelyn had a phone in her hand. "Now, Mrs. Nickens, you tell me when you are ready, and I will tell
Clarice to open the curtain. As I said before, Mr. Nickens will be lying on his back and a sheet will cover
him from feet to shoulders. You will be able see his
face clearly."

"I'm ready." Dolores's voice was surprisingly strong.
Elton stood at her side, with one arm around her so
his hands were lending support to both of her arms.

Evelyn put the phone to her ear. "Clarice, we are
ready."

The white curtains slowly began to open. The only
thing we could see was a white sheet draped over the
center of Willis's lifeless body. All at once the curtains
jerked completely open and Willis's head came into
view.

Dolores sobbed and her knees buckled, but Elton
had a secure grasp and he kept her steady. Deputy
Lascomb pulled a folding chair from the corner of the

room, and he and Evelyn helped Dolores sit. Elton took a bottle of water out of his pocket and insisted Dolores take a drink.

While everyone was distracted, I moved to the window for a closer look at Willis. The left side of Willis's body was facing the window. His eyes were closed and his face was ashen, his florid color long gone. I leaned against the window and stood on my toes. I was sure I saw a slight discoloration under his right eye, but no matter how I stretched or strained I couldn't see the right side of his face. Was it only a shadow? Or was it a bruise? And if it was a bruise, how did it get there?

"Jess, you're in my way." Dolores sounded drained.

I moved away from the window and stood against the far wall, deep in thought. If Willis had a bruise . . . Well, there was the heavy white river rock that didn't belong in the koi pond. I was becoming more and more convinced that Willis Nickens's death was no accident.

I caught Evelyn studying me. I gave a tentative smile and she came right to my side. "Are you all right, ma'am? Do you need a chair or perhaps some fresh air?"

Bingo! If I could get her alone and ask a few questions . . . "I am a bit light-headed. Perhaps I could go back to the waiting area . . ." I took a step toward the door.

Evelyn immediately said, "Why don't I walk with you?"

She signaled Lascomb, and then she and I walked down the hall. I sat in a chair while Evelyn hovered around me, offering water and even a cup of tea.

She looked relieved when, after a few minutes, I told her that I was feeling much better.

"Would you like to go back and say your good-byes to Mr. Nickens?"

I shook my head. "I think I will let Dolores say a private good-bye. One thing though: In the car on the way here, she repeatedly hoped that you would be able to tell us the actual cause of death. Did he have a heart attack, or—"

Evelyn cut me right off. "I am sorry, ma'am. The coroner's report is not finalized, and when it is it will have to go through proper channels. I wish I could help but I can't."

She pulled out her cell phone and said, "Clarice, it's time to close the curtains."

Elton had Dolores firmly in his grip and Deputy Lascomb was right behind them. Dolores held her emotions in check just enough that she was able to thank both Evelyn and Lascomb for their kindness without bursting into tears.

Elton got us settled in the car and promptly handed us each a bottle of water and opened one for himself.

"You were such a huge help, Elton. I am extremely glad you are with us today," Dolores said.

"It's completely my honor. Would either of you ladies like some fruit or a muffin?"

When we declined, he took off his jacket, folded it carefully, and placed it on the front passenger seat. Then he climbed into the driver's seat and started the engine. "We don't need to be heading out anywhere just yet, but I thought some air-conditioning might be the cooling off we all could use."

After a while Dolores said, "I guess it was the shock of seeing Willis lying there so still. In life he was a dynamo—always go, go, go. That was the reason Willis insisted we have separate bedrooms. Even in his sleep he would flail and roll from one side of the bed to the other all night long. Did you ever hear of anything like that?"

"Oh yes. In fact, back in Cabot Cove, Micah Wilson had to have rails put on his bed after one night, while sound asleep, he tumbled out of the bed and broke his shoulder."

"Willis was afraid that while he was asleep he would punch me with a thrashing arm or kick me with a flailing leg. I was willing to risk it, but he said he would never forgive himself if he injured me even by accident."

Dolores leaned back in her seat. "I guess we should be on our way. Elton, do you know where the Harrold Brothers Funeral Home is located?"

"Sure 'nuff. It's right along Colonial Drive. You want me to head on over?"

"If you would. I think it's time for me to get everything done so Willis can have the final honors he deserves. Don't you, Jess?"

"Of course. As long as you feel up to the task."

"Well, I suppose the staff at Harrold Brothers will take care of organizing, but it would help for me to have a list." She began ticking off on her fingers. "I'd like Pastor Forde to hold the memorial service over at Holy Mission Church. It's cozy and so peaceful. Willis and I were married there. Then flowers. Willis didn't care much about flowers, but I think he should have a few bouquets around him."

She thought for a moment, tilting her head to one side. "Elton, I have noticed Marla Mae has a way with flowers . . ."

"She does that, ma'am."

"Do you think she could be persuaded to team up with Toni Eggers over at Buds and Blossoms to create some understated but elegant floral arrangements to adorn the coffin?" Her voice started to crack.

"Miss Dolores, Marla Mae will do anything you need. You have only to let her know."

Dolores sniffled. "That would be awfully kind of her. I know Willis was demanding when it came to the staff, so I am doubly relieved that you think she'll help out."

I reasoned it was likely that Marla Mae would extend herself to do her best for Dolores and just ignore the way Willis had treated her in the past.

Dolores continued with her list of priorities. "I will need to decide on some charities for donations in lieu of flowers, and there is Willis's obituary to consider. Jess, you're a writer . . ."

I should have seen this coming. "Well, that's true—I am—but I write fiction. I invent stories from whole cloth. An obituary is factual, a testament to the life of the decedent . . ."

"Oh, bosh. I can tell you everything you need to know. Please, Jess. You'll get it right. I know you will."

"If that's what you want, Dolores. I will do my best." What else could I say?

If Willis was as prominent in the community as he seemed to be, it was likely a local newspaper had an "advance obit," a prewritten obituary they updated periodically that was ready to print at a moment's notice with only the addition of the final facts. I could start there.

"You're a good friend, Jess." Dolores sighed. "That was the one thing missing from Willis's life. He knew so many people but there is no one who I could point to as being his good, true friend. How sad is that?"

"Sad as that may be, Willis was lucky enough to be well loved by you and by Abby. Many people never have that close a connection with anyone."

I hadn't even noticed we were in the mortuary parking lot until the car had stopped and I heard Elton pop the locks.

Dolores looked around. "Oh, we're here. Elton, you are a treasure."

He looked over his seat back. "I try, ma'am. I truly do."

His face was so sincere that Dolores broke into a smile. I was happy to see it. I knew it was the first of many that would creep back into her life day by day, although I was sure she wouldn't recognize that now.

Jonah Harrold was the oldest of the three brothers who owned the funeral parlor, which was founded by their father and his younger brother. He proudly showed us oil paintings of the founding brothers hung inside the entryway, and then led us to his office.

We sat in plush high-backed chairs around a cherry-wood conference table with a herringbone inlaid top.

The room was painted bright yellow, and half a dozen vivid watercolor paintings of birds and flowers adorned the walls. I'd never seen such a cheery room in a funeral parlor.

"Mrs. Nickens, we were all sorry to hear about Willis. He and I belonged to the same chapter of the Rotary Club, and my brother Dillon served on the Community Hospital fund-raising committee with Willis for several years. He did so much good. It's a real loss to the service community." He stopped for half a beat. "And to you, of course."

"Thank you. I admit that I am lost, adrift, confused— all those things. I thank the Lord my good friend Jessica happened to be in town for a visit when the . . . accident happened. She helps bring me strength."

Jonah Harrold smiled at me, and returned his attention to Dolores. "May I ask where Mr. Nickens is at present?"

"He's at the Coroner's Office, and before you ask, I don't know when they will allow you to bring Willis here."

He looked perplexed but decided to let that drop rather than make further inquiries. I am sure he knew as well as I did that if Willis had died by accident, Harrold Brothers would have collected the body by now.

"I want to be prepared for when they do release him, so I thought I would come to discuss plans with you."

"Very wise, very wise indeed, Mrs. Nickens. If you would like to take a look at our facility and pick a room you think is suitable . . ."

Dolores interrupted. "First, I have a list of what I

have decided so far. I was hoping you would coordinate it all. Holy Mission Church, flowers from Buds and Blossoms, and Marla Mae Anderson will work with them to approve the arrangements. Jessica will take charge of the obituary, and we will be asking for charitable donations, so you won't be inundated with floral deliveries."

Jonah nodded. "My, you have given funeral plans a lot of thought in a very short period of time."

I detected a slight tone of suspicion in his voice, so I chimed in, "Actually, we discussed these arrangements in the car on our way here. I am a widow myself, so I was able to help Dolores decide what she needed to do."

If, as I suspected, Willis was a victim of foul play, I was sure the sheriff already had his eye firmly on Dolores. My intention was to distract the funeral director from any such thoughts.

Oblivious to the accusatory current swirling around her, Dolores said, "I am glad you mentioned the Community Hospital fund. Willis did work very hard on that committee. I think the fund should be one of the charities we suggest."

Jonah Harrold stood. "That's a grand idea. Now if there is nothing else that comes to mind, shall we take a look at the facility? Rest assured we'll meet your wishes when the Coroner's Office allows us to receive Mr. Nickens."

Chapter Eleven

Jessica Fletcher. Long time, no hear." Harry McGraw sounded as feisty as ever when he answered my call on the first ring.

When we had arrived home from Harrold Brothers, Dolores could scarcely drag herself into the house. Pleading exhaustion, she went directly to her room for a nap, which gave me time to call my favorite Boston private investigator. I was delighted to reach him so quickly. If he was working undercover or was otherwise embroiled, it would often take a few days for him to return a call.

"Hello, Harry. You're right. I have been remiss, but, well, I was on deadline with my last book; then I went to a mystery conference in Bethesda—such a great time—and for the past few days I have been staying with a friend in South Carolina."

"Jessica, South Carolina? Really? Isn't it like ninety

degrees there every hour of the day and night? We New Englanders don't like hot weather."

"Actually it's not nearly that hot, and the scenery is quite lovely." I looked out my window. "There's a gorgeous tree that grows down here called a crepe myrtle, and they are in full flower all around my friend Dolores's house, not to mention along the highways and byways."

"Better not let Doc Hazlitt or Sheriff Mort hear you praising trees unless you are talking about solid New England red maples. You know they both think you spend too much time on the road as it is."

Harry certainly had that right.

"And speaking of the road, when are you coming to Boston? I stopped by Il Cibo the other night for some gnocchi Bolognese and Angelo was asking for you. He claims you class up the joint, while I bring it down a peg or two."

I laughed. "Oh, Harry, Angelo is far too agreeable to say something like that."

"Which part, you being classy or me being the down peg? Anyway, I have a great invitation for you. The Boston Symphony has scheduled a very upper-crusty kind of concert with some major European opera singers—I didn't pay attention to the names, but you probably know them. I thought you might want to show up."

"A concert? With opera singers? Harry, that doesn't sound like anything you would enjoy."

"It's not, but it does sound right up your alley, Jessica. A friend of mine got the security gig and asked me to help out, so I can get you in for free. And we can visit Angelo for dinner. You know he'll make something extra special, like that chicken saltimbocca from his mother's old recipe, if his favorite Cabot Cove lady is in town."

"Well, that is an attractive offer, very hard to resist. I'll call you when I get home and see what we can do, but in the meantime . . ."

"In the meantime you need me to take a look-see at something or somebody. Am I right?" His drawn-out sigh gave the impression that my asking was a terrible imposition.

"Harry, are you ever wrong?" I could almost see his grimace morph into a grin.

I gave him a brief rundown of my visit with Dolores at Manning Hall and ended by telling him about Willis's untimely death.

"Untimely death, my eye. Just say it, Jess. The guy was murdered and you are on the case. Murder follows you like a gambler follows the ponies."

"Harry, I do *suspect* Willis was murdered. Neither the sheriff nor the Coroner's Office will confirm cause of death, at least not to me, not even to his widow. But Dolores is one of my oldest, dearest friends and I want to be prepared in case the sheriff comes knocking."

"Gotcha. So, how can I help? First tell me the dead guy's name and particulars so I can scratch it on a pad. That way I won't have to call you back a hundred times with questions like 'How do you spell the last name?' or 'Where did you say he lived?'"

"His name is Willis Nickens. His wife's name is Dolores."

Harry kept asking questions until he was satisfied

that he knew as much as I did about Willis and Dolores.

"One thing I don't get, Jess. If this guy is such a big-deal businesswise, how is it that you don't know exactly what kind of business he's in? How does a guy have no money worries but even his wife doesn't know exactly what he does? Sounds shady to me."

In truth the phrase "shady business" had crossed my mind when it came to Willis's finances.

"Well, the word 'investments' came up a time or two, and there was the mention of at least one real estate deal." I was as exasperated with my lack of knowledge as Harry was. Then I remembered. "Oh, wait. The Rotary. I recently heard that Willis was a member of the local Rotary Club, and he also served on a fund-raising committee for Community Hospital. Wouldn't his business affiliation be known in those organizations?"

"Now you're using your noggin. That'll be my way in, for sure. And once I am in, who am I looking for?"

"Willis has a business partner—at least they say they are partners, but whether there is one business or a dozen . . . His name is Norman Crayfield. I have no idea what his business interests are or even where he lives. Right now he's staying at Manning Hall—I did mention that's Dolores's house, didn't I? He was here when I arrived and shows no signs of leaving."

"Hold on—pen dried up."

Through the phone I could hear Harry shake his pen, drop it, and fumble through a drawer for another one. When he was ready, he asked, "Okay, who else?"

"I have been thinking. Willis's daughter died a few

years back, leaving a husband and a small child. Willis dotes on the little girl . . ."

Harry picked up my thread. "The kid will get buckets now that Grandpa's gone, and the kid's father will have control 'cause she's a minor. Father's name?"

"Clancy Travers. But that's all I have. He and his little girl, Abby, are staying at Manning Hall right now, but I do know they don't live there—Dolores called them houseguests. He'll be local, though, because Dolores talked about visiting back and forth quite often."

"The daughter's death—anything suspicious there?"

"I don't think so. From what I understand it was an aggressive brain tumor. Sad in one so young."

"Sad for anybody. Who else you got? Servants? This guy's gotta have servants who hate him."

"There are two. Lucinda Green is unflappable and has been with Willis since long before he married Dolores. Because of her, this place runs like a fine-tuned Swiss watch. I don't see any potential there. Marla Mae Anderson was terrified of Willis but lacks the resourcefulness to commit murder. Even if she killed him accidentally, she would likely have sat by the body and cried until someone came along so she could confess."

"I'll back-burner the servants on your say-so but they stay on the list. Who else you looking at?"

"There are a couple of neighbors, Tom and Candy Blomquist. They own a hotel named Jessamine House that is quite nearby. They approached Willis for a loan to renovate, and Willis kept them dangling even though I heard he was adamantly opposed to the deal. Now he's dead and the Blomquists are quite chirpy, confident the money is on the way."

"And you're wondering how that came to be. Could be a coincidence, but you know how I feel about coinkydinks . . ."

"Ain't no such thing," we said in unison.

"Harry, I did meet a person who hated Willis with a blazing passion so obvious that even a complete stranger like me could see it."

"Blazing passion, huh? Now that's the kind of suspect I can get behind. You got a name? Although I gotta say, Jessica, you see things most strangers wouldn't even notice."

"The lady in question is called Marjory Ribault. Apparently her family owned Manning Hall and the surrounding property for generations. When her father fell on hard times Willis swooped in and took away her family home. You should have seen her in the same room with him. She could hardly stand to look at him."

"So, other than a murder the sheriff won't verify and being surrounded by suspects everywhere you turn, how's South Carolina treating you?"

"I can tell you this, Harry: I have never been called 'ma'am' so much in my entire life."

I curled up in the comfy chair, looking out the window at the colorful tops of the crepe myrtle trees, and mulled over my conversation with Harry. I was completely frustrated by my inability to get any information about Willis's death from the sheriff or the coroner. I sincerely hoped they were merely following a strict governmental policy and not trying to keep

Dolores guessing as to what they knew and how they knew it. I was confident that even from as far away as Boston, Harry McGraw would be able to dig deep and learn whatever I needed to suss out a killer and protect Dolores. I did notice that Harry never asked me why I was so sure that Willis was murdered and that Dolores had nothing to do with the killing. That was the thing about Harry—his gut instinct about me was as precise as my gut instinct about Dolores. Between the two of us, she would be well protected.

I decided to go for a run. The day was too lovely to stay indoors, even with the crepe myrtles for company.

I put on my jogging suit and headed to the kitchen. Elton was sitting at the table, thumbing through a book. As soon as he saw me he stood. "Are you in need of a ride?"

"Not at all. What I need is a nice, leisurely run to get my energy back. I just wanted someone to know that I've gone out to explore the grounds in case Dolores needs me."

I looked at the book he'd left on the table. "If you don't mind my asking, what is that you're reading?"

He held up a brightly colored catalogue with MID-LANDS TECHNICAL COLLEGE printed in large letters. "I go to night school. I'm studying how to open and run my own business. I love what I do. Helping people safely get from where they are to where they want to be—what could be better? I'll tell you what: doing it on my own, without a boss making decisions for me. I know I can make them for myself."

"That is commendable, Elton. I wish you great luck

in pursuing your education. Also, I think we can safely say that Mrs. Nickens is thoroughly exhausted and we won't be going out later. Why don't you go home and get some extra study time in? Marla Mae will call you in the morning with tomorrow's schedule."

Elton gathered up his books and said good-bye. When he opened the back door Lucinda was on the other side with a basket overflowing with asparagus. She came in and set the basket by the work sink. "My cousin and her children just came back from fishing over on Lake Marion. Caught plenty of fine blue catfish, with more than a little to spare. Dinner tonight will be fresh catfish and fresh asparagus. Can't do much better than that."

"I can't wait. That sounds absolutely delicious. Do you have a farmer nearby who delivers vegetables?" I asked.

"No, ma'am. Way out back is our kitchen garden. It's been there for years. When Mr. Willis bought this place, he liked the idea of 'eating off the land,' as he called it, so he allowed me to cultivate and harvest. Asparagus is in season right now."

"I'm about to spend half an hour or so familiarizing myself with our gorgeous surroundings. Perhaps I will take a look at the garden. I promise not to disturb anything."

"Nothing there to disturb. If you go out the back door, pass by the putting green, and follow the path through the pine trees, you'll find the kitchen garden right in front of you."

The back door led to a small wooden porch with a cozy sitting area. I could picture relaxing at the picnic table and shucking corn or shelling peas under a cloudless sky.

I did some light stretching and then started off. As I turned the corner of the house, I came to a full stop. Both Clancy and Lucinda had mentioned a putting green, but this one would have fit right in at the Augusta National Golf Club. The green itself was manicured to perfection and must have been at least two thousand square feet, with three distinct holes marked by pristine white flags flying in the breeze. A sand trap was off to the left, and directly in front of me was a water hazard.

I couldn't imagine frustrated golfer Seth Hazlitt's reaction to a putting green like this. I took out my phone and snapped a few pictures so I could text them and get Seth in a tizzy.

I jogged through the pine trees, and came to the kitchen garden in a couple of minutes. It was much closer to the house than I'd expected. The tomato plants were staked alongside a row of carrots—always a good combination. A small, neatly labeled herb garden was set off to one side and surrounded by the same white river rocks that edged the sitting garden. Every planted area was meticulously weeded.

As I bent down to read some of the herb labels, I heard a rustling sound near the edge of the pinewood. I turned to see a woman pushing branches out of her path as she ran away. I pulled out my phone and snapped two blurry pictures, but even as I did

I realized that such a tall woman could only have been Marjory Ribault. But why would she have been skulking around the kitchen garden? I began to jog along the path she had taken. Perhaps this was one mystery I could solve.

Chapter Twelve

I reached a clearing in the trees and found Marjory Ribault sitting on a garden swing in front of a quaint cottage. She had a red bowl in her lap. When she saw me she stooped and pushed the bowl under the swing, but not before I noticed the asparagus tips peeking over the top.

"What brings you to the poor side of town?" Marjory asked. Although she tried to sound as if she was joking, there was a tinge of irony in her voice.

"Oh, I was out for a jog, following this path and that. The path behind the kitchen garden led me here."

When I said the words "kitchen garden" a guilty look flashed across Marjory's face but was instantly replaced by an expression of indifference. Could she possibly have been afraid I would cause trouble for her over a few asparagus spears?

I tried to help her relax by making a show of scrutinizing the cottage. "My, you have a lovely place here. So bucolic and peaceful."

"This is all I have left since Willis Nickens blackmailed my father. Or I think 'swindled' is a better word. We used to have a grand driveway here, and this was the gateman's house. Now Willis has forty-five acres and I have not quite two hundred square yards, with the house taking up most of it."

"I imagine that must be challenging for you." I glanced at the swing. "Perhaps we should sit for a while and you can tell me how it came to be."

She wavered for a few seconds and then made a decision. "Actually I'd like that. It would be such a relief to talk to someone who doesn't already have an opinion one way or another about Willis. Where are my manners? Please, come inside. I made some fresh lemonade this morning."

For such a rustic cottage, the kitchen was extremely modern, even including an in-the-wall steam oven, similar to one I had recently seen at Charles Department Store. Jim Ranieri, who owns the store with his brother David, assured me steam ovens are the up-and-coming appliance guaranteed to make food healthier and tastier. At the time, I settled for a new microwave. Someday I would have to ask Marjory how she liked her steam oven, but this was not the day.

We sat at a round pedestal table covered by a white cloth with a decorative trim of bluebirds in flight. Marjory's lemonade was delicious and I told her so.

"The secret is a light dusting of confectioners' sugar on the lemon halves before I squeeze them in a good old-fashioned hand squeezer. Takes away a bit of the tartness but doesn't make it sugary sweet like something out of a bottle."

"I'll have to remember to try that when I get back to Cabot Cove."

She nodded. "And whatever you do, don't use an electric juicer. Elbow grease does a superior job."

"In my experience that is true of so many things."

"Mrs. Fletcher . . ."

"Jessica, please."

"Jessica, the first thing I want to assure you of is that your friend Dolores had nothing to do with Willis's outrageous thievery. She is a sweet, warmhearted woman, and for the life of me, I never understood what she saw in Willis Nickens." She looked at me as if expecting an answer.

"Affairs of the heart . . . who knows?" I shrugged.

"I guess. Anyway, my family has lived on this land for generations. My father owned it, as did my grandfather and his father before him. After my mother passed, Dad and I lived a peaceful existence and, I am embarrassed to admit, I had no idea about money, where it came from or where it went. Unfortunately, my father got sick. Lung cancer. He was headed for a slow and painful death." Marjory started to tear up at the memory.

I reached over and gave her a sympathetic pat on the shoulder. "I am so sorry. That's so grueling for a family member to go through."

Marjory went on. "I didn't know that over the years Dad had had serious money problems and mounting debt. He took out private loans, with the property as collateral. It's a common practice among the old families. They call it 'helping each other out.' Then one day Willis showed up. Dad sent me out of the room but, naturally, I listened at the door. Willis was such a bully. I am sickened to this day that I was the pawn he used. He had bought up the loans and could call them due at any time. He said Dad had two choices: He could keep the house and leave me destitute and homeless when he died, or he could sign the house over to Willis. The debts would be canceled and Willis would set up a tiny trust fund so that I wouldn't starve. He actually said that to my father: 'You don't want your daughter to starve, do you?' Can you imagine?"

Although my acquaintance with Willis Nickens had been brief, I had no problem envisioning that he was capable of such despicable behavior. "That is truly reprehensible. If you don't mind my asking, how did you acquire this cottage?"

Marjory sniffed. "When my father told Willis I had lived here all of my life and could never live anywhere else, Willis didn't flinch. He'd obviously anticipated that roadblock and immediately offered to include this cottage in the trust—which is a revocable trust, I might add."

Revocable trusts seemed to be the core mechanism Willis used to bend people to his will. First with Clancy, now with Marjory. I wondered who else he controlled that way.

Marjory sighed. "Well, at least I have some privacy because Willis moved the driveway. Not for my benefit, of course. He said this approach didn't show Manning

Hall to full advantage. He wanted everyone who drove up to be in awe of his house, the house that should be my house."

The mention of the driveway triggered a notion lodged in my mind. "Speaking of the driveway, do you happen to have a clicker for the gate?"

"Sure, do you need one? I don't have a car right now but I keep a couple handy for guests, deliveries, and the like."

"Oh, no, thank you. The gate is so imposing; I was curious how accessible it actually is."

But I already knew the answer. Marjory confirmed what Elton had told me. So much for security. The clickers were treated so casually that anyone and everyone could easily get one and enter through the gate at will. The Blomquists were the only people in the house before Willis's death who hadn't actually stayed on the grounds the night he died. And according to Dolores they were frequent guests, so if one of them had managed to get their hands on a clicker it would have been easy to circle back for a midnight tête-à-tête with Willis Nickens.

As I made my way back to the house through the pine trees and past the kitchen garden, I remembered what Dolores had told me. She was so proud of her bold, decisive husband who had bought the house and asked her to marry him all in one day. Perhaps it would be for the best if she never learned how Willis had maneuvered to make Manning Hall their home.

Clancy Travers was focused on chipping a golf ball out of the sand trap. He had just begun his swing when Abby saw me and waved her forearm. "Mrs. Fletcher!

We went to the zoo. It was so much fun. Look, I have a koala tattoo on my arm."

Clancy's face morphed in frustration as the distraction completely crumpled his stance. He laughed. "I probably wasn't going to pop it with one shot anyway. I'm still working out the kinks of my new sand wedge."

I oohed and aahed over Abby's tattoo and listened attentively while she told me how koalas sleep most of the day and that makes them very cuddly. She asked if I knew where they came from and was impressed when I said, "Australia."

Clancy interrupted. "Okay, sweetie, why don't you check the hummingbird feeder and see if we need to make more nectar? Daddy wants to talk to Mrs. Fletcher for a minute."

Abby ran off toward a red plastic feeder that hung from a tall metal pole, and Clancy said, "She's making me nervous. At every exhibit she talked about Emily and Willis. 'Mommy read me a story once about koalas; Grampy said he would take me to see the tigers, but we didn't have time to go.' I don't know what to say, what to do." He spread his hands in a gesture of hopelessness.

"I'm sure it is a difficult time. Fortunately Abby still has Dolores, who is connected in her mind to Willis, and therefore to Emily," I suggested. Knowing Dolores's fear of losing Abby, I hoped to shore up her cause.

"How is Dolores doing? I gather today was tough for her. Seeing Willis . . . I remember with Emily." Clancy looked down. His grief seemed genuine.

"She did have a daunting time, but she is much stronger than she knows. She'll come through this. Of that I am certain." I tried to sound confident. In reality, I wasn't sure myself.

"I wonder—" Clancy paused, took a deep breath, then charged ahead. "Do you think it would help if Abby and I moved into Manning Hall permanently?"

I was rendered speechless. Surely it was too soon to consider taking such a step. Dolores might jump at the chance, thinking it would strengthen her relationship with Abby. But what was Clancy's true motive? Did he think he and Abby could live in Manning Hall rent free with an adoring and now-wealthy Granny Dolores? I had heard Willis tell Clancy that Dolores would be well provided for. Was this Clancy's way of ensuring his share? He could access the benefits of Willis's fortune without having to deal with the annoyance of Willis himself.

"I would think that would be something to be decided in a year or so, when Dolores has acclimated herself to life without Willis."

If my response disappointed Clancy, he didn't show it.

"That probably would be for the best. Dolores will need time, probably a lot of time." Clancy turned and waved to his daughter. "Come on, Abby. It's nearly dinnertime. We'd better get cleaned up."

As they began to navigate the circular walk to the front of the house I heard Abby fret, "I don't have to wash off my koala tattoo, do I?"

I smiled when I heard Clancy answer, "No, sweetie, you don't."

I headed for the back door, and as soon as I opened it the aroma of Cajun spices enveloped me, bringing back memories of my most recent trip to New Orleans. It would be fun to go back there sometime soon. Maybe in a few months I could talk Dolores into a girls' jaunt to the Big Easy. I tucked that thought away for now.

Lucinda was drying her hands on a dish towel. "I was beginning to wonder where you'd gone off to. Marla Mae brought Miss Dolores a dinner tray in her room. I suppose Mr. Clancy, Abby, and Mr. Norman will be in the dining room. Would you care to join them, or would you like a tray?"

Before I could answer, the chimes in the hall and the buzzer in the kitchen sang out in direct competition with each other. For my money, the chimes would always win.

Lucinda started toward the hallway, but I held up my hand. "You have enough to do with dinner. It's probably Clancy and Abby—they left the putting green and were walking to the front door at the same time I was coming to the kitchen."

Lucinda nodded. "Mighty kind of you."

Clancy must have already let himself in with a key, because when I opened the front door I was surprised to see Norman Crayfield standing on the veranda, pulling at the collar of his wrinkled tan dress shirt. "Oh, hi, Jessica. It is way too hot today for a button-down shirt."

The driver of a green sedan at the edge of the veranda tapped the horn in a friendly good-bye, and I saw Tom Blomquist at the wheel. Norman ignored the beep, but I waved good-bye, at least in part to let Tom know that I had seen him.

"You'll be glad you got back in time for dinner. There's fresh-caught catfish." I thought I would start the conversation on a genial note.

"That is great news. Nobody fries catfish like Lucinda—crispy outside and tender inside. And the spices! I hope she had time to make hush puppies. Mm-hmm." Norman smacked his lips.

He had me there. "Well, I'm not sure about hush puppies, but I know there will be fresh asparagus."

"Oh, there she goes, ruining a perfectly good dinner by adding healthy food." Norman laughed.

I purposely caught him unawares when I said, "So you spent some time with Tom Blomquist. Did you happen to reach an agreement about the funding for Jessamine House?"

Norman looked awkward, but his response was strong. "No, never. How could I do that without Dolores's consent? I'm sure we'll have plenty of time to address it after Willis is . . . well, after Willis is put to rest." He ran a finger around his collar again. "I'd best change this shirt before dinner."

He took the stairs two at a time, looking unexpectedly agile for a man his age.

No matter what Norman wanted me to believe about his business relationship with the Blomquists, Tom Blomquist's chirpiness the last time I had seen him made me sure he, at least, was convinced that Norman would tell Dolores that the deal had been struck and that Dolores would be too caught up in her mourning to object.

I also wondered how Tom's car had come through the gate. Plainly he had a clicker.

Marla Mae was in the dining room, setting the table for dinner. I told her not to set a place for me; then I walked back to the kitchen, where Lucinda was bustling about, seeing to the last-minute dinner preparations. "Did you decide where you want to eat tonight?"

I said I would like to eat in the kitchen if it was no bother. "It's cozy in here, and smells so good. I've had a long day and don't want to make small talk at the dinner table."

My request seemed to put her on guard, but she could hardly say no.

I washed my hands at the kitchen sink, and while I was drying them I said to Lucinda, "I saw Marjory Ribault down at the kitchen garden today. She'd pulled up some asparagus. Is that something you allow? Are you two friends?"

Lucinda put her hands on her hips. "Those asparagus stalks are in the garden because Miss Marjory's grandma planted them long before any of us were born. The entire kitchen garden was her grandma's work. I know for a fact Miss Marjory still does her share of weeding. What harm can it do to let her have a few fresh vegetables from a garden she has worked all her life?"

"No harm that I see. However, when some time has passed it might be a good idea for you to tell Dolores about your arrangement with Marjory regarding the kitchen garden."

"Yes, ma'am, I surely will. Your dinner is ready." Lucinda set a plate of catfish, asparagus, and hush puppies on the table.

As I pulled out my chair I looked at the hush puppies and thought Norman was sure to be delighted—but not as delighted as Tom Blomquist would be if he got the money he so sorely desired.

Chapter Thirteen

I woke up to the sound of a woodpecker hammering in a nearby tree. I leaned across the desk to look out each window but couldn't see him, so I guessed he was in the pines rather than the crepe myrtles. As I straightened, I noticed the text icon on my cell. I had two messages, both from Harry McGraw, who either was a very early riser or, more likely, hadn't yet been to bed when he sent them.

3:08 AM: Quartermaster Industries W.N. and others. Talk when I have more

It hadn't taken Harry long to find at least one business with Willis Nickens's name attached. This might be an excellent starting point for unraveling Willis's finances. I wondered if Dolores knew anything about the company and Willis's relationship to it.

I eagerly tapped on the second text, which read:

3:10 AM: M.R. 2X collared for shoplifting. Still digging

Marjory Ribault had played the financial innocent. She'd claimed to have no idea about the family money, how it came in or how it went out. Yet she'd been arrested for shoplifting more than once, which made me think it was quite possible that she knew far more about money than she let on.

I texted back to Harry, Thanks, can't wait to talk.

I wasn't sure what Dolores had on our schedule for today, but I hoped we'd have some quiet time for a serious chat. I sat in the blue wing chair for a few minutes, drawing up a mental agenda.

First, and most immediately, Dolores needed to insist that the sheriff or the coroner tell her what caused Willis's death and when they would release his body so she could plan a funeral to honor his life and get her own future on track.

Second, she and I needed to discover as much information as we could about Willis's business interests, without using Norman Crayfield as our source. Harry had sent me one place to start. I wondered if Willis had as many business interests as Dolores seemed to think, or was Quartermaster Industries the umbrella for them all?

Third, we needed to devise a way to keep her connection with Abby strong, without allowing Clancy to impose on Dolores's good nature. I was sure he thought Dolores would be a much softer touch than

Willis ever was, and I didn't want to see her relationship with Abby become contingent on Clancy getting a huge piece of the money pie.

After completing my stretches and taking a shower I decided to forgo my morning jog in favor of breakfast with whoever might show up in the dining room. Perhaps I could learn a thing or two.

I put on my black pencil skirt and a short-sleeved mauve blouse with tiny pearl buttons, sure it would be a comfortable outfit for whatever the day might bring. My feet could use a rest from the pumps I had been wearing almost nonstop, so I was glad I'd brought along a pair of black flats.

Clancy was in the dining room pouring a cup of coffee. "Marla Mae just brought out French toast and scrambled eggs a few minutes ago. She'll be bringing sausage and bacon along in a minute or two."

"Sounds like we have delicious choices this morning." I poured my own coffee and a big glass of water.

"Lucinda is wasting her talents here. She could be a chef in any of the finest restaurants in South Carolina. I don't believe she has ever prepared a meal that didn't turn out perfect."

"I'll be happy to pass along that compliment to Lucinda for you, Mr. Clancy." Marla Mae set a tray on the breakfront, lifted the top, and pointed. "Extra-crispy bacon to the right, less so to the left. The sausage has morsels of kale and apple. Lucinda has it special ground by Mr. Archer. His farm is up the road a ways, by the railroad museum. His sausage is worth the trip—you'll see."

She was nearly out of the room when she said, "Mrs. Fletcher, I forgot to say Elton called. He's wondering what time he will be needed."

I set my coffee and water on the dining table. "Hmm, I'm really not sure. Best for him to stay home until I talk to Dolores, and then I will let you know. Tell him I said to study. He'll understand the message."

"Studying is what that boy does best." Marla Mae laughed and headed back to the kitchen.

I put a piece of French toast, a small serving of eggs, and one sausage on my plate. When I sat at the table, Clancy said, "Jessica, that will hardly keep you going until midmorning, never mind lunch."

"After I've eaten this, perhaps I will want another bite or two," I said. He didn't know how hard I would have to exercise for every extra bite.

"Before you go home you will have to ask Lucinda to make you some shrimp and grits. Oh, and her—" Clancy stopped at the sound of high heels tapping across the foyer floor.

Dolores came in, gold bracelets jangling. Her cream-colored silk blouse and black skirt were perfectly tailored. As always she looked stunning, makeup perfect and every hair in place. "Good morning. How's breakfast?"

Clancy hopped up and pulled out a chair. "Delicious. Why don't you take a seat, and I will fix you a plate?"

Dolores sat down, thanked Clancy, and then said, "So, Jess, did you have a good night's sleep?"

"I did indeed. I hope you did as well. Between

dealing with grief and taking care of the myriad chores regarding Willis . . . rest is extremely important at a time like this," I said.

"I agree. I'm barely out of bed, and I am worn to the nub already. We have lots to do today. Thank you, dear," she said as Clancy set a plate down in front of her. "French toast! My favorite. Lucinda is such a gem."

"I was just saying the very same thing to Jessica," Clancy chimed in, and when neither of us responded he tried two or three more conversation starters, but Dolores ate in silence and I followed her lead.

Eventually he drained his coffee cup and said, "Well, if you'll excuse me, ladies, I'll see if Abby is awake yet."

As soon as we could hear Clancy walking up the stairs, Dolores whispered, "Have you seen Norman yet this morning?"

I shook my head. "Only Clancy."

Marla Mae came in and began to clear the table, and Dolores repeated her question in her normal voice.

"Earlier, Mr. Crayfield went for a walk. I don't know that he came back yet." Marla Mae stacked the dirty dishes in a basin.

"Thank you," Dolores said. "Please close the door on your way out."

As soon as the door snapped shut, Dolores leaned closer and lowered her voice once again. "Today, Jessica, you and I are going to ransack Willis's office. I am determined to find out everything about all of his business arrangements—and I mean all. Norman keeps fawning over me, but I am sure that's because he knows he is stuck with me, at least for now. I don't trust him to have my best interest at heart. He's all about himself."

I tried to phrase my words carefully. "Dolores, I agree that Norman Crayfield is not your best ally, but at the moment I think discovering exactly what happened to Willis is more important than finding out every nuance of his finances. Until we hear from the sheriff or the coroner you need to be more concerned about cause of death than your inheritance."

"Please, Jess, humor me." Dolores pulled a key from her pocket and stood. "Let's go through Willis's office and get the search behind us. Once I know what's what, I promise to hound the entire government of South Carolina if that is what it takes to find out how Willis died."

I hoped it wouldn't come to that.

When Dolores opened the door Marla Mae was waiting in the foyer. "Miss Dolores, might I clean up the dining room now?"

"That will be fine." Dolores took a few steps and then stopped "Marla Mae, Jessica and I are going to spend the morning in Willis's office. We do not want to be interrupted for any reason. Is that clear?"

"Very clear, ma'am. Will that be all?"

"Yes, thank you." Dolores stood in front of the door to Willis's office. She took a deep breath, raised her chin, and threw her shoulders back. With one hand on the ornamental brass doorknob she inserted a key into the lock below it. *Click*.

She was barely in the room when she involuntarily

took a step backward. "Until we came in to lock the windows and doors the other day, I had never been in this room without Willis being present. It feels unnatural to be here."

Dolores inched her way to the leather desk chair where Willis had been sitting the day I arrived. She touched the headrest lovingly, and then grasped one of the chair arms as if holding Willis's hand.

After a while she turned to me. "Ready, Jess?"

"Of course. What would you like me to do?" I was ready to help in any way that would make Dolores feel satisfied.

"Let's start by opening the drapes and letting the sunshine brighten up this place. And then we'll get down to work." She flipped open the laptop sitting in the middle of the desk and hit the power button. "Do me a favor and open the French doors. The air in here is a little stale."

I pulled the drapes wide open, and sunlight flooded the room. I cracked the doors a few inches, and the scent of jasmine from the vines clinging to the outside wall swept the mustiness from the room. I was eager to discover any information this office held about Quartermaster Industries, but I waited for Dolores to start looking around in earnest so I could follow her lead.

I watched as she began to open the desk drawers. "Aww, Jess, look at this." She held up a menu. "The Garden Eatery. It's where Willis and I had lunch on our first date. And look—he wrote across the top: 'Dolores 1 pm.' I had no idea he was such a romantic."

Her tone quickly changed when she opened the

bottom drawer. "That son of a gun. I repeatedly told him he was not to smoke his stinking cigars in the house. Look at this."

She held up a large glass ashtray, and a decorative beige cigar box with bold white letters on a red background. **ROMEO Y JULIETA**.

"Well, you did say he was a romantic, and I guess that brand of cigars proves it," I ventured.

Dolores shot me a look and then burst out laughing. "I guess you're right. No point getting mad at a man who appreciates Romeo and Juliet." She reached down into the drawer once again and came up with a spray can of air freshener. "And at least he tried to cover up his transgression."

She hugged the can for a moment, and then said, "Okay, I'm good. Let's get to work. I'll take the computer. Would you do me a favor? Dig through the file drawers. Open whatever strikes your fancy and see what that mystery-writer nose of yours can sniff out."

The drawers were made of heavy mahogany, with handles made of dull bronze. I needed two hands to pull the first one open. An outsized tab in front of the file folders was neatly labeled A–F, with smaller tabs identifying the folders arranged within. I moved along the row of drawers, and the large tab in the third one announced that it held folders in the range from "M" to "R," exactly what I was looking for. I flipped through to the rear of the drawer and found the word QUARTERMASTER on the tab of a surprisingly thin folder. I tucked it under my arm and then began to read the names of the rest of the file folders, and my eyes went wide when I saw one labeled NORMAN'S

SCREWUPS. I pulled it out of the drawer and was surprised by how thick it was. Inside I saw dozens of
photocopies of business contracts, letters, and invoices. Most of the paperwork had handwritten notes,
which I guessed were written by Willis, and without
exception, every note seemed to indicate a mistake
Norman had made.

I was about to show the folder to Dolores when she
gave a little squeal.

"Jess, am I reading this correctly?"

I bent over her shoulder, read the e-mail she was
looking at, and asked, "Who is Marcus Holmes? Is he
a lawyer or financial adviser of some sort?"

"He's a lawyer and has represented Willis in everything from our purchase of this house to a lawsuit
regarding a car accident Willis had a few years back.
I don't know if he handles business deals, but he is
definitely Willis's personal attorney."

I nodded. "This e-mail is dated two weeks ago, and
Willis specifically says that he wants to sit down with
Mr. Holmes to review Abby's trust with a view to
making you sole trustee. We have to find out if this
meeting took place. Perhaps Willis changed the terms
of the trust."

Dolores shook her head. "Seriously? I can't believe
he would do that without asking my permission, or at
least telling me it was on his mind."

I said as gently as I could, "You did say Willis was
a charge-forward kind of man. And we both know he
was quite sure you loved Abby as if she was your
own."

Dolores sighed. "True. Well, I'll call Marcus this

afternoon and ask about the trust. Actually I guess he and I have a lot of things to discuss."

I certainly agreed. I was about to put the Norman folder on the desk for the two of us to examine when there was a knock on the door and Marla Mae called, "Miss Dolores?"

Exasperated, Dolores replied sharply, "Marla Mae, I told you we would be busy in here. No interruptions."

"It's Sheriff Halvorson, ma'am. He's waiting on you." Marla Mae put as much apology in her tone as she could.

Dolores popped out of the chair and clapped her hands. "Finally, Jess, finally. He's come to tell me I can take Willis to Harrold Brothers and have him rest in peace. Oh, and I have to call Pastor Forde . . ."

"Ma'am? Are you coming to see the sheriff?" Now Marla Mae sounded nervous.

"Yes, yes, we are. Please tell the sheriff we will be right with him, and ask Lucinda to prepare a pot of tea and some scones, or cookies, whatever she has. You can bring it to the library in about ten minutes."

As certain as Dolores felt that Sheriff Halvorson was here with good news, I was far less confident. If there was nothing troublesome about Willis's death, wouldn't the coroner simply release his body?

I slipped the two folders I was holding into the front of the first file drawer so I wouldn't have to search for them again. We stepped into the foyer and Deputy Lascomb was standing by the front door. He wished us good day and said that the sheriff was in the library. Dolores clenched my arm, and we found the sheriff standing in the middle of the room. No more browsing through the books and pretending he was making a social call.

He pursed his lips and wagged his jaw from right to left. "Mrs. Fletcher, must you keep turning up? I asked to see Mrs. Nickens."

"I know that, Sheriff, and it does worry me, but I merely have one simple question," I said.

"Mrs. Fletcher, I am not inclined to answer any more of your questions. Please excuse us." And he pointed to the door.

Dolores loosened her grasp on my arm. "It's okay. I'll be fine, Jess, really."

I wish I had believed that was so.

Chapter Fourteen

I was frustrated beyond belief. I closed the library door behind me and saw Deputy Lascomb at his post by the front door. Nothing ventured, nothing gained. I took a few steps in his direction and he acknowledged me at once.

"Mrs. Fletcher." He touched two fingers to his eyebrow in a kind of salute, and then reached for the door to open it for me.

"Oh, no, I'm not going out—I just had a question . . ." I stopped directly in front of him.

"Questions and answers are above my pay grade, ma'am. I think I told you that before." He stood straight and crossed his arms.

"Yes, you did, and I respect your loyalty to the sheriff. But my question isn't about the case." I hoped for any sort of hint in his response.

"Well, as long as it's not about the case, I suppose

we can talk a bit." He uncrossed his arms and loosened his stance.

But I already had some of what I needed. By referring to it as a case, the deputy confirmed that there was an ongoing investigation into the death of Willis Nickens. Now the sheriff was behind closed doors with Dolores, which sent a surge of anxiety coursing through me. I knew that could not bode well for her.

Still, I continued a polite conversation. "I was wondering about the fish."

"The fish, ma'am?" He seemed puzzled.

"I stopped by the pond yesterday and it is quite empty. I was wondering what happened to all those beautiful koi that were in it before . . . before Willis's unfortunate . . . accident."

My use of the word "accident" relaxed him completely.

"No need to worry. In a case like this, where we find a dead person in a small body of water, it is common practice to call the Department of Natural Resources. They scoop out the fish and quarantine them for some amount of time to make sure they are all healthy."

I pressed my hand over my heart and gave him a warm smile. "That is a relief. Such beautiful creatures. I am glad they are being well cared for."

"Yes, ma'am. I expect Sheriff Halvorson is explaining that all to Mrs. Nickens, if he hasn't already done so. She needn't worry about her fish one bit."

And there it was, the opening that might help me wriggle a few morsels of information out of him.

"How thoughtful of you to realize how many things

Mrs. Nickens has on her mind right now. I understand that Willis had business interests spread far and wide. I can't imagine how Dolores will be able to deal with all that high finance." I shook my head as if I was pondering an insoluble problem.

Deputy Lascomb cleared his throat. "Now, that's a problem most people would love to have."

"Oh yes, I'm sure. Tell me, has your office spoken to any of Willis's business associates, lawyers, accountants, or the like?"

I could see he was deciding how, or if, he should answer. I pressed further in as casual a tone as I could muster. "It's just that any contacts or information that your office gleans could be of great help to Dolores when she begins to wrestle with the family finances."

My question must have sounded innocent enough, because the deputy responded, "Sheriff Halvorson don't think it's necessary to look all around Mr. Nickens's business, ma'am. He already has a focus, and he's a man who locks down a focus pretty quick, if you get my meaning. Now I may have said too much, so I kindly ask you to move along before the sheriff comes out."

"I understand." I raised my voice slightly, in case the walls had ears. "Thank you for letting me know those beautiful fish are being taken care of."

I started to walk back to Willis's office. While I waited for the sheriff to finish talking to Dolores, I wanted to go through the Quartermaster folder in the hopes of discovering . . . well . . . anything I could.

My plan was derailed by Norman Crayfield, who was coming down the stairs. His well-pressed chinos and hot pink golf shirt were a step up from his attire of the past few days. I wondered if he was going somewhere. "Jessica, I'm so glad I ran into you. Follow me to the dining room. I got a text from Clancy. There are muffins straight from the oven, and I do believe it is time for a midmorning snack."

"Oh, that sounds like a wonderful idea." Sure as I was that Lucinda's muffins would be scrumptious, it was the thought of an opportunity to speak informally to Clancy and Norman that truly whetted my appetite.

Clancy waved us into the room with a knife in his hand, and went back to slathering butter on a muffin. "Oat bran with almonds and raspberries. There is quite an assortment here. I am not sure how Lucinda does it, but I am so grateful that she does. There's both iced and hot tea on the sideboard. Take your pick."

I looked around. "Where is your sweet daughter this morning?"

Clancy had just taken a bite of muffin. I waited for him to swallow and wipe his mouth with a napkin. "She's in the kitchen learning how to make corn bread. Honestly, Lucinda and Marla Mae spoil her rotten. The day we arrived Lucinda made chocolate pudding from scratch because it's Abby's favorite."

Perfect. A time for adult conversation. I poured myself a cup of tea and sat at the opposite side of the table from the two men. As soon as I saw blueberries among the muffins on the plate, I took one. If they were anything like Lucinda's blueberry scones, I was in for a treat. My first bite confirmed that I had made an excellent choice.

"Hmm-mmm. Heavenly. I didn't realize how peckish I was. This certainly hits the spot." If we were going to have a serious conversation, I might catch them off guard in this relaxing atmosphere.

Clancy beamed. "I know exactly how you feel. Next, try a cinnamon apple muffin."

"Clancy, please—I still have half of this one left to eat." It was a tempting offer, but I managed to resist.

"I was just being helpful," he replied.

"Oh yeah, we are nothing if not helpful around here." Norman chuckled.

And I had my opening.

"Well, in fact, there is a way that you both could be quite helpful to me. You could tell me about Willis," I said.

They exchanged a look, and then each of them leaned back in his chair as if willing the other to go first.

To ease their discomfort, I tried again. "You see, Dolores has asked me to write Willis's obituary and perhaps a eulogy, yet I am the one person here who hardly knew him. We'd only just met. Sorry as I am for everyone's loss, I do wonder what he was really like. And who better to ask than you two, his business partner and his son-in-law. You can give me a glimpse of the two sides of Willis Nickens, the personal and the professional."

That did the trick.

Norman said, "Of course we'll help. How fortunate for Dolores to have a writer of your stature among her friends. We'll tell you the stories and you can arrange the words perfectly. You have to mention that Willis was one dapper dresser. Everything he wore was pressed and polished. I am sure he is up in heaven complaining to the angels that he looks ridiculous wearing a tuxedo with his ratty old brown suede slippers. I'm sure he's begging Saint Peter for a change of shoes." Norman chuckled. "Clancy, why don't you tell Jessica about Grampy Willis?"

Clancy told a particularly endearing tale about how, after Emily died, Willis often visited Abby to tell her a bedtime story. And the stories always involved a heroine named Emily.

Norman followed up with a far less endearing narrative involving a ruthless Willis who saw every financial downturn as an opportunity to buy up private mortgages for pennies on the dollar. Then he would demand full payment or foreclose on the property, hold, and sell. It reminded me of Marjory Ribault's story. Sure enough, Norman mentioned it.

"In fact, that's how he was able to buy Manning Hall. Sharp negotiator was our Willis." Norman appeared to be quite proud of Willis's ability to profit from other people's misfortune.

Clancy picked up the thread. "Oh, he could be a mean 'un, all right. Remember Arabella?"

"Arabella?" I asked.

"Arabella is Abby's godmother and was Emily's best friend ever since third grade. Willis never liked her. Didn't like the whole family—some fuss or another from decades ago."

I certainly understood those silly perpetual feuds. I knew a couple of families in Cabot Cove who hadn't spoken for three or four generations. No one even remembered how it all started. They just followed the tradition and snubbed one another mercilessly.

"Anyway," Clancy continued, "Emily was the only person who could ever stand up to Willis, and she did so consistently when it came to Arabella. She was maid of honor at our wedding, and a frequent guest at our home. The two remained close until the day Emily died, and it was on that very day, while we were all still at the hospital having said our final good-byes, that Willis told Arabella she was persona non grata, and was no longer welcome to visit Abby."

I was aghast. "But surely you could have . . ."

"I did what I could, which was absolutely nothing. Willis controls the purse strings, and that ensures that Willis gets what Willis wants," Clancy said sourly.

"Hey, no more glum stuff." Norman slapped Clancy on the back. "Jessica needs happy stories for the obituary and funny ones for the eulogy. We have lots of those stories. My personal favorite—remember the time Willis almost broke his shoulder with a golf club because of the fire ants?"

Clancy nodded, and within seconds Norman had us both in stitches. I had no problem envisioning an enraged Willis Nickens hopping up and down on one foot while trying to brush fire ants from inside the HyperFlex golf shoe on his other foot. The whole time he was yelling, demanding a do-over, claiming the ants had struck just as he swung and missed.

"He kept screaming, 'Mulligan! Mulligan!' I can see it to this day." Norman was practically doubled over with laughter. "And then in sheer frustration he threw his club in the air and it spun back and landed on his shoulder. He had quite a welt, I can tell you."

Clancy chimed in, "He threatened to have the groundskeeper fired. And then he decided to have the golf pro fired, too. The more we laughed, the crazier he got."

"That is a brilliant story. From the little bit I saw of Willis the day I arrived, that story, how you say he acted, describes him perfectly but with great humor."

Norman went on. "And of course you cannot leave out the great romance, Willis and Dolores. I am sure she told you all those loving details."

"Yes, she did. We had several burn-the-midnight-oil phone calls about her new beau, who gradually became her love, and then her beloved husband. Norman, if you had to stand up and say something about the two of them as a couple, what would you say?"

Norman looked pensive, and then I saw that look on his face, the same look my students used to get when they were sure they had figured out the exact right answer and eagerly raised their hands. "I would say that Willis was a rudderless ship until Dolores came into his life."

I was amazed by his eloquence. "Oh my, that is lovely, Norman. Dolores will be so very pleased."

Abby came running into the room. "Daddy! Daddy! There are butterflies in the backyard but Miss Lucinda and Miss Marla Mae don't have time to watch me run after them. Could you . . . could we . . . ?"

Clancy pretended to be stern. "Where's your manners, young lady?"

Abby stopped in midrun. "Good morning, Mrs. Fletcher. Good morning, Mr. Crayfield."

As soon as we both responded in kind, she looked at Clancy as if to say, *Now can we go?*

Clancy got the message, and he hurried behind Abby as she skipped joyfully away.

Norman stood and said, "Well, I have places to go and all that. I'll see you later, Jessica."

He strode past Marla Mae as if she were invisible. She began to clear the dishes. "How were those muffins, Mrs. Fletcher?"

"Tell Lucinda I asked how she works such magic with blueberries."

"She'll be glad you enjoyed them."

"Tell me, has there been any word from Dolores? Is she still in the library with Sheriff Halvorson?" I asked.

"Yes, ma'am. Early on I did bring in a pot of Irish breakfast tea and a plate of muffins but neither of them talked while I was in the room. Miss Dolores looked a tad upset, but that's how she's been since Mr. Willis . . . And the deputy is still by the door. I did manage to give him a muffin but didn't get any words back other than a thank-you. Tight-lipped, he is."

"Don't I know it? I think I'll go back to the office and begin to work on some of the files. I suspect that's how I can be most helpful to Dolores. Please let me know the minute she comes out of the library."

I wouldn't feel comfortable sitting at Willis's desk, so I sat in a visitor's chair and opened the Quartermaster file, intending to learn what I could so I'd be ready to compare notes with Harry McGraw when we finally reconnected.

"Jessica, oh my goodness, there you are." Dolores dashed into the room and slammed the door shut. Her face was flushed and she was wringing her hands.

I tossed the folder on the side table and led her to a chair.

"Sit down and take a few deep breaths. Then you can tell me everything that happened with the sheriff. Do you want me to get you a glass of water?"

Dolores waved me off. "No. No, thank you. I am really fine, just kind of shocked. He asked me the same stupid questions, but the shock was . . . Oh, Jess, Sheriff Halvorson said that Willis was murdered! Can you imagine? It happened sometime around midnight. Someone hit him with one of those white rocks from the sitting garden. They found the rock in the pool."

None of that surprised me. I wondered only why it took so long for the sheriff to tell Dolores, and why he didn't want me in the room as a support for her when he was bringing such horrible news.

Dolores's next sentence made it perfectly clear: "He also said . . . he said coming to the house today was a courtesy on his part but from now on whenever we speak it would have to be at his office because—oh, I can hardly say the words—Sheriff Halvorson is declaring me a person of interest. Me! A person of interest in Willis's murder."

Her voice broke and she erupted into tears.

Chapter Fifteen

I pulled a couple tissues from my skirt pocket and Dolores took them gratefully.

"I don't understand. Why would anyone want to harm Willis, much less kill him? And why on earth would the sheriff think it was me? I loved him. I wanted us to spend the rest of our lives together. And so did Willis."

I waited until her tears diminished, then said, "Dolores, I know you realize this is serious. The sheriff told you that you are a person of interest so that you can prepare yourself for what is to come. I suggest you hire the best criminal lawyer you can possibly find."

"Marcus Holmes is the only lawyer I know. Do you think he can help me?"

I shook my head. "From your description he handles civil matters, business affairs and such. However, I'm sure he can recommend a criminal attorney . . ."

Dolores bolted from her chair. "Only a few days ago my life was picture-perfect; now, on top of my life being in ruins, I'm accused of being a criminal. Jess, I can't deal. I just can't." She began pacing in a circle.

"Settle down. I will take care of finding a lawyer, and then we'll go to the kitchen and ask Lucinda for a nice pot of tea and perhaps some sandwiches or snacks. How does that sound?"

I could tell by the way Dolores shrugged her shoulders that she was humoring me when she said, "I guess."

"Now, where would I find Marcus Holmes's phone number?" I asked.

"Center desk drawer. Willis has the tidiest address book. You'll find Marcus easily."

I opened the drawer and the black leather book was dead center. I looked under "H." No luck, but he was the very first entry on the "L" page. I guess Willis believed that Marcus's profession was more important than his name.

A young man answered the phone on the second ring. I gave my name and explained I was calling on behalf of Dolores Nickens and wished to speak to Mr. Holmes. He put me on hold; a minute later he picked up the call to say he would be right back, and put me on hold again. I was tapping my toe impatiently as I watched Dolores sink lower into her chair, becoming muddled by the panic that was setting in minute by minute.

At last I heard the phone line come alive. A young lady asked, "Is that Mrs. Willis Nickens?"

And before I could say anything more than "Hello," she put me on hold. But a few seconds later, a man said, "Dolores, I am so sorry about Willis. I meant to call sooner, but the truth is, I didn't want to intrude."

Talk about confusion. "Mr. Holmes?"

"Why, yes, Mrs. Nickens . . ."

"I am not Dolores Nickens. My name is Jessica Fletcher and I am calling on Dolores's behalf."

"Oh, I see. Well, what can I do for you, Mrs. Fletcher? I promise you I will render any and all assistance to Mrs. Nickens during this, er, terrible time."

"I am glad to hear you say that, Mr. Holmes, because your assistance is exactly what she needs. We have only recently learned that Willis Nickens was murdered . . ."

"What? No! How is that possible? I mean, who? A burglar, something like that?" He was so flustered he was stumbling over his words. "Are you absolutely sure? Of course you are."

I wished he would stop talking and let me get to the point.

At long last he began to wind down. "Who would say something like that if it wasn't true . . . ? Er, of course you're sure. How can I help you, Mrs. Fletcher?"

"Mr. Holmes, I am sorry to tell you that—quite erroneously, I assure you—Sheriff Halvorson has decided that Mrs. Nickens is a person of interest in the inquiry regarding the death of her husband."

There—I couldn't make it any starker. I was hoping to shake him into action. Instead, my words had the exact opposite effect: His bluster began anew.

"Great Scott! Well, you do realize that I am not a practitioner of criminal law. It would be malpractice for me to even advise . . ."

I interrupted his rambling. "Mrs. Nickens is merely asking for you to recommend an attorney who *does* practice criminal law and who *could* advise her in this situation."

I could feel him relax right through the phone. "Of course. Of course, that makes perfect sense. And for everyone's protection it is probably wisest to delay the reading of the will until this is all sorted out."

I didn't like the sound of that one bit, but right now Dolores had more important things to worry about. "Mr. Holmes, *do* you have a recommendation? Someone we can call today?"

"Why, yes. I believe Francis McGuire is the very man. He is bright and confident and will protect Mrs. Nickens fiercely. It was nice to speak to you, Mrs. Fletcher. I only wish it was under better circumstances. Please hold on, and my assistant will provide you with the attorney McGuire's contact information. And, er, please give Dolores my warmest regards."

Click. I was on hold once more.

The assistant was quick, and I hoped accurate. I wrote down the contact information for Mr. McGuire, and then cajoled Dolores to come with me to the kitchen. She fumbled with the key until she got the door locked. I hoped a snack and a few minutes of quiet time would calm her nerves.

Lucinda was bent over a cookbook while Marla Mae was folding table linens. Both stopped and stood at attention when they saw Dolores.

"I was wondering if Dolores and I could sit at that picnic table outside the back door and share some tea and whatever sandwiches might be available." I looked directly at Lucinda, sure that she would know exactly what would best suit Dolores.

Lucinda met the challenge. "As a matter of fact, I just put a pitcher of sweet tea in the refrigerator. Miss Dolores, would you prefer a prosciutto and asparagus finger sandwich or a blue cheese and walnut? Shall I make two of each?"

Dolores nodded and smiled her thanks. We walked through to the backyard and sat at the picnic table.

Dolores said, "Great idea, Jess. I don't know why I never come out here. I know Willis considered this to be part of the servants' quarters, and I guess I went along. But look around. How wonderful it is to watch the birds sail from tree to tree on a sunny day. The world doesn't look quite so bad from here, does it?"

"No, it doesn't. Just stay resilient, and I'm sure that you will get through this. In fact, I promise."

Lucinda brought out a tray of sandwiches and fruit, followed by Marla Mae carrying a pitcher of sweet tea and some glasses filled with ice.

As they were arranging the table, I asked them to stay for a moment. "Dolores wants you to know that the next few days likely will be filled with commotion, and there will be lots of disruption to the daily schedules. I know you two can handle anything that is thrown your way, but it is important that you prepare yourselves. It is probable that the sheriff's office will want to interview you at some point. At a time like this it would be usual for guests like Norman and

Clancy to go to their respective homes, but for now it's almost certainly best that everything stay as it was the night Willis . . . died." I decided not to use the word "murder" just yet.

Lucinda took a step closer to Dolores. "Miss Dolores, Marla Mae and I have talked about this. Not gossip, mind you. Just sort of planning for the future. We know there might be hard times ahead. We see the sheriff coming back and forth . . . We hear rumors. Well, ma'am, we are on your team. Just tell us what to do, even what to say, and we'll be happy to do it or say it."

I saw the tears begin to form in Dolores's eyes, and before she could get all weepy again I became businesslike. "That is so nice of you both. Just tell the truth, and all will be fine. In the meantime, Marla Mae, if you could, call Elton and ask him to come over. Tell him that beginning today we would like him to come each morning and stay for the entire day in case we need to go somewhere in a hurry."

Dolores started to object, but I cut her off. "You know that you are in no condition to drive."

I turned back to Marla Mae. "Tell Elton to bring along his study materials, and he can set up in the library and do his schoolwork when he is not driving. As a bonus I am sure Lucinda will bake a treat or two should he get hungry."

Marla Mae grinned. "You are offering Elton the use of a library along with Lucinda's baked goods. I can tell you that boy will be happy as a hog in a wallow."

I smiled uncertainly until Dolores said, "Jess, down here that means he'll be *really, really* happy."

We sat enjoying our surroundings and sipping sweet tea. I took a bite of a blue cheese and walnut sandwich on what tasted like homemade sourdough bread. I encouraged Dolores to eat something. After she finished half of a prosciutto and asparagus sandwich, I felt that she had settled down enough for us to have a serious conversation.

I poured some more tea in each of our glasses.

"Dolores, I don't want to pry, and under normal circumstances it would be none of my business, but . . ." I hesitated.

Dolores looked at me expectantly, ready for whatever I might bring up, so I plunged ahead.

"I believe that you and Willis once had a misunderstanding so egregious that you locked yourself in your room for more than a day. I am sure the sheriff will want to know the cause of the argument and how it was finally resolved. I thought perhaps you wouldn't mind telling me about it before you have to tell the sheriff."

"Oh, that." Dolores discarded it with a backward flap of her hand. "It was such a major fight at the time. I think it was twice as difficult because we had been a couple a remarkably long while without having a serious disagreement."

Dolores leaned back in her chair. "I know what everyone thinks of Willis—his bluster, his ego, and his need to win, all traits that could turn people off completely. But he needed all that exterior crustiness to feel in control of his life. I think the death of his first wife, Claudia, broke him emotionally. He adored her, and losing her was something he couldn't control. He spent nearly twenty years focusing on the things he could control, especially money and power. Then his beautiful daughter, Emily, died. Again he was affected by something out of his control."

I had not looked at Willis's persona quite that way. It never occurred to me that there was underlying damage that fed his need to be in charge. But Dolores had, and I supposed she thought her love could help him heal.

She took a long sip of tea and continued. "As a second wife, I wasn't sure what to expect. I did have some fear that Willis would either consciously or unconsciously compare me to Claudia and I would fall short. All during our courtship it never happened, and by the time we married I was relaxed, secure that Willis loved me and that I was not competing with a woman I'd never met."

Dolores described conquering something that I couldn't even imagine. I thought her ability to recognize the problem and face it head-on was remarkable, and I said so.

"One day Willis showed me a hand-tooled leather jewelry box, which I thought he'd bought especially for me until I lifted the lid. You can imagine my shock when I saw the name Claudia inscribed in gold on the inside. Even worse, there was jewelry, lots of expensive jewelry. Willis wrongly thought that he could just transfer the diamonds and emeralds from one wife to another. I practically threw the jewelry box in his face. I asked why he hadn't given it to Emily."

"Yes," I said, "I would wonder that myself. They were her mother's jewels."

"As I'm sure you could tell, there was no love lost

between Willis and Clancy. Willis never trusted him and always hoped Emily would end the marriage. But if that happened the jewels would be part of a divorce settlement, and that would have driven Willis insane. Of course, after Emily's untimely death . . ."

I was getting a clear picture. "Willis kept the jewels, and when you married he thought they should become yours."

Dolores nodded. "Exactly. He even offered to have the stones reset for me. He'd actually made an appointment for us to visit Morgana's, the most exclusive jewelers in the state of South Carolina, to see what they could design for me. Can you imagine?"

Actually, I could imagine. Willis Nickens was nothing if not a take-charge kind of man. Once he got an idea, I am sure it would be hard for him to let it go. I still wasn't quite sure where the fight came into the story. "Dolores, what led to the huge battle?"

"Honestly, Jess, haven't you heard a word I said? It was the jewelry. How could Willis expect me to take those expensive gems and have them put in what he called 'modern settings' when he had a perfectly adorable granddaughter who should inherit her grandmother's jewelry intact? When she is grown she can make her own decisions as to settings and all that. Maybe a grown-up Abby would actually prefer to have her grandmother's jewelry in the original settings. You know how tastes change from generation to generation and back again."

Now I was thoroughly confused. "But the argument? I still don't see a cause for an argument."

"That's because you didn't get to know Willis well

enough. He had an idea that he thought was brilliant and he wouldn't let it go. I told him that his mistrust of Clancy was clouding his judgment. He told me I did not know anything about dealing with duplicitous people. I reminded him that I'd had *two* duplicitous husbands before I met him. And it went on from there." Dolores laughed. "I locked myself in my room and only Marla Mae was allowed to enter. He cracked in the middle of the second day."

Now I was laughing, too. "I suppose you won?"

"Yes, I did. The whole enchilada, as they say. We agreed that he would hold on to the jewels and present them to Abby on some significant day—perhaps a special birthday, college graduation, engagement—a day to be determined in the future."

I thought back to what I had overheard during Willis and Clancy's heated discussion the night Willis died. It was no wonder Willis had been so confident that Dolores would always put Abby first. She had certainly proved herself.

"And now?" I hated to bring up Willis's death, but that had changed everything.

Dolores's face clouded. "I would have to check, but I think Willis made arrangements that if anything happened to him, Abby would receive the jewels on her twenty-fifth birthday. I think some bank is the custodian until then. Something like that. Marcus will know."

"Yes, I am sure Marcus can answer a lot of our questions. One I have is about a folder I found in Willis's file cabinet. Have you ever heard of Quartermaster Industries?"

Chapter Sixteen

Before Dolores could answer we heard a tap on the kitchen door, and then it opened. Elton stuck his head between the door and the jamb, just far enough that I could see his blue and green striped bow tie.

"Don't mean to disturb." His broad smile was infectious. "I just want to let you know that I have set up in the library, and that is where you'll find me, at your service, whenever needed."

I was sure Lucinda had provided a delicious lunch, but, half teasing, I asked, "Did you manage to find something good to eat in the kitchen?"

"Sure 'nuff. I had a fried catfish sandwich on thick slices of Lucinda's homemade sourdough bread. Mmm-hmm. Don't get better than that. Oh, Mrs. Fletcher, Marla Mae said you left your cell phone on the kitchen counter and it pinged a text message just now. You want me to get it for you?"

I looked at Dolores. "Would you mind excusing me for a few minutes?"

"Not at all. Go ahead—I'll just sit here and enjoy my surroundings. I wish Willis and I had done more sitting and less socializing."

The text was from Harry McGraw.

Jess, even if your friend has to split the guy's estate with a dozen other people she would still be set for life. Call me.

I thought, for privacy's sake, my room would be the best place to make the call. I told Marla Mae I was going to slip upstairs for a few minutes, and she promised to keep an eye on Dolores.

I was slightly drowsy from our relaxing lunch in the warm sunshine of the back porch, so my comfy wing chair looked extra inviting. I was afraid I would fall asleep if I sat down, so I walked back and forth, and while waiting for Harry to answer his phone, I pulled a pen and an old receipt out of my purse in case I needed to jot down a word or two.

He picked up and, without preliminaries, said, "Jess, you are surrounded by a merry band of criminals. If I was you, I'd get out of Dodge ASAP."

That was enough to make me ask him to hold on while I opened the door to my room to make sure no one was listening in the hallway. Of course there wasn't a soul, and I blamed Harry for activating my Spidey senses.

"That's some way to start a conversation, Harry. You have me looking over my shoulder for spies and scoundrels. What on earth are you talking about? Who are these criminals?"

"Remember a few years back, here in Boston, we were all surprised to see how many people were connected to the gangster Whitey Bulger and his crew?"

I had no idea where Harry was going but I tried to follow along. "I'm sure the entire country remembers. It was front-page news for months and followed up on for years."

"Well, your Willis Nickens had quite the crew around him. Gotta say, they don't seem quite as dangerous as Whitey's gang"—Harry chuckled—"but still, a questionable group."

My patience had run out. "Harry, what are you talking about? *Who* are you talking about?"

"You got my text about the shoplifter, right?"

"Marjory Ribault. Yes. Yes, I did. She does seem to have some . . . issues, I guess you would say, regarding money."

"Issues? Jessica, she ain't some old lady stealing a few cans of Fancy Feast to feed her cat. The first time she was grabbed, it was for filching a bracelet worth— get this—seven thousand dollars. Daddy got her off by paying for the bracelet and promising she'd get 'treatment,' if ya know what I mean."

I knew exactly what he meant and, personally, I thought a bit of therapy would do Marjory a world of good. "What about the second time she shoplifted?"

Harry cleared his throat. "Mind you, we only know about the first and second time she got *caught*. What she got away with before and after, we have no idea. Anyway, the second collar was for snatching a pair of

high-end sunglasses at the eye doctor's office. She
went in for reading glasses and came out with a two-
hundred-and-fifty-dollar pair of sunglasses hidden in
her coat. The optometrist's assistant saw her slip the
glasses into her pocket and followed her outside, demanding the dame pay up or return the glasses. It
turned into a shouting match, with a bit of shoving on
your pal Marjory's part, and at some point someone
called the cops. The optometrist is an old family
friend, so she got off with a slap on the wrist. That's
all she wrote."

I was having a hard time believing that Marjory
could murder anyone—she seemed more likely to
turn her back, as she had the other night when Willis
was looking for a bridge partner—but if she had actually assaulted someone, that did put a whole new spin
on her personality. "Oh my, Harry. She certainly is a
troubled woman. But I don't see murder in her persona. I hope I'm not wrong."

"Next in our lineup, we have Clancy Travers. Seems
like our boy forgets he shouldn't drive after he's had
a few scotches. He's got one DUI conviction and one
case pending."

Now that was something I considered appalling.
"And he has full responsibility for his nine-year-old
daughter, who should never be in a car if her father is
driving while under the influence. No wonder Willis
was riding him so hard."

"You're assuming the old man knew. That I couldn't
confirm."

"But if Willis did find out he might have tried to get

custody of Abby, and wherever Abby goes, so goes her trust fund."

"True. You want to know about the next crook?"

"I can't wait to hear." Harry was so full of information, I was having trouble taking down notes. "Wait a sec—let me get another piece of paper." I opened the desk drawer, pulled out a sheet of pristine stationery meant for elegant thank-you notes, and poised my pen to record more criminal activity. "Go ahead."

"This Norman Crayfield—he is something of a playboy. Likes to party. Been locked up a couple of times. Small potatoes. He got nailed once in a sweep of a bordello in Charleston and has a couple of arrests for being on the premises of after-hours booze-and-gambling joints both inside and outside of Columbia. All misdemeanors. None particularly recent."

"I can't say I am surprised. Mr. Crayfield likes to play the role of rapscallion."

"Get ready, Jess—here comes the big one. Candace Parker Smith, aka Candace Parker, aka Parker Smith. Served two years in Georgia, at Whitworth, for kiting checks."

"Kiting, did you say?" I wasn't sure I'd heard him correctly. "What does that even mean?"

"Jess, you write mysteries for a living. In all those books didn't anyone ever play the check-kite game? You know, deposit a check from account one into account two. Account one doesn't have the money to cover the check, but for a day or so account two doesn't know it . . ."

"Oh, I know what you mean. I once had a character

who did what my research called 'playing the float.' It's harder to do now, with all the electronic banking."

"Exactly. Anyway, this broad, who you know as Candy Blomquist, was something of an expert until she finally got caught in Georgia about twenty years ago. Far as I can tell, she's been either clean or careful ever since."

"And her husband, Tom Blomquist?"

"So far, not so much as an outstanding parking ticket, but I'll keep looking. Oh, and I'm sure it will be a comfort to your friend the widow Nickens to know that her husband had no record whatsoever."

"That certainly will be a comfort, but it's not the information that Dolores needs to know this very second. In your text you said that, well, Dolores will never have money problems again?"

"Yeah. I'm still working on the money angle, Jess, but it does look like Willis Nickens was loaded with a capital 'L.'"

"And Quartermaster Industries? What have you learned about that?"

"I learned it exists and Willis Nickens owns it. But it's a privately held company, and the kind of info that public companies make available to potential investors is not easily obtainable with a click or two on the Internet, so I am tracking as much as I can through some of my sources, both the legit ones and the not so legit."

That was a bit of a jolt. "But, Harry, you said Willis had no criminal record, so why would you need to check with your less-than-legitimate friends?"

"Jess, you're a smart lady. You must know that

crooks and con men understand more about high finance than your average bank manager. They need
creative ways to hide their money, and most times the
straight business guys are all too willing to help. Anyway, there's no harm in asking around."

"I do see your point, although I always worry that
you will get yourself into some sort of trouble."

"Goes with the territory, Jess, goes with the territory.
And what about you? How are things at your end?"

"More than a little hectic, I'm afraid. I did find a
Quartermaster folder in Willis's file cabinet but hav-
en't had a chance to go through it. Maybe I'll get some
answers there. My major concern is that, though it
took a while, now the sheriff has announced that Willis was murdered—"

Harry broke in. "I don't know why he ever doubted
you, Jessica Fletcher, Girl Detective. Once you decided
it was murder, the sheriff should have just said, 'Of
course it was murder,' and got on board."

I could practically see him grinning right through
the phone.

I said, "If only, Harry. The worst part is that he has
named Dolores as a person of interest. The fact that
anyone, anyone at all, would think she could ever harm
her husband has driven Dolores to deeper and deeper
lows. I am having trouble keeping her on track."

"Don't worry, Jess. In a couple more days, we will
have this all worked out. I just have to do a little more
digging."

"Seriously, Harry, I know you are the best in the
business, but I didn't expect that you would find out
so much so soon."

"It's gonna cost you. You'll have to spend a week-end in Boston so we can visit the opera and have dinner at Il Cibo. Angelo will never forgive me if I don't produce you soon."

I thought that was a price I'd certainly enjoy paying, and I told Harry so. "Of course, I also want to spend some time at Gilhooley's. I haven't seen Cookie in ages. If you run into him, please give him my regards."

"As it happens, I got a guy on the hook for a game of eight ball tonight, and Cookie will be serving the poor sucker the beer he'll be crying in."

"Oh, Harry, are you so sure your challenger will lose?"

"Jess, he's playing against me. Obviously he'll lose." Harry chuckled and clicked off the phone.

I left my room to go back to Dolores and met Marla Mae coming up the stairs. "Miss Dolores was wondering where you got to. She sent me to fetch you, tell you she is waiting in Mr. Willis's office. Something about a lawyer."

Francis McGuire. I checked that I had his phone number in my cell and went downstairs.

Dolores was sitting in the leather chair behind Willis's desk. "Funny, this chair always seemed so big to me, larger than life, but I guess that was because Willis was sitting in it. Now it's just a perfectly normal desk chair."

I knew exactly what she meant. The significance of so many things, so many places, completely changed after my husband, Frank, died.

I closed the door and sat down opposite her at the

desk. "Before we call Mr. McGuire, is there anything you want to talk over with me, perhaps to get your thoughts straight?"

Dolores looked pensive for a few moments, and then shook her head. "I can't imagine anything I would need to tell the lawyer other than that I loved my husband, someone killed him, and no matter what Sheriff Halvorson thinks, it wasn't me."

"Then we are ready." I reached for the desk phone. "Once I have the lawyer on the line I'll put the call on speaker." Remembering how long it took to get through to Marcus Holmes, I cautioned Dolores, "It may take a while for me to get Mr. McGuire on the phone. We may even have to wait for a callback, but either way, we need to be prepared for the next time we hear from the sheriff."

The receptionist had a crisp no-nonsense persona. When I told her I was calling Mr. McGuire on behalf of Dolores Nickens, she immediately asked, "Is Ms. Nickens presently being detained by law enforcement?"

"No, she is not. I hope it won't come to that."

"In that case, may I ask your relationship to Ms. Nickens and the purpose of your call to Mr. McGuire? Is Ms. Nickens incapacitated in some way?"

I was beginning to understand her screening process. "My name is Jessica Fletcher. My dear friend Dolores Nickens is sitting here with me and is available to speak with Mr. McGuire. I merely placed the call."

"Thank you. Please hold." Before I could finish whispering to Dolores that Mr. McGuire's office seemed very professional, the phone line opened again.

"Francis McGuire here, Mrs. Fletcher. How is Mrs. Nickens doing this afternoon?"

"Mr. McGuire, I am going to put the phone on speaker so Dolores can tell you herself."

I pressed the button and nodded at Dolores, who said, "Good afternoon. This is Dolores Nickens."

"Mrs. Nickens, Marcus Holmes told me to expect your call and explained your current circumstances. I am so very sorry for your loss." He sounded remarkably sincere for someone who didn't know either Dolores or Willis.

Although I was afraid his kind words would have Dolores crying again, she held it together, thanked him, and said, "Sheriff Halvorson has named me a person of interest in the investigation of my husband's death. I did not kill him."

McGuire's response was lawyerly to the nth degree. "We can have that conversation at a later time. For now I need you to know that, as of this moment, I am your counsel of record. You are not to speak to anyone from the sheriff's office about this case without me present. If they approach in any way with what appears to be even the most inconsequential questions, you demand that I be present. Is that clear?"

When Dolores assured him that it was, he went on. "I'll be at your house first thing tomorrow morning and we will map our strategy going forward. Get a good night's sleep, Mrs. Nickens. Tomorrow the hard work begins."

Chapter Seventeen

I had a number of things I wanted to do, so I was relieved when Dolores decided she would go to her room for a rest. I was sure she felt that the world was crashing in on top of her. And in many ways it was.

I went to the library, where Elton had his nose buried in a book. Always a gentleman, he stood when I entered the room. "Are we on the move, ma'am?"

"Not yet. I wanted to check in. I have a few things to do, but later on I may want to go to Jessamine House. It's actually a hotel. Do you know it?"

"Doesn't pop right to mind but I can find it and be ready to drive there whenever you want."

"Elton, you are the best."

I headed back to Willis's office to read the Quartermaster file, but of course Dolores had locked the door. When she came downstairs later I would have her unlock it so I could get the two folders of interest and put them in my room. I was sure there was information inside each of them that would help resolve my curiosity about exactly how Willis ran his businesses and who, besides Dolores and Abby, might benefit from his death.

Stymied by my research material's being temporarily unavailable, I decided that going for a short jog to clear my head was my best option. I realized that if I could manage to run into Marjory Ribault, so much the better.

I changed into my jogging suit and headed outdoors. I didn't realize how much the stress of recent events was tying my body in knots until I stood on the veranda and took several long, deep breaths. I once had a yoga instructor who swore by the mantra "Inhale fresh air. Exhale stress."

I did a slow jog around the side of the house toward the putting green, and sped up when I veered off through the pines toward the kitchen garden. Then I slowed to a casual walk when I followed the rocky path to Marjory's cottage.

I knocked on the door twice, harder the second time. When she finally opened it, Marjory had a butcher's apron wrapped around her body and a smudge of chocolate on her cheek.

If she was surprised to see me, she didn't show it.

"Jessica, how nice of you to stop by. I don't get many visitors. You are just in time to try one of my mocha cupcakes with chocolate frosting. Can you do with a cup of tea?"

She was so cordial that knowing my mission would

make her uncomfortable gave me a fleeting sense of guilt. Still, my decision had been made, so I panted as if I was seriously out of breath and replied, "I may have overdone my afternoon jog. And who could turn down homemade cupcakes?"

From the moment I walked through the door of the cottage I could smell that homey scent of fresh baked goods that always permeated Lucinda's kitchen. It seemed the two ladies had more in common than vegetables.

Marjory set two cups with saucers on the table and motioned me to sit. She put a plate of cupcakes within easy reach and followed it with a pot of tea. "I hope you enjoy oolong. It's my go-to cuppa in the afternoon, a little bolder than green, which is my favorite for evenings," she said as she filled my cup.

"I never met a cup of tea that I didn't savor. This smells wonderful."

Marjory offered milk and lemon and was pleased when I opted for lemon. "I personally believe that milk is only appropriate with black tea, and I'm amazed that so many people pour it in all types of tea. Why, I have even seen people add milk to a cup of white tea, which is far too delicate for any kind of additives. Well, at least that's my opinion."

I nodded. "I completely agree. White tea is so mild, a splash of milk could kill it."

Marjory smiled politely. "Milk kill tea? That is an odd way of putting it. I guess you mystery writers always think in terms of murder and mayhem."

Flustered, I took a bite of my cupcake, which was

delicious. When I said so, Marjory confided that her secret ingredient was the slightest dash of turmeric, sifted twice through the flour. She claimed it strengthened the coffee flavor so it wasn't overpowered by the chocolate.

"Well, it certainly works. This is delicious. And I was so in need of a pick-me-up. I am glad that when I saw the cottage I thought to knock."

"Tense day?" Marjory's tone was offhand, but she peered at me carefully, as if she was looking for an answer rather than lending support.

I pretended to hesitate, as if I was not sure whether I should speak. And when Marjory inclined an ear closer, I said, "I am so worried about Dolores. I suppose you heard . . ."

"Heard? Heard what?" Marjory's face expressed a mixture of curiosity and alarm. "Is she all right?"

"Physically, yes. She is perfectly fine, but emotionally . . ." I looked down at the table and shook my head ever so slightly. "You didn't hear this from me, but I'm sure that the word has already spread around some quarters, so I may as well tell you . . ."

Marjory was leaning so low across the table that her chin threatened to knock the lid right off the teapot.

I lowered my voice as if afraid of being overheard, even though we were completely alone. "It's Sheriff Halvorson. He's declared Dolores a person of interest in Willis's murder."

Marjory's head snapped up and she stared at me, wide-eyed. "Willis was murdered?" It was a convincing expression of innocence. But it could be meaningless. She might have rehearsed it, waiting for this moment.

"According to both the coroner and the sheriff, yes, Willis was definitely murdered."

"And they think Dolores . . . Why, that's . . . that's ludicrous. Willis Nickens was an evil, brutal man but Dolores loved him. I never understood how she could, but I am sure she did. Anyway, she's such a sweet lady. I don't think she could swat a fly, much less hurt a person, especially one she cared about."

"I agree completely. We all have to hope and pray that the real killer is caught and that Dolores comes through this crisis unscathed." I held out my cup. "May I have a bit more tea?"

I stayed long enough to finish a cupcake and promise to try the turmeric trick the next time I was making anything mocha.

When enough time had passed, I stood up. "Thank you so much for letting me unburden myself. I feel so much better."

"Please, Jessica, stop by anytime. That's what friends are for, and this tragedy has certainly made our friendship warm up faster than it otherwise might have."

I was sure what she really meant was: Come over anytime you have more news about the goings-on at Manning Hall.

When I got to the pine trees I turned, and Marjory was still standing in the doorway. We both waved good-bye, and after she shut the door, I began a mental countdown. Ten, nine, eight . . . , and I wondered what number I reached before she picked up the telephone. I didn't have to wonder who she would call. I already knew.

I jogged to the back door of Manning Hall, and when I let myself in, the kitchen was all abuzz.

Abby was at the table sharing milk and cookies with Elton, who was regaling her with a story about Martians and moon men that had her giggling between bites of chocolate chip.

Marla Mae said, "Good to see someone is up and about." She ticked off on her fingers. "Miss Dolores is still upstairs. Mr. Clancy went home for a few changes of clothes, although he knows full well that we have a perfectly good washer and dryer here. As for Mr. Crayfield, he did mumble something about business and the office."

"Willis's office? The one here in the house?" I was rattled. Did Norman have a key? If he found the folders I wanted to read, I might never see them again.

"No, ma'am. Some other office."

That was a relief. It was imperative that I get those folders out of the office and hidden in my room the minute Dolores came downstairs.

"Mr. Crayfield is always talking about going to the office or coming from the office. Sort of like Uncle Jasper." Marla Mae snickered.

"Uncle Jasper?" I had no idea who he was, but expected I was about to find out.

"When we was children, old Uncle Jasper and a few of his cronies used to spend a large part of their days sitting on the side porch of Turner's Feed Store playing checkers and taking the occasional sip of hooch. They claimed to be spending their time talking smart and solving all the world's problems. Called that rickety porch their office. You reckon Mr. Crayfield has a porch somewhere?"

I couldn't help but chuckle. "Now, that wouldn't surprise me at all."

Dolores walked into the kitchen, looking tranquil and refreshed. "Sounds like there's too much fun in this kitchen." She bent down and kissed the top of Abby's head. "Is that true, princess? Is there too much fun?"

"Oh, Granny Dolores, didn't you tell me lots of times we can never have too much fun? Mr. Elton is telling me about moon men and Miss Marla Mae is talking about funny offices. Miss Lucinda is chopping potatoes—I was counting the times the knife hit the wooden board. Thirty-seven."

Every adult in the room looked at the child in amazement.

Dolores said, to no one in particular, "What is that old saying about little pitchers?"

"They have big ears," Abby shouted gleefully.

We adults couldn't contain our laughter. Dolores sat down and tugged on one of Abby's ears. "Yes, they do. Now tell me, are you willing to share a cookie with me?"

Abby passed the plate of cookies and pointed to a cookie in the center. "Take that one, Granny Dolores. I think it's the biggest. Daddy went to our house to get some clothes. I wanted to go with him so I could get Marilyn, my glitter monkey. I want to introduce her to Fluffy." She pulled the wooden rabbit out of her pocket. "Daddy said I should stay here and he would bring Marilyn back for me. I hope he doesn't forget."

Dolores and I exchanged a look. We both wondered why Clancy wouldn't want to take Abby with him if he was only going home to pick up a few things and coming right back. There were so many odd mysteries in this small group of people.

Lucinda invited Abby to go with her to the kitchen garden. "We need some nice ripe tomatoes and a few carrots for tonight's salad, and I think you are the right woman for the job."

Abby raised her arms muscleman-style. "Yes, I am. And don't forget that we have Fluffy. Rabbits are excellent at eating carrots, so they must be excellent at pulling them, don't you think?"

As soon as Lucinda, Abby, and Fluffy went out the back door, Elton excused himself to head for the library, but not before reminding us he was ready to drive at a moment's notice.

Marla Mae was cleaning dishes off the table when Dolores spontaneously grabbed her wrist. "I hope that Willis, wherever he is, knows that he has left me in good hands. You and Lucinda have done so much to help make this horrible time bearable. I hope you will consider staying on after . . . after everything is settled."

Marla Mae flushed with pleasure. "Yes, Miss Dolores, I will indeed."

Dolores turned to me. "And you. Jessica, how can I ever repay your many kindnesses? This was supposed to be a get-together with lots of gossip, reminiscing, and shopping. Glad as I am that you are here, I know this isn't what you expected."

This was the first time since I'd given her the terrible news that Dolores seemed to be aware of what was going on around her. I took that as a sure sign she would be able to cope with the coming days.

"I am glad to be here, especially under the circumstances. Having friends and family around me when Frank died was a great comfort." I changed direction. "Now, I need a small favor from you."

"Anything, Jess."

"Could you unlock the office? I left a couple of things in there and I'd like to get them."

"That's an easy one." Dolores slapped her pocket. "The key is right here."

As we walked from the kitchen, she lowered her voice. "So, what do you think Clancy is really up to? Picking up some clothes. Ha."

"Now that you mention Clancy, there is something I have been wondering about." I nodded my head toward the office door. This was a discussion that needed privacy.

Dolores unlocked the door, and I made sure it was firmly closed behind us. Rather than chance my getting lost in our conversation and missing out on reading the files, I went directly to the first file drawer and pulled out the two folders. It was a major relief to see they were right where I had left them. Dolores watched me put them on a side table and take a seat in a guest chair.

"What is so special about those file folders?" she asked.

"I don't know, exactly. They seem to have something to do with Willis's businesses and I thought there might be some information that would help the sheriff."

"I have more important problems." Dolores crossed her arms and started to pace. "I'm afraid Clancy is going to cut me off from seeing Abby. That would be just like him. And it would break my heart."

"Oh good heavens, no. I doubt he will do that, at least not until all of Willis's financial affairs are settled. Clancy is shrewd enough to want to know where he stands before he does anything rash. I do have some questions about Clancy but they have nothing to do with your relationship with Abby. I am curious about . . . well, about his drinking."

Dolores glanced around the room as if she expected someone, perhaps Clancy himself, to have sneaked in while we were talking. She took a step toward Willis's desk chair but then opted for the visitor's chair next to mine. She looked perplexed. "His drinking?"

"Dolores, please, it may be nothing. But I did notice that at dinner the night I arrived he seemed to imbibe rather heavily."

"Well, he may have had a bit too much to drink but he was staying over, so what would it matter?"

"There's more. In fact, if Willis knew he may have told you and I am starting a big fuss for nothing." I took a deep breath. "Clancy has been arrested twice . . ."

Chapter Eighteen

Arrested? Dear Lord. Will he have to go to jail?"

"I don't know. Both arrests were for drunk driving. He was convicted once and is awaiting adjudication for the second arrest."

"Drunk driving! How could he possibly drive under the influence? He drives Abby everywhere. School. Playdates. Dance class. How can he put her in that kind of danger?"

"We don't know any details yet. It is quite possible that he drinks when he is out socially at places where Abby isn't with him, or wherever." That sounded lame even as I said it.

"Even so, he could kill himself and leave Abby an orphan. I don't even know what guardianship arrangement Clancy has made for her. Now that Willis is gone and Clancy has no family to speak of, I should step forward. I'll do that right now, as soon as he comes back."

Dolores was ready for action much sooner than I had anticipated. I should have realized that if she thought Clancy's drinking would affect Abby, she would move with lightning speed.

"Dolores, please, slow down. There's a lot to consider before you run off and talk to Clancy. For one thing, he is going to wonder how you know."

"How do I know? You told me, not five minutes ago. That's how I know." She pondered for a couple of beats, and then asked the obvious question. "How did you find out?" She looked at the file drawers. "Did Willis have copies of the arrest records squirreled away?"

"Not that I know of. I haven't finished looking through the file drawers, but so far I haven't seen anything about Clancy's drinking." I was a little embarrassed to admit how I'd found out. "I have a friend. His name is Harry McGraw and he's a private investigator. I asked him to look into, er, certain things for me and he stumbled across Clancy's arrest records."

"Whoa. That was some stumble. Is your friend local? Can we meet with him?"

"No, Harry works out of Boston, but he is exceptionally good at what he does." Harry would appreciate that description. I took a deep breath, and laid out my idea about how this should be handled. "Obviously I had to pass the information on to you as soon as I learned of it, but, now that you know, I wouldn't advise you to go charging after Clancy about his arrest records. Personally, I think you should hang on to that information. It may be quite useful when you and he are trying to come to terms with how much contact he will allow you to have with Abby now that Willis is . . . gone."

Dolores looked at me blankly; then a smile lit up her face. "Jessica Fletcher, you are a sly one. Clancy's drunk-driving record gives me . . . leverage."

"That's exactly how I see it. For now keep it up your sleeve, until it will be advantageous to bring it into the light."

Dolores clapped her hands. "With everything happening so fast, my major worry has been about losing Abby, and now, thanks to you and your PI friend, I have—leverage!"

"Dolores, I know that's what you continue to be most upset about, but I assure you that a sheriff who thinks you are, quite possibly, a murderer is a more compelling problem." I couldn't put it more bluntly. Dolores was running out of time. "Deputies with an arrest warrant could knock at the door any moment. We need to be prepared."

Dolores dropped her chin and hunched her shoulders. "But isn't that why I hired Mr. McGuire? To straighten this all out?"

"As your attorney, Mr. McGuire will protect you from hurting yourself in interviews with the sheriff or the government attorney. He also will be sure that no one on the law enforcement side crosses legal boundaries, so to speak. Our job is to be ready."

Originally I'd hoped to get Dolores energized enough to take an active part in her own defense; now I was asking her to go a step further.

"Ready? Ready for what?" She seemed thoroughly confused, and I couldn't blame her.

"In a perfect world, with enough time we might be able to figure out who killed Willis, but for now I will settle for finding possible motives for someone else, anyone else, to have killed Willis. In fact, the more suspects we can find, the better off you will be. Sheriff Halvorson is content to focus on you. We need to change his focus."

Dolores frowned. "My life is beginning to sound like the plot of one of your novels. So, tell me, how do we do that? How can we create 'suspects'? If there was evidence of a stranger being on the property that night I'm sure the sheriff would have found it." Her brown eyes grew wide. Her mouth formed a perfect O. "No. You can't mean we have to look at the family and friends who were here with us that evening."

I nodded. "I'm afraid that's exactly what I mean."

Dolores sighed. "But it isn't possible. None of them would ever, could ever . . ."

I stopped her right there. "We don't know what any of them may or may not have done, but we do know the sheriff thinks you killed Willis, and we *certainly know* you are completely innocent."

"Thanks for the vote of confidence, Jess. I suppose you're right. What do you need me to do?"

I picked up the thinner of the two manila folders on the side table. "First off, tell me everything you know about Quartermaster Industries."

Dolores was puzzled. "I've never heard of it."

"Are you quite sure? Willis never mentioned it, even just in passing?"

"No. Never. The name means nothing to me. Why do you ask?"

"According to Harry, Quartermaster Industries is a company that Willis owned. It is quite valuable, and Harry tells me it's been difficult for him to uncover information because it is privately held. But we have this." I held up the folder, pointing to the name on the tab. QUARTERMASTER INDUSTRIES. "Shall we take a look?"

Dolores said, "That folder seems kind of skimpy. Must be a very small company."

I glanced at the first page and gasped. "Dolores, Willis never told you *anything* about the company? Are you sure?"

"Positive. Why would he?"

"Because, according to this document, Willis owned fifty-one percent of Quartermaster, Norman Crayfield owns ten percent, and you own thirty-nine percent."

"What? That's not possible. Let me see that." Dolores grabbed the paper from my hand.

I pointed. "There's your signature, and Willis's. Your signatures were witnessed. Don't you recall any of this?"

"Honestly, I don't. Let me see the date. Yes. This does make some sense, I guess. You know Willis had arranged for us to go on an extended honeymoon. We visited Australia and New Zealand, and then spent a luxurious week at the Ko Olina lagoons on Oahu."

"I remember you sent me pictures, but . . ."

Dolores waved at me to be silent. "Because we were going to be gone for so long, Willis wanted everything to be in order legally. He mentioned health care, the ownership of the house. You know, married-people stuff. So, two days after the wedding, on the day before we left for a monthlong honeymoon, we went to Marcus Holmes's office and signed scads of paperwork."

"And you didn't look at any of it? You just signed whatever was put in front of you?"

Dolores raised her eyebrows and gave me a look. "When you put it that way, I sound like a dolt."

I backtracked immediately. "Not at all. I am just beginning to understand that Willis wanted you protected with regard to all his assets as soon as possible after the wedding. So he had the lawyer set up everything for you both to sign. It came across as though it was routine housekeeping. Am I correct?"

"Exactly right. What else is in the folder?"

I held up a sheaf of white papers edged in blue. "Receipts for a storage facility. Do you know anything about a storage locker in a place called Seven/Twenty-four Storage?"

Dolores shook her head. "Never heard of it. I guess Willis rented space there."

"Correction: You and Willis rented space there. Your name is on the most recent receipt."

"Honestly, Jess, how many secrets did this man have?"

"If Willis was truly keeping secrets, your name wouldn't be on anything. I am sure over time you will know all there is to know."

"I guess so, but didn't he realize that he was going to leave me in a mess?"

"Now, now, Willis didn't plan it this way. I'm sure

that given more time he would have told you"—I gestured toward the file cabinets—"about everything that he kept here."

"I know, but still . . ." Dolores stood up and stretched. "Anyway, what do you think he kept in storage?"

"There is only one way to find out."

"Please don't tell me to ask Norman—you know I can't abide his slobbering all over me now that Willis . . ." Dolores said.

"Good heavens, that's the last thing I would suggest. Just because he has a ten percent interest doesn't mean Willis confided in him."

"All along I thought Willis and Norman were full partners, fifty-fifty in everything. I wonder if this is their only joint business interest. If so, perhaps I could buy Norman out and be rid of him."

I didn't think it would be nearly that simple. I cautioned, "Let's not make any decisions. I was thinking more along the lines of visiting the storage facility to see what's in it. We may find answers to any questions you have."

Dolores stretched again. "Let's put that on the agenda for tomorrow. Right now I need a nap before dinner."

"Of course. You must be exhausted. There's no rush. We can visit the storage locker whenever you are ready. Do you mind if I hold on to these folders?"

"Help yourself. I am going to lock this office up tighter than a drum, so anything you want, get it now."

Dolores went upstairs, and since I knew exactly

how I wanted to use my free time, I headed to the library to ask Elton to be ready to leave for Jessamine House in about twenty minutes. When I got to my room I looked around for a place to conceal the files. For the first time I wished I had a key to lock my door. After failing to find a good hiding spot in the bedroom, I put the files side by side on the bathroom floor and placed the fluffy bath mat on top of them.

True to his word, Elton had the directions to Jessamine House down pat. When we turned into the driveway I could see instantly why Tom was so proud of the house. It was a two-story white clapboard building. Two curved staircases led from the left and right sides of the driveway to a wider set of stairs that ended on a wraparound porch with rocking chairs and garden swings scattered about.

I told Elton I would be no more than half an hour. In response he held up one of his schoolbooks. "Take your time, Mrs. Fletcher. I have plenty to do."

As I reached the top of the steps Tom Blomquist opened the wide double doors.

"Ah, J. B. Fletcher. We are honored. Welcome to Jessamine House."

Tom ushered me into the lobby, where several guests were sitting under ceiling fans, their broad leaf blades circling languidly. Candy was moving among them with a teapot in one hand and a pitcher in the other, offering refills.

"Ah, you're just in time for a mint julep. Or would you prefer tea? Candy," he called to his wife, "look who is honoring us with her presence, our dear friend the famous author J. B. Fletcher."

He got precisely the reaction he was looking for. The hotel guests reacted to the word "famous," skipping entirely over the word "author." Heads turned as they looked around for whatever movie star or country singer they hoped to see—all except one woman, who nudged the man sitting next to her on a wicker settee. "Harvey," she said in a stage whisper, "it's her. The lady who wrote that racing book you loved so much. You know, with the crown in the title."

She looked at me and raised her voice. "You must remember. You wrote it, didn't you?"

It wasn't the first time I'd been asked to identify one of my books for an avid reader. I said, "Are you referring to *The Triple Crown Murders*?"

"That's it." Harvey jumped from his chair and began pumping my hand furiously. "It's a pleasure to meet you, ma'am, a country-fried pleasure." Then he dropped my hand and went back to huddle with his wife in excited murmurs.

Satisfied that was all the reaction to be had, Tom escorted me to a quiet nook and we sat in catty-corner chairs.

Candy came over with a dainty porcelain teacup and saucer in hand. "It's good to see you, Jessica. Here. I didn't think you were the mint julep type, but if I am wrong . . ."

"No, this is absolutely fine. I have to say, Jessamine House is even lovelier than you described it. The outside staircase alone . . ."

"Yes," Tom said. "The staircase and the large porch are two of our major selling points. Anyone can make rooms look like they're from the 1800s, but the outside character of a house . . . Well, Jessamine House carries the indelible mark of two-hundred-year-old architecture."

"Oh yes, it gives exactly that impression." I took a sip of tea, hoping he would take the conversational lead.

"I'm sorry I didn't have time to stop and say a proper hello the other day when I dropped off Norman. But we had new guests expected to register. After I drove off, I thought to myself, where are your manners, honking like a high schooler? Shame on me."

"Don't be silly. I did wonder, though, how you were going to get through the gate."

"Easy peasy." Tom reached into his pocket and pulled out a set of car keys. Hanging from one link was a clicker exactly like the others I'd seen for Manning Hall's gate.

When I appeared not to recognize it, he explained, "Old Willis had a lot of clickers made for the gate. So many people need them: the staff, the gardener, and naturally his houseguests."

"Naturally." I nodded but managed to keep a befuddled look on my face.

"It's Norman. He and I often play snooker of an afternoon. Norman likes to have a bourbon or two, and I am the designated driver." He tapped lightly on his stomach. "Ulcers, you know. So when Norman stays at Manning Hall, he often gives me a guest clicker so we can come and go to Tiny's Billiard Parlor, or wherever else, totally under the radar."

"I understand. No one likes to have to clock in

and out when they are a houseguest. That can be so tedious."

Candy came to our corner of the room. "Jessica, don't let Tom talk your ear off. He promised to help our one permanent resident, Mrs. Coyle, package some of her 'collectibles' and then take her to the post office to mail them to her niece in Ohio."

"Ah, I had forgotten all about that. I'd better run. Nice to see you again, Jessica." And Tom rushed off.

"My official duties as tea pourer and bartender are over for the day, so why don't I show you around?" Candy waved me out of my chair.

I stood and hooked my arm in the crook of her elbow. "Lead on."

"Shall we start in the gardens? They are so pleasant this time of day. Are you ready?"

I was more than ready. "Sounds lovely. While we're there you can tell me if the name Parker Smith rings a bell."

Chapter Nineteen

Candy pushed me away and spun around until she had completed a full circle. She was in absolute shock. Her eyes darted around the room as if she was afraid someone was coming for her with handcuffs. Her words were nearly inaudible: "Shush. To the garden. Now."

She nudged me toward a set of French doors that led to the porch. We walked down a side staircase into a delightful section of the garden where trellises of climbing roses and clematis were surrounded by patches of fragrant lavender. Under normal circumstances it would have been a lovely spot for a private conversation, but our talk was going to be far from normal.

Candy walked all around the edge of the garden, peering over bushes and behind trees to be sure there was no one within hearing distance. When she came back to where she'd left me standing, she said, "I think it's best if you tell me how you found out."

Determined to keep her off guard, I said casually, "I have friends, and my friends have friends. Word gets around."

"Let's take a seat." Candy indicated a white wrought iron bench far from the porch. Her hands were shaking so badly that she clasped them together, fighting for control.

Once we settled in, she looked me straight in the eye and, her voice full of conviction, said, "Parker Smith is dead and buried. I can tell you that for certain."

"I am curious about one thing. Did Tom ever have the opportunity to meet her?" I asked.

"No. Of course not. Parker Smith and her alter egos existed decades ago. After a few devastating scrapes with the law I learned my lesson and changed my life. Then I met Tom. Everything else is ancient history. As if it never existed." She looked at me, her eyes filled with worry. "You didn't tell Tom, did you?"

"Good heavens, no. It's not my place to tell him, but after all these years, don't you think you should? In my experience, keeping secrets in a marriage is never a good idea. It often leads to upheaval or tragedy. Think how hurt Tom would be if he found out about your past from someone else."

"Believe me, Jessica, that is my most constant worry. By the time he and I met I had concealed the fact that I used to be a swindler for such a long time that it seemed natural to just ignore it. Then as I grew to love Tom and wanted to share my life with him, a man who is so decent and kind, I was terribly afraid that if

I told him about my past he would leave me. It has always been the elephant in the room, but an elephant I sincerely hoped Tom would never see."

I found that to be an extremely interesting statement, so I asked, "And when you found out Willis had died in rather odd circumstances, were you at all afraid that the sheriff would want to interview and investigate everyone who was at Manning Hall on the night Willis died?"

"If you are asking if I was afraid the world would find out about Parker Smith, yes. Yes, I was. And I was most afraid that Tom would find out and hate me for the liar I am, maybe even leave me."

We sat in silence for a few moments, and then Candy asked, "Did Willis know? I was always afraid that he would discover my secret and use it as a weapon in one of his torment sessions. In fact, when he wouldn't give us the loan for this place I was afraid he'd found out and didn't trust us. Didn't trust me. With my history, who would lend me a dollar, never mind thousands of them? It seemed that Tom would not be able to fulfill his dream, and I was afraid it would be completely my fault."

"Candy, are you saying that you knew Willis was going to deny the loan?"

"Oh yes. Tom and I both knew. Since they're friends, Norman told Tom in the strictest confidence."

"But when we were playing bridge after dinner, Willis bullied Tom so deliberately that I was puzzled Tom allowed it. At first I assumed he was just being a gracious guest, but once I learned about your asking

Willis for financial help of some sort, I determined Tom didn't want to jeopardize your chances."

"It was a tricky situation. Willis kept telling Norman that he was going to deny the loan, but Willis never told Tom and me. Jessica, we'd approached every possible source and been turned down. A private loan from Willis was our last chance. So when Norman told us, completely off the record, that the loan was a no go, we decided it was best to keep sucking up to Willis on the off chance he would change his mind. Then he died. So now it's a completely new ball game."

I said, "It certainly is. You and Tom went from the certainty that Willis was going to deny your loan to the real possibility that when the dust settles, Dolores will grant it."

"When we heard about Willis—I mean, it was a great shock, as you can imagine, but for us there was a silver lining. We were sure Dolores would be much easier to work with and we'd be able to get a nice loan at a decent rate. But now that the sheriff is looking at her for Willis's murder . . ." Candy clasped her hand over her mouth.

That was what I had been waiting to hear. "I suspect you heard that from Marjory, and she swore you to secrecy in the bargain."

"Yes," Candy answered in a tiny voice. "I feel terrible. Please don't tell her I slipped."

I stood up. "You needn't worry. All your secrets are safe with me."

"Thank you, Jessica, and please, if there is anything

we can do for Dolores, anything at all, just call us and we will come a-running."

I walked along the garden path to the driveway, deep in thought. I'd told Marjory about Dolores's being a person of interest in the hope that she would pass that knowledge along to the Blomquists. I hoped it might rattle them, and sure enough, it had. They'd gone from being confident that Dolores would help them financially to being unsure of Dolores's status in relation to Willis's estate. And Candy went from worrying about her past becoming common knowledge to having it safely tucked away because the sheriff was busy looking in a completely different direction for Willis Nickens's killer.

If either of them thought killing Willis would be a solution to their problems, well, as it turned out, even after his death they were still in major turmoil.

By the time I got to the car, Elton was standing next to the open passenger door.

"Do you have a next stop in mind?" he asked as I settled into my seat.

"Actually, I do. I'd like to talk to Sheriff Halvorson again, if I can get a few minutes of his time. Let's go to his office."

We'd barely gotten to the main road when my cell phone rang. Seth Hazlitt.

"Woman, where did you get these pictures of such a fancy putting green? Here I thought you were staying at the home of an old college friend and comforting her after a loss. Next thing, I find texts from some fancy country club all over my phone."

I couldn't help laughing. "Seth, that putting green

is on Dolores's property. Her husband, Willis, was an avid golfer."

"More like a *rich* golfer, I would say." Seth harrumphed. "Ayuh, Jessica, Doris Ann over at the library is wondering, do you have any idea when you might be coming home? She says the furniture committee is sure to run amok and spend too much money for unsuitable tables and chairs without its most level-headed member."

"I wish I could give you a date, but for Dolores's sake I want to stay for the funeral, and the coroner hasn't released the body yet."

"Jessica, that's not a good sign. Not at all."

"I know, and I've yet to tell you the worst part. The sheriff has declared Dolores a person of interest, which means it's likely he's not looking too hard at anyone else."

"Well, that settles it. I'll tell Doris Ann not to make any committee meeting plans. You won't be home anytime soon. And, Jess, you take care of yourself. Keep a watchful eye."

"Thank you, Seth. That is exactly what I intend to do."

Elton turned into the driveway of the Sheriff's Department. "I'd feel better, ma'am, if you allowed me to park the car and escort you inside."

"Actually, Elton, I'd prefer you to wait here at the curb." I smiled. "The sheriff tends to get annoyed by my very presence, so this may be the time we really do need to make a quick getaway."

Elton looked alarmed. "When I said that the last time we were here, I was joking. You look serious."

"Not really, although, as I said, the sheriff does tend to lose patience with me. For some reason my very existence seems to push his buttons."

"I can see why that would be. You are such a good friend to Miss Dolores, the sheriff sees you as getting in his way."

"Well, when you put it like that . . ."

"I hear a lot of talk when I drive people around, and one thing I have learned is that the talk goes much smoother if you try to see how the other person views things. Sheriff Halvorson is not at all interested in your opinion, but you might do well to understand his."

"Elton, you are a genius. I just might change my approach."

Deputy Remington was sitting behind the counter. Bright sunlight streamed through the window and reflected off the wide blond streaks in her hair. She looked like an angel with a halo.

"Mrs. Fletcher." She greeted me with a smile. "How can I help you today?"

"I'm flattered you remember me."

"Everyone who was in this lobby the last time you were here remembers you. It's rare that Sheriff Halvorson changes his mind, and yet . . . that day you managed to get him to do so. I hope you aren't looking to see him again. He's not here at the moment." She clicked a key on her computer and the screen changed. "Let's see. He is at a meeting of the Professional Women's Association over at the Marriott Courtyard. I'm sure he'll be sorry to have missed you," she said with an impish grin. "Is there anything I can do?"

I thanked her and said I would try again. In the meantime I knew exactly what I planned to do.

Elton was leaning on the fender of the Escalade. He straightened up and said, "Happy to see you're not being escorted out of the building."

"Well, let's give it another try. The sheriff is at a meeting at the Marriott Courtyard. Do you know where that is?"

"It's right down the road, no more than a few hops by a high-jumping frog." Elton opened my door. "I expect you'll want to go find him."

"Well, it won't do any harm to try."

True to his word, Elton pulled into the hotel parking lot about five minutes later.

The hotel lobby was spacious, with white floor-to-ceiling columns lending an air of discreet elegance. I was about to ask the desk clerk where I could find the Professional Women's Association when I saw Sheriff Halvorson walking right toward me in the midst of an entourage of four or five people. I stepped in front of him.

"Excuse me, Sheriff . . ."

"Mrs. Fletcher, what are you doing here?" He wrinkled his brow. "If you are looking for the professional women's group, they are in the meeting room off to the left. Nice crowd they have today."

Wishful thinking on his part. Before he could walk away, I lowered my voice and said in a confidential tone, "I have some information. It may help your case."

"Jim, I'll meet you at the car," he said to the man on his left, who immediately herded the others out to the parking lot.

I kept Elton's wise advice uppermost in mind. Rather than insisting that he was making a terrible mistake, I said, "I'm afraid you may be blamed for a blunder that is no fault of your own."

He took me by the elbow and moved me into a corner behind a row of blue easy chairs. "Ma'am, I have to ask, what are you talking about?"

"Sheriff, when there is an estate as large and diverse as Willis Nickens's is likely to be and there's a recent bride who suddenly becomes a new widow . . . well, I am sure that your compatriots are searching high and low for evidence that will link her to the murder."

Sheriff Halvorson was losing patience. "If you're going to try to convince me that Mrs. Nickens is not a likely suspect, all I can say is that you are wasting your breath."

"Oh, not at all. But I do have some information you may find helpful. I overheard a conversation between Willis Nickens and his son-in-law, Clancy Travers, mere hours before Willis died.

"Willis apparently had a trust set up for his granddaughter, and he was explaining to Clancy that he was going to change the trusteeship from Clancy to Dolores. I've also learned that Willis added Dolores to the ownership of some of his companies. Clearly he trusted her."

"Mrs. Fletcher, even if I thought this information had some bearing on the case, why would I take your word for any of it?"

"Oh, you don't have to take my word. Speak to Marcus Holmes. He was Willis's attorney, so he would have handled all the paperwork. Then ask yourself if a man as shrewd as Willis Nickens would trust his wife with everything, including his beloved grand-daughter's fortune, if he had even an iota of doubt about her love and fidelity."

I thanked the sheriff for his time and courtesy and headed for the door. I knew I hadn't sold the idea to him totally, but I could see by the look on his face that I had planted a seed of doubt. I hoped it would give me the time I needed to clear Dolores's name.

Chapter Twenty

I automatically rolled away from the sunlight streaming through the bedroom window, only to bump my nose against a piece of cardboard. I opened one eye and saw the manila folder labeled NORMAN'S SCREWUPS lying on the pillow. I'd fallen asleep last night reading Willis's comments on odd pieces of business letters and memos, even a contract or two.

I glanced at the clock and saw I had time for a quick jog before breakfast. I was tying my Nikes when my phone signaled a text. Harry.

Haven't forgotten about you. Still looking around. More info to come.

Harry was nothing if not thorough. It would never enter my mind that he wasn't fully investigating any case that crossed his path. It wasn't in his nature to leave things undone.

I went out the front door, leaving it unlatched, and took a slow jog around the gardens. Then I ran down the driveway to the gate, which was securely locked. On my way back I stopped at the koi pond. The chalk marks had faded, and the pond looked rather forlorn without the colorful fish swimming about. A frog sat on the rear timber beam, and jumped into the pond for a swim as I stood there. I wondered when the Department of Natural Resources would return the koi they'd removed, or if Dolores would have to restock. Even the water irises looked lonely.

After I showered and changed into tan slacks and a blue and tan man-tailored shirt, I went downstairs. I heard voices coming from the dining room, but I walked toward the kitchen.

"Good morning, everyone."

Elton stood, pulled on the napkin that was tucked into his shirt collar covering his green and gray plaid bow tie, and dropped it on the table. Lucinda was busy at the stove. I assumed Marla Mae was in the dining room.

"I wanted to let you know that a Mr. Francis McGuire will be visiting this morning. He's a criminal attorney who is going to help Dolores navigate any future conversations with the sheriff or his deputies. She will meet with him in Willis's office and is not to be disturbed."

Lucinda said, "I'll be sure and tell Marla Mae. What about Mr. Clancy and Mr. Norman?"

I shrugged. "I see no reason for them to be told who Dolores's visitor is. If they ask directly, please refer them to me. And Elton, please sit down and finish your breakfast. Is that a corn muffin I see?"

"Sure 'nuff. The best one I ever tasted. I'll be in the library shortly, ma'am, and available for whatever you or Miss Dolores might need."

"Later today we'll be going to the Seven/Twenty-four Storage facility. Here—I'll text you the address." I entered the address from my memo pad into a text box, and in a few seconds Elton's phone pinged.

Lucinda said, "Would you care to have some breakfast here?"

"Not today, thank you. I think I will join whoever is in the dining room."

From behind me Marla Mae said, "Good morning, Miss Jessica. That would be Mr. Clancy and Abby."

As I entered the dining room, I heard Abby ask, "And if anyone at school asks me why Grampy died, what can I tell them? I'm not sure myself. Did he drown in the pond? Or fall and hit his head? I know he wasn't sick like Mommy."

Clancy saw me in the doorway and smiled. He seemed to be relieved that I was interrupting. "Abby, where are your manners? Say good morning."

"Good morning, Miss Jessica. Guess what. I'm going back to school today. Daddy says I can't stay home forever, although I wouldn't mind that at all."

"That's wonderful news. Do you know I used to be a schoolteacher?"

Abby's eyes opened wide. "No! Really? You said 'used to be.' Do you miss being a teacher?"

"Sometimes I do miss it. I particularly miss the energy of the interactions with my students. And I bet these past few days your teacher has been missing you."

"Oh, I didn't think of that. Mrs. Creighton probably does miss me. I raise my hand a lot and always do my homework. Before we leave I'd better go get Fluffy so I can show him to my friends Rosa and Eileen. We eat lunch together." Abby dashed out of the room.

Clancy said, "Jessica, I had no idea you were a teacher. So what would you advise me to tell Abby about why Willis died?"

"Well, to children most adults are already impossibly old. I would just tell her that if asked, she should say her grampy was old and tired and it was time for him to go to heaven. That should do it."

I heard the *click click* of high heels in the foyer, and then Dolores came into the room. She was wearing a short-sleeved black dress and strappy black sandals with heels higher than those of any shoes I'd worn in years.

"Good morning. Jess, look at my drop pearl." She leaned forward and touched a silver chain at her neck. "Isn't it gorgeous? Willis gave it to me on the anniversary of our first date."

"It's lovely. Clancy was just telling me that Abby is going back to school this morning."

Dolores said, "That's probably a good idea. At the rate we're slogging along, I can't even guess when the funeral will be. School will keep her busy."

Abby burst into the room. "Granny Dolores, look. I am taking Fluffy to school to introduce him to my friends."

"I'm sure your friends will be happy to meet him. Now, where's my good-morning kiss?" Dolores leaned down and Abby gave her a sweet kiss on the cheek.

As soon as Clancy said, "Let's go, or we'll be late," Dolores's face morphed from smiling to frantic.

She held up a hand. "Are you driving?"

Clancy looked puzzled. "Of course. It's much too far to walk."

Dolores recovered slightly. "I only meant we have Elton on standby. Perhaps you'd like him to take you both. That way he could bring you back."

"That's a very kind offer, but I have some errands to run, so I'd rather take my own car. Come on, princess— we don't want to be late."

Abby turned to wave good-bye as she skipped out of the room behind her father.

Dolores leaned on the dining table for support. "I can barely breathe. Is this how it's going to be from now on? I'll have my heart in my mouth every time Clancy takes Abby in the car? I know he drinks too much. *He* knows he drinks too much. I have to do something, but I am not sure what."

I put my arm around her. "Dolores, I am sure there's a solution—"

She cut me off. "A twelve-step program is the only solution I can see. You tell me how I can force him to join one and follow the rules. He's a grown man; he should know better."

There was a light tap at the door, and Elton stuck his head in. "Excuse me, ladies. Marla Mae said to tell you that Mr. McGuire is at the front gate. I'm going down to let him on in."

"Oh dear, I am not nearly ready. Let me go splash some cold water on my face and redo my makeup."

"Dolores, you look fine."

"Jess, I need a minute to gather my thoughts."

"Why don't you go to Willis's office and take your minute? I'll greet Mr. McGuire and offer him coffee, and then I'll bring him to meet you."

"Oh, would you, Jess? That would be grand."

We walked into the foyer, and Marla Mae stood there ready to answer the door. Dolores darted into the office, and I asked Marla Mae if she'd seen Norman Crayfield that morning.

"Mr. Crayfield—he's a strange one. In and out at all sorts of hours. I saw him drive off the grounds early this morning. When I was coming to work he was driving out the gate." The chimes rang out and Marla Mae opened the door.

Francis McGuire was younger than I had thought from our phone conversation, perhaps mid-thirties, certainly no more than forty. He wore aviator glasses, a bright yellow golf shirt, and khakis. I noticed he had on brown leather loafers but no socks. The only thing lawyerly about him was his Gucci messenger bag, similar to those I had seen high-powered men in expensive suits carrying on their shoulders when I was in New York City last month.

"Good morning, Mr. McGuire. I'm Jessica Fletcher . . ."

"The old college friend. Yes. Mr. Holmes told me about you." He made it sound more like Marcus Holmes had warned him about me.

I remained pleasant. "Please come with me. Mrs. Nickens is waiting in the office."

He took a step backward. "Let's get one thing straight, right from the start. I need you to realize that Mrs. Nickens and I must be completely alone when we speak."

"Of course you do. Any third-party presence would negate the lawyer-client privilege of confidentiality."

He did the closest thing to a double take that I had ever seen, so I continued. "I have no intention of staying with you and Mrs. Nickens. I am merely acting as her hostess. Would you care for a coffee?"

I led him to the office, and while I introduced him to Dolores, Marla Mae brought in a tray with coffee and muffins. When I said good-bye, Dolores looked as though she was losing her last friend in the world.

I gave her a hug and said, "Tell Mr. McGuire the truth and everything will be fine. I'll see you later."

Ever since Willis was murdered, I'd been nervous about Dolores's ability to cope. I'd lived through the shattering experience of losing a husband myself, and the circumstances of Dolores's loss, the uncertainty, were devastating enough without being named a person of interest by the local sheriff. I sincerely hoped Francis McGuire could keep the wolves at bay.

The house was quieter than usual, although I suspected if I walked down to the kitchen I would find some cheerful conversation with Lucinda and Marla Mae. Instead I decided to bring the NORMAN file down to the dining room so I could finish my research and still be within shouting distance should Dolores need me.

The file title made me think this might be the folder Marla Mae had seen Willis throw across the room. I opened it and spread the contents on the dining room table. Apparently I hadn't gotten far when I fell asleep last night. I picked up the yellow pad I had stored behind the papers, and the only note I had written was *Sort by company*.

I followed my own directions, and in short order I had twelve piles of two or three papers each related to different companies. I plugged the names of the first few companies into my phone one at a time, but each Internet search came up empty.

I decided to read everything carefully and take notes in the hope that I could discover whatever information the papers contained. The first pile included two invoices, one dated this past January and one dated two years ago. The company name on the invoices was Dresher, Inc. Willis had scribbled, REALLY? on the older one and WHO CAME UP WITH THESE NUMBERS? on the most recent.

The third piece of paper in the pile was a letter from Marcus Holmes advising Norman Crayfield that Dresher Inc. was in danger of bankruptcy. Across that one Willis had written, JERK!!!! and underlined it twice.

I assumed that the letter had something to do with Norman because it was in this folder, but I was pleased to see Marcus Holmes was involved. He'd be a resource for Dolores when the time came to go over Willis's business dealings, and perhaps he could explain these papers.

By the time I went through the third pile, I could tell that everything on the table was going to be indecipherable to me, but at least I would have the information in orderly fashion to discuss with Dolores. On several

Willis had scrawled in black marker: NORMAN, WE COULD HAVE DONE BETTER or NORMAN, DO BETTER NEXT TIME.

I suspected that when Willis wrote "do better" he meant "make more money."

I picked up the second paper in pile number four and a name caught my eye. "Clancy Travers." Now things were getting interesting. It was a letter from Marvin Pappas, CEO of Coliseum Investments Inc., who was complaining about a meeting he'd had with Clancy Travers when he'd expected to be meeting with Willis. Mr. Pappas felt snubbed and demanded a personal meeting be set up immediately. I looked at the date of the letter. It was written nearly three months ago. I wondered if the meeting ever took place. Willis had written across the top of the page, NORMAN, EXPLAIN.

I heard voices in the foyer; then Dolores called my name. I stepped out of the dining room and she looked calmer than she had since before I discovered Willis's body.

"Jess, there you are. Mr. McGuire would like a word."

"Mrs. Fletcher, I understand you write mysteries for a living."

"That's certainly true."

"Mrs. Nickens tells me that you have, in the past, contributed to the resolution of a real-life murder or two."

I am always a little flustered when the topic comes up. It usually results in my being told to back off, but that was not the case with Mr. McGuire.

He handed me his business card. "If you come across anything that might point to a suspect other than Mrs. Nickens, please call my office immediately. If I am not available, ask for Michael Clark. I wrote his name on the card. You can trust him as you would me."

Mr. McGuire bade us good day and left, telling Dolores he would be in touch.

Dolores clapped her hands, her gold bracelets clattering up and down her arm, as she took a little skip across the foyer. "Oh, Jess, I feel better than I have since . . . since you came to my room to tell me about Willis. For the first time I believe this nightmare will end. And with you on the case . . ."

"Dolores, you and I have a lot of work to do. This isn't a television detective show. This is your life. Now, come into the dining room and tell me what you discussed with Mr. McGuire."

Chapter Twenty-one

Dolores looked at the papers spread on the dining room table. "What's all this?"

"I'll explain in a minute, but first tell me what Mr. McGuire said." I was extremely curious how he had handled the interview.

"Well, the first thing he asked me was whether or not I had murdered Willis. Can you imagine? He said he was bound by law, that everything I told him was in complete confidence, and then he asked, straight-out, if I killed Willis. I started to cry and almost walked out of the room.

"He reminded me that he was not accusing me of anything but needed to know the truth so we could mount the best possible defense should it come to that."

I nodded. "Yes, that is standard lawyer talk. I write sentences like that in my books all the time."

"Once I told him that I didn't kill Willis and I have no idea who did, he shifted his focus and asked if I knew anyone who had reason to want Willis out of the way—permanently." Dolores spread her palms open wide. "I couldn't think of a soul. I mean, sometimes Willis was cranky, but who would kill him for that?"

I didn't have the heart to tell her that kind of murder happens more often than she could imagine. "What else did Mr. McGuire say?"

"You already heard the rest. He repeated what he told us on the phone—I shouldn't talk to anyone without him present, that kind of thing. So now, tell me, what is all this?" Dolores waved her hand across the table, causing a few papers to flutter.

I picked up the folder. "These papers are the contents of this folder that I found in Willis's file cabinet. As you can see it is titled 'Norman's Screwups.' I have tried to organize it, but so far most of it doesn't make any sense. There are papers about companies that seem not to exist. And here"—I picked up the letter from Coliseum Investments—"is a letter that mentions Clancy."

"This doesn't make any sense." Dolores shook her head. "As far as I know Clancy has nothing to do with any of Willis's business ventures. Maybe Mr. Holmes will know."

I phrased my next question carefully. "Dolores, do you have any idea how Clancy earns a living?"

"Honestly? I'm not sure. I know he owns a musty antique shop that belonged to his grandfather. Not furniture. Small items, like tableware, men's pipes, and tin lunch boxes from the 1950s—that sort of thing. He buys and sells through a few websites."

"Do you think he makes enough selling antiques to support himself and Abby?"

"Who knows? He inherited the house they live in from Emily. It was a wedding present from Willis, so Clancy owns it free and clear. And although he didn't receive the contents of Emily's trust fund, he did get odds and ends of investments she owned. Then there is Abby's trust."

"From what I overheard Willis say, we know Clancy had access to the trust, but we have no idea how that all works." I realized that was another question for Marcus Holmes, who, unfortunately, had already shown reluctance to talk to Dolores as long as she was a person of interest.

I started to gather up the papers and put them back in the folder. "Dolores, do you feel up to going to the storage locker today?"

"Jess, after speaking with Mr. McGuire, I believe you are absolutely right. We have to find out if someone else, anyone else, had a reason to kill Willis. We need to create what he called a suspect pool. Mr. McGuire told me that a jury would consider Willis's financial assets to be my motive and that no one in the world has ever thought being alone and asleep could be considered any sort of an alibi. When he put it like that . . . So, yes. By all means, let's see what is in that locker."

We were in the Escalade less than fifteen minutes before Elton pulled into the parking lot of the storage facility. A cheery white and yellow customer service counter was inside, to the left of the front door. On the countertop was an old-fashioned call bell next to a sign that read PLEASE TAP ONLY ONCE FOR HELP.

Dolores elbowed me and said, "How many customers couldn't resist the urge to hit the bell with a tap-tap-tap-tap-tap-tap before they put up the sign?"

I hit the bell once. "Well, for us one tap will do."

A middle-aged woman with a pen stuck in the grayish brown bun at the nape of her neck came through a door next to the file cabinets. She wore a yellow and white striped jacket that matched the wallpaper behind the counter. Her name tag identified her as Sue Ellen.

"Welcome to Seven/Twenty-four. How can I help y'all?"

Dolores pulled the latest receipt from her purse. "My husband and I have a storage space here. I'd like to access it, please."

Sue Ellen took the receipt and tapped a few keys on the computer. "That would be one of the big lockers— room number 124. Your husband's been in now and again but I see this is your first visit. I hope you find the space to your liking. It's one of the best we have. May I see your driver's license?"

Dolores passed her license over the counter, and Sue Ellen pushed it through a slot in a small gadget next to the computer.

"There you go, ma'am. Now we have your license attached to the file. From now on when you come in, we'll just pull it up and see that you are you, and off you go, no fuss, no muss."

"Excuse me, but does anyone besides Mr. and Mrs. Nickens have permission to access their space?" I asked.

"Not a single person. Mr. and Mrs. Nickens are the only ones for now, but"—Sue Ellen turned to Dolores—"you can add another person at any time you've a mind to. Also, I wanted to say that you're a lucky lady, ma'am. Lots of men come and go through here and the wives are none the wiser about what all is stored in the lockers and rooms. In my years I've seen everything from motorcycles to porn collections. But Mr. Nickens is a straight-up man. No secrets. I remember he came within a day or two of your wedding to add you to the account. Gave me a big tip and all. That's how I remember."

Sue Ellen reverted to business. "Now, you go straight down this hall and make a left. Toward the end of the corridor you will see room 124. When you want to go in, tap the three-digit code on the door; a yellow light will come on, which will send me a signal to click the master lock. Then the green light will come on, and you're in."

Dolores looked perplexed, and I could see she had a question or two, so I took her arm and hurried her down the hall.

"But, Jess," Dolores said, "we don't know the code."

"Oh, I am sure we do." I was confident. "Willis was not the type of man to waste his time devising a secret code. He would unquestionably follow a safe and simple route. I promise you he chose a code you could come up with in no more than two or three tries. Here we are."

We stopped in front of the door and I indicated the keypad. "Try the first three digits of your birthday."

Nothing.

"Now the first three digits of your wedding date," I instructed.

Dolores raised an eyebrow but didn't voice her skepticism; instead she hit the numbers, and the yellow light glowed.

In a few seconds the green light came on and, filled with excitement, we opened the door, only to be instantly deflated.

Willis's storage area was a room that looked about ten feet by twelve feet. An old metal desk and a chair filled one corner. The rest of the room was packed with four-drawer file cabinets, some with two or three cardboard boxes piled on top.

"What on earth?" Dolores walked over and leaned on the edge of the desk. "What could all this mess possibly be? It looks like Willis held on to every piece of paper he ever touched."

"It certainly does. I suspect at least some of these cabinets hold files for Quartermaster Industries." I looked at the cabinets. None of them had identification tabs on the outside. Clearly this was not going to be as simple as I thought.

Dolores began opening the desk drawers, which were loaded with pads, pens, clips, staples—all the usual office paraphernalia. The center drawer had a telephone book. I picked it up and opened to the letter "L" and there was Marcus Holmes under "L" for "lawyer." This book was likely an exact replica of the one in his home office.

Dolores opened the bottom drawer and didn't seem to be surprised when she found a couple of cigars and an ashtray. "At least Willis ran true to form."

I held up the phone book. "He certainly did."

"What am I going to do with all this?" Dolores was clearly overwhelmed.

"Unless we want to sit here day after day for the next several months, I suggest you arrange to have it moved to the house, where you can go through it at your leisure."

"To Manning Hall? You want me to bring these dirty, dusty cabinets and decrepit boxes into my home?"

I ran the tip of my finger along the top of a cabinet and acknowledged she had a point. "Well, for now perhaps I will take only a few files from the cabinet nearest Willis's desk. They're probably the most current."

When I went to open the top drawer, I saw the handle was thick with dust. Wrong assumption on my part. But it did give me an idea. I scanned the cabinets one by one. Right in the middle of the room was a cabinet with no dust whatsoever on its drawer handles. It was either brand-new or frequently used. The bottom three drawers were empty, but the top drawer held about a dozen file folders; all had papers inside. None of them labeled.

I grabbed a handful of files and said, "Okay, here is the plan. Am I correct in assuming you trust Marla Mae?"

"Very much so. She and Lucinda both."

"What about Elton?"

"I have no reason not to. He has been so good to us."

"Well, with your permission I will call Elton and have him meet us at the front desk. You can have Sue Ellen put him on the access list and he can bring Marla Mae over to give this place a thorough cleaning. Then we can decide what to do with all this."

It took about three minutes to persuade Elton that it was perfectly legal for him to be on Dolores's storage facility account and under a minute for Sue Ellen to swipe his license through the recording gizmo and say, "You are good to go, Mr. Anderson."

So in less than five minutes we were in the car and on our way back to Manning Hall. Dolores and I toasted each other with bottles of water we'd taken from the cooler.

"Well, that was exhilarating." Dolores began to giggle. "Just like the good old days at Harrison College. Remember the time, as part of our sorority pledge, we had to pick a professor who didn't know us, had never taught us? Then we had to go into his office and convince the secretary that we *were* his students and get an excusal slip from her for some made-up absence."

"How could I forget?" I laughed. "We picked Professor Marsden in the music department because he was so old and befuddled we thought it would be easy to convince his secretary that he'd forgotten to give us our excusals."

Dolores said, "And we had the secretary—Oh, I can't remember her name. Mrs. Kiley, Kelly, something like that. Anyway, we had her nearly convinced. She actually had her hand on the excusal-slip pad when who walked in but old Marsden himself, who asked in his usual crusty snarl, 'What are these two doing here?'"

I nodded. "Oh, I well remember. The secretary held up the excusal slips and looked at Marsden for permission. And he said—"

Dolores jumped in with a pretty good imitation of the professor. "He said, 'What are you waiting for? Give it to them and get them out of here. It's for a pledge to some sorority or another.' We were stunned."

"That's for sure. I never doubted any of the, shall we say, more mature professors again."

Dolores said, "Neither did I."

I brought the files I'd taken from the storage facility to my bedroom and slid them under my suitcase. I checked my phone, hoping I had another text from Harry, but no such luck. Then I took a few moments to freshen up before I went to meet Dolores in the kitchen.

Lucinda looked up from the sandwiches she was making. "Deviled ham on home-baked wheat bread, in case you're wondering. Miss Dolores is out at the picnic table. I believe that is fast becoming her favorite rest spot."

"Possibly so. And when all the houseguests leave Dolores will be alone, so she may spend even more time there. Hopefully she won't get in your way."

"Wouldn't mind if she did. Back in the town house it was just me and Mr. Willis for all those years, and when he married, well, naturally I worried how the new wife would treat me. But Miss Dolores has been nothing but kind. She was the one who insisted that this house was too big for me to manage on my own. Something Mr. Willis never gave a thought to. When I told her Marla Mae, a friend of my niece, was looking for work, she hired her on my say-so. Said it was important for me and my coworker to get along. That's how thoughtful Miss Dolores is."

"Lucinda, when I go home to Cabot Cove, I will feel much better knowing that I am leaving my friend in such caring hands."

Dolores was sitting at the picnic table. "Hey, Jess, look at that black-and-white warbler." She pointed to a bird whose striking color combination made him highly visible on the branch of a distant pine tree. "This is their nesting season, and they are one of the few bird species that hide their nests on the ground. Abby told me that they do so to prevent the eggs from falling from a nest high in a tree, but I am not sure if she assumes that or if it's true."

I poured myself a glass of sweet tea from the pitcher on the table. "Speaking of Abby reminds me of her father. I am so curious why he, instead of Willis, attended that meeting with Mr. Pappas."

Dolores sighed. "I've been so surprised by what I've learned about him in the past few days. Who can tell with Clancy?"

At that exact moment, casually carrying a putter and some other golf clubs over his shoulder, Clancy Travers came around the side of the house. "Did I hear my name being taken in vain?"

Chapter Twenty-two

I leaned over and whispered to Dolores, "One thing at a time. Let's just ask about Pappas for now. Save your leverage for later."

Dolores considered for a moment and then became an amiable hostess. "Clancy, would you like a glass of sweet tea? Jessica has something she would like to ask you."

Clancy sat down and said, "Jessica, if this is about the eulogy, I have been thinking and I promise to come up with more stories."

Before Dolores could ask what he was talking about, I said quickly, "No, it's something else. We have been going through Willis's papers and came across an irate letter from a Mr. Pappas of Coliseum Investments. He was upset because Willis sent you to meet with him instead of attending the meeting himself.

Dolores and I couldn't imagine why on earth Mr. Pappas was so upset."

Rather than being demanding I decided to go for perplexed, and it worked.

Clancy groaned. "Oh, I remember Mr. Pappas—or as I call him, Mr. Pompous. He lives and works in California someplace but came east for a wedding in Atlanta. Since he was going to be so nearby and he and Willis had never actually met, Pappas decided to come to Columbia and have a lunch meeting with Willis. Trouble was, Willis and Dolores were on their honeymoon when Pappas texted from Atlanta."

"Why didn't Willis tell the man that we were on completely different continents?" Dolores asked.

"You know that wasn't Willis's style. His motto was 'Never let a business opportunity slip by,' or at least that's what I always imagined his motto to be."

I said, "And he assumed Mr. Pappas would have some business to discuss rather than this being strictly a social call."

Clancy nodded. "And here is a sentence I would never dare say while he was alive: Willis was wrong. Pappas thought that the geography of his nephew's wedding made it easy for him to meet Willis and have a friendly lunch. He had nothing more on his agenda. But when I showed up, Pappas hit the ceiling. I explained about the honeymoon, but even after I told him I was Willis's son-in-law he was furious at Willis for, as he called it, 'blowing him off.' Pappas couldn't understand why Willis wasn't straightforward. All he had to do was text back that he was out of town."

"How did you get involved in the first place? Did Willis send you to the luncheon?" Dolores asked the question that was on the tip of my tongue.

"You know he would never involve me in anything remotely connected to the business. He thought I was a complete idiot. The first time Willis heard that I had represented him was when he got the letter from Pappas. This entire snafu falls squarely on Norman's shoulders. You see, Willis sent Pappas's text to Norman and told him to represent the company by meeting with Pappas."

I could visualize the catastrophe in the making. "Norman had other plans that day?"

"He sure did. And she must have been a real hot number, because he paid me a thousand dollars to go to lunch with Pappas and be congenial. And we figured by the time Willis came home Pappas would be back on the West Coast and long forgotten. To be honest, Norman's been helping me out over the years by having me represent the company at useless meetings and paying me off the books so Willis never knew."

"But this time Mr. Pappas wrote a letter," I said.

"Yes. And Willis went ballistic. He blasted me from here to kingdom come. Told me I was never to go near any of his business associates again. I thought he'd take a similar piece out of Norman's hide, but since mine was the name in the letter, he sent for me first. With Willis round two was never as bad as round one, so Norman just did a little genuflecting and the incident passed."

Clancy squinted at his phone. "It's getting late. I

have to pick up Abby and drive her from school to dance class."

I put my hand on Dolores's arm, but it was too little, too late.

"Tell me the truth," Dolores demanded. "Did you drink any alcohol today?"

Clancy began to squirm. He leaned so far back that I feared he would fall off the bench he was sitting on. "No. Of course not. It's the middle of the afternoon. Why would you even ask such a question?"

Dolores stood up and planted her hands firmly on her hips, her voice getting louder with every word. "Clancy, you know why. You have multiple DUI arrests that you have been hiding from the family, and all the while you are putting our Abby in jeopardy."

Clancy crumpled like a punctured tire. "I would never." He stopped, and started again. "I would never jeopardize Abby's safety. Never!"

"And what about your own? The poor child has lost her mother and now her grandfather, and you risk your life every single time you get behind the wheel after you've had one too many. You won't be happy until she's a full orphan."

Clancy slashed back, "You'd love that, wouldn't you? Then you'd have Abby all to yourself."

"At least when I drive her anywhere I will always be sober. Maybe you should stay here and I should pick her up from school."

"Clancy, Dolores, stop it right now." I was beginning to fear they would come to blows. "I personally think you are both too upset to get behind the wheel of a car. We have Elton and a roomy Escalade at our disposal. Why don't you let him drive the two of you to the school? And for goodness' sake, act as though you like each other. It's important for Abby to see the two people she loves getting along."

Neither answered me.

After a long silence I said, "Do I have to go along to keep you from arm wrestling in the car?"

Dolores broke first. "Clancy, we can hash this out later but for Abby's sake we should be civil, and perhaps our going together to pick her up from school would be a start."

Clancy shrugged, which I hoped meant *Why not?* but he didn't answer.

Dolores said, "Besides, I think Abby will love the captain's chairs in the Escalade. Don't you, Jess?"

Before I could agree, Clancy said, "Okay, for Abby's sake I'm in, but very soon we'll have to have a long talk about how our relationship proceeds from here."

Dolores said she would look forward to it and went off to find Elton.

Clancy got up and gathered his golf clubs.

Before he left, I took the opportunity to say, "That was very gracious of you."

"Well, the fact is, after my first conviction for drunk driving I had to pay a fine and was sentenced to one hundred hours of community service, instead of spending thirty days in jail and having my license suspended. I was lucky the judge took my circumstances into account and reduced it to a restricted license because I am a single parent. I was allowed to drive Abby to activities and to visit relatives, do the food shopping, things like that."

"And that's how you kept Willis from finding out."

"Willis and everyone else. But time went by, I got sloppy, and one night coming home from a—well, I may as well say it—coming home from a date, I got pulled over for a burned-out taillight and out came the old Breathalyzer. My lawyer says I am definitely going to lose my license this time. I'm only glad that Willis isn't here to see it." Clancy smiled wryly. "He would lambaste me, although I am chagrined to see that Dolores seems quite capable of filling that role. Looks like Willis married the right girl. And I'd better get to the car before she comes looking for me."

I sat for a few minutes enjoying the serenity. Dolores and Clancy certainly had far more issues to work out than I'd realized. But if they both put Abby's best interest first, I was sure it could be done.

Then I noticed Marjory Ribault, wearing a red cape and carrying a small basket, walking along the path through the pine trees. The scene reminded me of the fairy tale about Little Red Riding Hood.

I offered her a glass of sweet tea, and while I poured she put her basket, which was full of blueberries, on the table and took a seat.

"There are blueberry bushes on the other side of my house, and they are laden with fresh fruit. Lucinda likes to use them in her baking."

I said, "I've been fortunate enough to sample some of her baked treats. She works magic with blueberries."

Marla Mae came out from the kitchen. "Here, let me refill that pitcher. Would y'all like a snack? We have sugar cookies and brownies."

I passed, but Marjory opted for sugar cookies and asked Marla Mae to bring the blueberries to Lucinda. We sat enjoying the cool afternoon breeze.

Marjory said, "I could hear Dolores clear over at the blueberry bushes. I couldn't tell what all had her upset but I could hear the rage in her voice. I certainly wouldn't want to get on her bad side."

I stayed mute.

After a while, Marjory tried again. "Was it about the jewelry?"

Now I was startled. Did she mean Claudia's jewelry? That was such a private fight between Willis and Dolores that even Lucinda didn't know the cause; how could Marjory?

"I don't know what you mean." Playing dumb usually got more information than most other tactics.

"Willis's first wife, Claudia, had about a million dollars in fine jewels, which should have gone to Emily but somehow never did. Well, to hear Clancy tell it, every time Emily asked her father about the jewels, he put her off for one reason or another. Clancy was getting quite frustrated, and then Emily died, and well, Willis still has the jewelry, or I suppose it's more accurate to say Dolores has it now. The jewelry should have gone to Emily, and then to Clancy for the little girl. Such a shame."

I was in a position to know it wasn't a shame at all, that Dolores had made sure Abby would get her grandmother's jewels, but I pretended to be aghast.

"Are you sure about this? Are you certain this jewelry actually exists?"

Marjory bobbed her head repeatedly. "Oh yes, quite sure. Clancy drank one too many martinis during a fairly large dinner party here at Manning Hall. He got flippant with Willis a time or two, and before real trouble could start Candy and I brought him out to the sitting garden to clear his head, and that's when he told us. He was quite emphatic, even . . . indiscreet."

"Indiscreet? In what way?"

"Well, he said his antique business—which, frankly, I always thought was more of a hobby—wasn't doing well and if he had the jewelry he could take out loans against it. That way he wouldn't have to hit up his daughter's trust fund so often."

I was shocked. "Oh my, he was absolutely reckless in revealing such personal information. Besides you and Candy, was anyone else there? Is it possible other people know about his financial woes?"

"Well, somewhere in the middle of Clancy's rant Norman came out for a cigar. He is the one who finally got Clancy to stop ranting. I believe his exact words were 'Shut up, you fool. You've said far too much already.' And of course there's Tom—I'm sure he knows. Candy tells him everything."

That's what you think floated through my mind.

"And speaking of Candy, I am a little . . . not exactly worried, but close—let's say concerned."

"Really? Why are you concerned?" I feigned ignorance. "I stopped by Jessamine House yesterday, and she seemed fine when I saw her."

"You're probably right. She just doesn't seem herself

since Willis died. She's always on edge. I guess we're all in turmoil. Everyone was so upset by the shock of Willis's death, and now the sheriff has deemed it a murder." Marjory shivered. "Well, that makes it bone-chilling. Positively bone-chilling. I mean, one minute we were all together, and within hours Willis was dead, and someone made it happen."

Obviously Marjory didn't know the secrets of Candy's past.

She stood. "Well, that's enough doom and gloom for one day. I'd better get home. Jessica, it was lovely to have tea the other day. Please stop by anytime you are out for a jog."

The kitchen door opened and Abby called, "Miss Jessica, come see the big surprise."

And the door slammed shut. *Well, she's here and she's laughing, so Dolores and Clancy must have pulled off the ride home from the school pickup line without any angst or confrontation.*

I entered the kitchen and it was filled with smiling people. Clancy, Dolores, and Elton were standing in front of the kitchen table while Lucinda and Marla Mae stood near the sink.

"Close your eyes," Abby commanded.

I did as I was told. She took my hand and led me slowly toward the table, giggling all the way.

"When I count to three, you can open your eyes. One . . . two . . . three . . . open," Abby shouted.

Everyone started to clap and laugh. On the table sat what I thought was a chocolate sheet cake until I read the sign next to it that declared it to be COLA CAKE in big letters.

"It's snack time," Abby proclaimed. Dolores began cutting the cake while Marla Mae offered hot tea, sweet tea, and coffee to the grown-ups. Lucinda put a healthy-sized glass of milk on the table in front of Abby.

Everyone crowded around to watch me take my first-ever bite of cola cake, and they cheered when I pronounced it delicious.

"Can I crash this party, or is it by invitation only?" Norman Crayfield had come down the hallway and stood in the kitchen doorway.

Dolores grabbed his arm and pulled him into the room. "Come, join us, please. We're celebrating Jessica's first taste of cola cake, but not her last, I'm sure."

"Most certainly not my last!" I agreed.

Norman folded his arms. "I can't imagine what Willis Nickens would think of this: family, friends, and servants all carousing together. Not his kind of party, that's for sure."

And in a flash the joy dissipated. Norman had managed to remind everyone of the pall Willis had often cast on social occasions. Only Abby didn't notice. Her mouth delightfully covered with chocolate, she held up her plate. "First one finished."

Chapter Twenty-three

Marla Mae cut a piece of cola cake and handed it to Norman, who smiled his thanks and said, "Jessica, I, for one, am doubly delighted you are here. Of course I'm happy for your gracious company, but it's been an age since I had some of Lucinda's delicious cola cake."

Clancy said, "Norman, I was looking for you earlier, hoping we could spend some time on the putting green, but I understand you left early this morning. What were you up to today?"

Norman held up his fork, using it like a pause button, giving him time to swallow his cake—or, I thought, perhaps to decide what his answer would be.

"Business, buddy boy, always business. I have to step up now since . . . That reminds me, Dolores— there is absolutely no rush, but I can go over any details about how we run the business whenever you are comfortable doing so. There's not a lot you need to know, but I am at your beck and call." He smiled, quite satisfied with himself. It was evident that Norman was hoping his version of mansplaining would convince the world, or at least Dolores, that business decisions should be left to him.

I wondered what he'd say when he found out that Dolores was the major shareholder in Quartermaster and that she intended to act the part once everything got sorted.

The house phone rang, and Lucinda immediately answered the kitchen extension. She put her hand over the mouthpiece and said, "Miss Dolores, you'd best take this call in your office."

I didn't miss that it was no longer "Mr. Willis's office." Score one for Dolores.

Clancy and Norman huddled in a corner, talking about golf. Elton asked Abby about her day at school. She started out by telling him how much her friends liked meeting Fluffy.

Lucinda moved to the pantry doorway and signaled me to follow. Her tone was both low and serious. "That was Mr. McGuire's office on the phone. Perhaps you should . . ."

"Say no more."

I slipped out of the kitchen and hovered in the foyer until Dolores opened the office door. I ushered her back inside.

"Apparently I have an appointment at the Sheriff's Department to be interviewed at ten o'clock tomorrow morning. Mr. McGuire will meet me in the Grits and Gravy Café at nine thirty. He said we don't need privacy because we won't be talking about substance.

He simply wants to give me a few pointers on demeanor."

I said, "He certainly seems to be good at what he does. By meeting first, having a light conversation and perhaps a cup of coffee, he's hoping to help you be less nervous, more prepared for the rigors of the interview."

"Jess, would you mind . . . ? Do you think you could . . . ?"

"Accompany you? Of course, I'd be happy to."

"Well, I'm sure they won't let you into the interview. You should bring a book or something. You might be in the waiting room for a long time."

I put my arm around her shoulders. "Don't worry. I'm sure I'll find something to do. And since we are going to be out, why don't we make a day of it? Why don't you see if you can get an appointment with Marcus Holmes for tomorrow afternoon?"

"That's a great idea. If we can get all the lawyer nonsense out of the way in the same day, then we can relax for a while."

I didn't say a word. I was fairly certain Dolores would not be able to relax in the near future, but she was in such a cheerful mood I decided to change the subject.

"How did you and Clancy manage riding together to pick up Abby?" I asked.

"Clancy was civil but frosty toward me. It helped to have Elton in the car. Clancy asked him a question about some sports team or another and in a few minutes they were chatting like old friends. By the time Abby got in the car we were behaving like a normal family, with the recent spat forgotten." She stopped, then picked up the thread. "Of course, it's not forgotten. I know I'm going to have to do something about Clancy's drinking. But that's for another day."

The bigger problem, as I saw it, was that in time Dolores would have to accept that Clancy was the only one who could do anything about his drinking problem, but I decided it was wisest not to point that out right now. Dolores had enough on her plate.

"Dolores, if you don't need me for anything, I'd like to spend some time going through those folders we brought home from Willis's storage room."

"I actually promised to help Abby with her homework, but if you need me just give a holler. When it comes to Willis's business activities I need to start learning the ropes, as they say."

"Don't be silly. Abby comes first." I started to leave, and then had a thought. "There is one thing that you can do, however. When Clancy and Norman are out of earshot, find out if Marla Mae would be willing to clean the storage room, and arrange a time for Elton to take her to the storage facility and sign her in."

"I'd forgotten about that," Dolores said. "You are a wise woman. There is no need for Clancy, Norman, or anyone else to know the storeroom and those files even exist."

I opened my windows wide, and was lucky enough to catch the same jasmine-scented breeze that had been so relaxing when we sat in the backyard. I pulled the files out from under my suitcase and set them on the desk.

Before I began to read the files I checked my phone again, hoping to hear from Harry McGraw. No luck. There was a text from my nephew Grady's wife, Donna. She hoped I was enjoying my visit and was wondering if on my way back to Cabot Cove I would be able to stop by New York City for a day or two. My grandnephew Frank had been asking when Aunt Jessica was going to come to visit again.

I texted back that my plans were in flux but I would let her know as soon as I could nail down my travel arrangements.

The folders from the storage room all looked reasonably new, and none of them were labeled. I wondered if they were just rest stops for papers until Willis got around to putting them in their permanent homes, whichever beat-up folder in one of the dustier file cabinets that might be.

I opened one folder. Inside I found two pieces of paper. One contained a phone number for a man named Carlo, with the words *New Rotary Pres.* written beside it. The second was a receipt for a rather substantial donation Willis had made to a Rotary service project supporting hospitals in underserved communities. Laudable, but of no use in my search for murder suspects.

I didn't find anything useful in either of the next two folders. I was getting frustrated and decided that I would look in one more folder before I would go to the kitchen in search of a cup of tea.

The next folder yielded half a dozen pieces of paper held together by a binder clip. The top page was a blank sheet torn from a legal pad, as if to protect the other pages from prying eyes. A phone number was scribbled in pencil on the inside of the folder. Apparently, in spite of his neatly kept telephone books, jotting down phone numbers in odd places was something Willis did fairly often.

I pressed open the binder clip and the blank page from the legal pad slipped away. The second page looked like a legal document, typed in single space, signed and witnessed at the bottom.

I looked at the signatures. Willis Nickens and Randall Carbonetti. The third signature was from a notary public signing as witness.

The page was number four of a document and it was stapled to page two, which had a few paragraphs and a short list of names. One name was highlighted in yellow. Thomas Blomquist.

Pages one and three were missing. As I read the two pages in my hand, it was evident that Tom Blomquist and the other people on the list owed money in some way to Mr. Carbonetti and that Willis had bought the loans.

I wondered if this was more of the practice I kept hearing about, that of families lending money to one another to keep the old houses in the hands of the even older families.

So it wasn't just a matter of Tom and Candy wanting to borrow money from Willis to modernize Jessamine House. Even without a new loan, they were already indebted to him for an undisclosed amount, and I had a feeling it wasn't a small sum. The final pages were also torn from a legal pad. There were all sorts of math calculations scattered around, which made them look like scrap papers from an exam in basic accounting.

After what I considered to be my big find, the last folder was extremely disappointing. The only page was a list of telephone extensions for the employees of a company called Available Options. It meant nothing at all to me, and I was about to drop it back into the folder when a name caught my eye. Randall Carbonetti.

Now the question was, did Willis buy the company, buy a subsidiary, or perhaps just buy some free-falling assets? And I knew just the person who could tell me.

I grabbed my phone and punched in Randall Carbonetti's number. On the third ring a young woman answered.

"Hello. I'm Mrs. Fletcher, special assistant to Mrs. Willis Nickens, calling for Mr. Carbonetti." I was hoping she would hear "Mrs. Willis Nickens, calling for Mr. Carbonetti" and lose my name, as had happened when I called Mr. Holmes's office.

Luck was with me. The next thing I heard was a deep voice. "Mrs. Nickens, Randall Carbonetti here. I must tell you how sorry I was to hear about the untimely loss of your husband. If there is anything I can do, please don't hesitate to ask."

"Actually, Mr. Carbonetti, there is something you can do. My name is Jessica Fletcher and I am calling on Mrs. Nickens's behalf."

"Oh, I . . . guess I misunderstood." He was trapped and he knew it. "What can I do to assist Mrs. Nickens?"

"In going through Willis's papers we found a folder that had some information about Available Options and a notarized document signed by you and by Willis. Unfortunately several pages are missing, so it's unclear—did Willis buy the company from you?"

"What kind of scam are you running, lady? Why would I sell my company to anyone?"

I hurried to explain before he hung up. "Please, this isn't a scam; it is merely a matter of lost pages from a contract you and Willis signed. Mrs. Nickens cannot decipher exactly what Willis bought."

Mr. Carbonetti drew a sharp breath. "What pages do you have? Is there a date visible?"

"Let me see. Yes, I have a signature page. You and Mr. Nickens both signed and dated it, as did the notary."

Once I told him the date he immediately let his guard down. "Hold on a second—let me check."

I listened to computer keys clicking, and then he was back. "Okay, I have it. You say you lost part of the paperwork?"

"Well, I only have pages two and four . . ."

He sniffed. "That sounds like a photocopy error. Should have copied both sides, and with pages one and three missing I guess the document doesn't make much sense."

"No," I agreed, "it doesn't."

"Well, how's this for a solution? I will explain exactly what the paperwork represents, and then I'll messenger a complete copy to Mrs. Nickens first thing in the morning."

"That sounds perfect."

"How much do you know about Available Options, if I may ask?"

"Not a thing," I confessed. I was getting more curious by the minute. I wished he would get to the point.

"We are a private loan company. We lend money based on collateral: jewels, houses, coin collections, antique cars, pretty much anything that has substantial value."

"I see." Or at least I was starting to.

"In our line of work, cash flow is of paramount importance." He stopped, waiting for my reply.

"Paramount. Yes, of course." I hoped that would satisfy him, and apparently it did.

It took forever for him to get to the point. "To keep our coffers full so that we can continue to provide our services to our highly appreciated clientele, we occasionally sell off some of our longer-term loans to, I assure you, only the most discerning investors, one of whom, I am happy to report, was Willis Nickens. Our records do indicate such a transaction occurred on the date you provided."

I pried a little further. "So the individuals listed on page two owed money to Available Options, and now they owe it to Willis Nickens."

"That's it exactly."

"Mr. Carbonetti, I have one final question. Are there loan books of some sort? I mean, how do the people who received the loans know whom to pay?"

He cleared his throat and then said, "Our process is described in the pages that are, unfortunately, missing from Mrs. Nickens's copy of the loan agreement. Here is the short version. Each loan is due in a lump sum plus interest on a date certain. An investor such as Mr. Nickens buys the loan from us at the value of the original loan plus a small premium. When the loan comes due, the loan recipient pays Available Options and we pass the payment to our private investor. All completely legal and aboveboard."

"So as these loans come due, Mrs. Nickens will receive payment?"

"Certainly. Well, at least once the estate is settled. Will there be anything else?"

"You've been very helpful, Mr. Carbonetti. I will be sure to tell Mrs. Nickens."

"Thank you, Mrs. Fletcher. Remember to look for the messenger tomorrow."

I dropped the phone in my lap, astonished by what I had learned. The conversation left so many questions. Did Candy know about the loan? Did Tom even know that Willis now held the loan? And I was wildly curious about what valuable asset Tom had used to secure it.

Chapter Twenty-four

Rain splattered against my windows in large, heavy drops. No jogging for me today. *Well,* I thought as I did my stretches, *it will be a busy enough day, filled with lawyers and legal stress.* I wondered if Dolores had any yoga or aerobics DVDs. It would probably do us both good to exercise once we got home this afternoon, although, as she had since our college days, Dolores would resist my efforts to get her moving.

I checked my phone but there were no middle-of-the-night texts from Harry. I was counting on him to come up with something—and soon.

My tan travel suit seemed a perfect choice for a long day. I could go jacket on, jacket off—depending on weather changes. A short-sleeved dark blue cotton sweater was a nice complement to the suit and would be comfortable should the weather turn to eighty and sunny later in the day.

I went downstairs and headed directly for the kitchen.

Lucinda gave me a broad wink. "Blueberry scones this morning."

"Why, that's enough good news to chase the rain away," I said. "Is Marla Mae around?"

"Right behind you, Miss Jessica." Marla Mae came into the kitchen. "I just finished setting out breakfast in the dining room." She walked over to the stove and picked up a plate covered with a cloth. "Lucinda put these scones on the stove top to keep them warm. Said I was only to bring them out special when you come down."

"You two are a dream team. I am becoming so spoiled that I will be hard-pressed to poach my own eggs when I get back to Cabot Cove."

The ladies flushed at the well-deserved compliment.

Then I segued to the reason I wanted to talk to them. "A package of documents is being messengered to Dolores today. They are extremely important and extremely private. I would appreciate your handling it with discretion."

I watched as they exchanged a look and came to a decision.

Lucinda said, "On the bottom shelf of the pantry, behind the canned goods on the right-hand side, there is a carved-out square in the wall. Used to be where the milkman put the bottles. I imagine that was when he still came around in a horse-drawn wagon. Anyway, the outside is well boarded up, can't even tell it was ever there, but on the inside it makes a nice hidey-hole."

"Ah, the secrets of old houses. I'm sure that will do quite nicely."

A few minutes later I was alone in the dining room, nibbling on a scone slathered with a generous amount of butter. I heard the clicking of Dolores's high-heeled shoes, and she spun into the room like a Miss America contestant whose turn it was to show off her gown in front of the audience.

She stopped in midtwirl and held her hands up as if surrendering to the long arm of the law. "What do you think, Jess? Is this what the well-dressed convicts will be wearing on the prison runway this year?"

Dolores had on a black fitted blazer over a light gray blouse and a black and gray plaid skirt. She had limited her gold bracelets to one on each arm, and her gold button earrings matched a pendant hanging from a chain around her neck.

"You look flawless. Are you nervous about today?" I asked.

"Not as much as I thought I would be. I have been through so much since you told me . . . about Willis that I am practically numb. I mean, recognizing that I am tied to Norman for my entire financial future, finding out that Clancy drinks to excess and then drives when he does it, not to mention whatever is in all those file cabinets in the storage unit. Honestly, Jess, there is no more room inside me for worry."

"I understand—believe me, I do—but," I cautioned, "it is critical for you to be at your best, your most attentive, when you meet with the sheriff. Take your cue from Mr. McGuire and answer all questions with a minimum amount of information."

"I guess it pays to be a mystery writer. You seem to know exactly how this is done," Dolores said.

"I suspect that in real life it is far more difficult than what I put on paper. Why don't you have a cup of coffee and a scone? We have plenty of time."

Dolores started to fidget. "Actually, no. I'd rather get out of here, even if we ride around for a while and are early for my meeting with McGuire. I don't want to run into Clancy or Norman. I couldn't bear to make small talk today."

"Oh my, of course. That makes perfect sense. Why don't you get your purse and whatever else you need, and I'll find out if Elton is here and ready to go? I'll meet you in the kitchen."

"We are spending an awful lot of time in the kitchen lately. I hope Lucinda doesn't think we're in the way. I wouldn't want to lose her and Marla Mae," Dolores fretted. "Lucinda was with Willis for years. She might not like the change."

I smiled, thinking of my recent conversation with Lucinda. "Trust me, Dolores. I don't think you have to worry about anything on that score."

Holding an oversized umbrella above our heads, Elton ushered us to the car. He said, "The cooler is packed and ready. Lucinda piled on the snacks and drinks in case the day goes extra long."

Dolores said, "We have time before my meeting at the Grits and Gravy. Elton, would you mind taking us on a short ride through downtown? The least I can do is show Jessica the outside of all the touristy places I thought we'd visit while she's here."

"Don't bother about me. I am glad that I'm here for you now. This is the time you need a friend around."

"That's very true, and I am grateful." Dolores gave

a wan smile. "But you have to promise me that a year or so from now, when this is all over, you'll come back and we can have the girlfriend visit I planned for us."

"All you have to do is invite me," I said.

"Consider it done. Now look out the window. To our right is the Columbia Museum of Art. I had hoped I'd get to show it off. The collection is eclectic and organized by themes. One room has ultramodern pieces, and you walk to another room and find a portrait of George Washington by Charles Willson Peale. Small as the building appears from the outside, I could roam inside for hours."

Elton made a left turn and I saw a bright red marquee with gold letters: S. H. KRESS & CO.

"That can't be right. It must be the only Kress five-and-ten left in the entire United States."

Dolores laughed. "That sign fools every tourist. When the building owners took it over, they decided to leave it up. They claimed it is a tribute to a once-great company, but most people think they just want to make sure the site is noticed. The real entrance is around the corner. It's now a terrific Brazilian steak house. Excellent food, with even better service."

"Miss Dolores, sorry to interrupt, but it might be time for us to start heading to your meeting," Elton said.

Dolores agreed, and it wasn't long before we were sitting in a quiet corner booth in the rear of the Grits and Gravy Café with Francis McGuire. I needn't have been concerned by his informal clothes and offhand demeanor when he came to the house. Today he was all business, from his slim-cut chambray suit to his

Cartier wristwatch, easily identifiable by its Roman numerals.

Our short ride through downtown had relaxed Dolores completely, and she treated McGuire as if he were a guest she needed to entertain, telling him anecdotes about how Willis courted her. Then she began to tell the story of building the koi pond. That was when he stopped her.

"Mrs. Nickens, we only have a few minutes. We have to get to work. You are a grieving widow under suspicion for her husband's murder, not a socialite out with friends. This will be a weighty interview, not a polite conversation. You must treat it as such."

I thought that was extremely harsh, but Dolores nodded meekly. "Okay. What do you need me to do?"

McGuire handed me a piece of paper. "Mrs. Fletcher, if you wouldn't mind asking Mrs. Nickens these questions, she and I will answer in the same way we'll do at the interview."

He looked at Dolores. "No matter what is said, you will not speak until I have spoken. Is that understood?"

"Yes," Dolores said. "I understand."

I had to laugh as I read the first question. "Mrs. Nickens, how old are you?"

I thought for sure Dolores was going to say, *You know darn well how old I am. Our birthdays are only a few months apart.* But she was obediently silent and looked at McGuire for direction.

Mr. McGuire said, "That question is irrelevant to your investigation. Mrs. Nickens declines to answer."

He pointed to the paper in my hand, so I moved to question two.

"Mrs. Nickens, what is your favorite television show?"

McGuire waited to see what Dolores would do. When she remained silent, he said, "My client will answer the question. Mrs. Nickens."

Dolores said, "It's hard to choose. I love pretty much everything that comes up on *Masterpiece* on the public television station. You know, like *Victoria*, and *Sanditon*, and—"

McGuire said, "Please stop, Mrs. Nickens." He looked as though he wanted to cover her mouth with his hand.

"But you said I could answer."

"I did, but this is key. Answer as economically as possible. The less you say, the less they can throw back at us later. Now try that answer again."

Dolores thought for a moment, then said, "*Masterpiece* on the public television station."

McGuire nodded his approval.

We continued to role-play until it was time to leave for the meeting. McGuire seemed satisfied with Dolores's performance. I could have told him she was always a fast learner.

"I'll be waiting for you by the front door of the Sheriff's Department." He snapped up the check for our coffees and his tea and stuck a few bills under his saucer for the server. "Take your time. By the look of things, it will be a long session."

A few minutes later Elton pulled the Escalade in front of the Sheriff's Department, and, true to his word, the lawyer was waiting on the other side of the glass front door.

Dolores grabbed my hand. "Oh, Jess, now I am getting nervous."

"No need. You'll have Mr. McGuire guiding you the whole way. You'll be fine. Come. I'll walk in with you."

"Do you ladies want me to wait right here?" Elton asked.

"No," I said. "I have a feeling this is going to be a much longer wait than the last time you and I were here. You'd best park in the visitors' lot, and if you need me, I will be in the lobby."

Deputy Remington gave me a friendly wave, then changed over to fully professional as soon as I introduced Dolores and her attorney.

The deputy tapped a few keys on her computer, nodded to herself, and said, "Lieutenant Hall from the Investigative Division will be with you in a few moments. Please have a seat."

Dolores clung to my arm and I could feel tension rising within her, so I whispered, "I have been thinking about root beer floats."

"Carmody's Ice Cream Parlor on the last day of finals," Dolores said. "Do me a favor and call the house. Ask Lucinda to make sure we have plenty of root beer and plenty of ice cream. If not, tell her we will pick it up on the way home."

A middle-aged man wearing navy blue slacks and a tweed jacket stopped at Deputy Remington's station. She pointed to us.

As he walked our way I said, "You'll be fine, Dolores."

Francis McGuire stood and offered his hand.

"Lieutenant Hall, may I present Mrs. Nickens and her friend Mrs. Fletcher, who'll be waiting for us?"

"Just routine. Shouldn't take long." The lieutenant smiled at me as if to say, *Don't worry about your friend— I left my rubber hose at home.*

I sat for a while, thumbing through an ancient issue of *Newsweek*. Every time I glanced at my watch it was barely five minutes later than the last time I'd looked. And then I thought of something useful I could do.

I approached Deputy Remington, who was busy studying a chart on her computer. When she looked up, I said, "I was wondering if you could help me with something."

She gave me a friendly smile. "Of course. The restrooms are right off that alcove in the back of the lobby sitting room."

"Thank you, but that wasn't what I had in mind." I tried to sound apologetic.

She dropped her smile. "Well, if it's about the, er, death, you know I can't . . ."

"Actually, it's about the fish."

That caught her short. "Fish?"

"Yes. I understand that the Department of Natural Resources took . . . I guess you would call it custody of the koi that populated the pond where Willis died. I am sure it would cheer Dolores—Mrs. Nickens, that is—to have the fish back. Is there any way you could find out when that might happen?"

The deputy looked at me long and hard, and then came to the conclusion that what I was asking was harmless enough. "Just give me a minute, Mrs. Fletcher."

She tapped away at the keyboard and scrolled through a couple of pages.

"Found 'em." She enlarged a document and ran her finger across the screen. "No sickness, no internal objects on the X-rays, no poison. Looks like you're in luck, ma'am. Those fish are clean, healthy, and scheduled to be returned to Mrs. Nickens's home sometime tomorrow."

"Thank you, Deputy. Dolores could use some good news, and you have provided it."

Back in my seat I realized that, more important than telling Dolores that the colorful fish would soon be on their way home, I'd better remember to tell her about Available Options and Randall Carbonetti. She needed to be up to speed when we got to Marcus Holmes's office, where, hopefully, she would begin learning about Willis's business activities. If we were lucky, Mr. Holmes would be a shortcut so we wouldn't have to read every single paper in the storage locker. I did want to get back to Cabot Cove again sometime before next winter's first snow.

Chapter Twenty-five

I glanced at the cover of a copy of *Time* magazine sitting on the end table, only to see it was even older than the *Newsweek* I'd flipped through earlier. Someone had left a newspaper on a chair, and I tried that. The banner said it was today's edition of the *State*. The paper was filled with world and local news, homegrown gossip, and plenty of advertisements. One full page from the governor's office explained the dos and don'ts of hurricane preparation. Although hurricane season in South Carolina doesn't start until June first, according to the governor, it is never too early to begin preparation. I scanned every page, and there was nothing about Willis Nickens's death, and more important, not a word about his wife's being a person of interest.

I became increasingly restless so I stood for a while, and then began pacing back and forth. Everyone who had been waiting in the lobby when I arrived was long gone, and a small number of new people had come in for either aid or information. I had reached the tapping-my-toe state of impatience when Elton came in and handed me a paper bag.

"Water, ma'am. Thought you might be feeling parched. Any word on Miss Dolores?"

I shook my head. "She and Francis McGuire were called inside immediately after we arrived. I didn't expect us to be here this long."

"It has been a while. I wish there was something we could do to make Miss Dolores feel better when she comes on out."

"There is. I nearly forgot, Dolores wanted me to check with Lucinda to make sure we have plenty of root beer and ice cream at the house. She's planning a root beer float party when we get home. Perfect end to a stressful day."

"I can call Lucinda for you, ma'am. And we can stop for supplies if needed."

"Thank you. I appreciate that. And while you are pitching in, I was wondering if you could help with something else. I know Dolores spoke to you and Marla Mae about cleaning the storage room file cabinets when it is convenient."

"We are planning to get that done fairly soon."

"Eventually Dolores will want the files and cabinets moved from the storage unit to somewhere at Manning Hall. Would you be able to hire a truck and find someone to help you move them? Naturally, Dolores would pay you both and cover all expenses."

"My friend Quinton, who works with me at Success

City, has a brother-in-law with a truck. We borrowed it once to move another driver's family from one house to another. I'm sure we could borrow it again. Quinton and I can easily move some cabinets for Miss Dolores. She only needs to call on us when she is ready."

At that moment I heard my name being called from near the front desk. "Miz Fletcher. What are you doing here?"

I almost didn't recognize Deputy Lascomb because he was dressed in baggy denim shorts and a baseball jersey that read ZEKE'S ZOMBIES. He noticed I was staring at his shirt and he pointed to the logo with both index fingers. "Cool, right? Sheriff says we are like the walking dead: We sneak up on the other team and whomp! They're goners."

"It certainly is a catchy name for a, I'm guessing, softball team."

"Yes, ma'am. The season starts next week, and we have a preseason game against the fire department tonight. It's a practice game for both teams but I can tell you now, we're going for blood." He glanced over at the desk. "Is Remington taking care of you?"

"Yes, she has been very helpful. In fact, she was able to find out that the koi are coming home tomorrow."

"Well, that's good news. I know you were worried about those poor little fish." His tone was not quite mocking. "So I suppose you'll be on your way, then."

"Actually, no. I'm waiting for Mrs. Nickens. She is meeting with Lieutenant Hall."

His entire demeanor changed from happy-go-lucky

ballplayer to deputy on the case. He stiffened, gave a half wave, and rushed off into the inner sanctum.

"That was weird," Elton said. "He made a complete one-eighty in a split second."

"In a way, and I think it indicates that being called in to a meeting with Lieutenant Hall means Dolores is a serious suspect. It's possible things are about to get a lot worse. Elton, can you wait here in case Dolores comes out? I don't want her to be alone for even an instant, but I need to make a quick phone call."

"Sure 'nuff. Happy to."

I found a spot under a tree where I could have some privacy but still keep my eye on the front door in case Dolores and Elton came out.

Harry McGraw's voice mail picked up immediately.

"Harry, it's Jessica. Things are getting urgent here. I'm spending the day with Dolores, but if you have anything that you think can help her, please call me tonight."

I was walking back to the building when Dolores came out, flanked by Elton and Francis McGuire. She looked flustered but not completely done in. As I got closer I heard McGuire say, "You were really a trouper in there, Mrs. Nickens. From my perspective you are a dream client, following my lead consistently."

Dolores gave him a gracious smile. "I had an excellent coach. But I am inclined to wonder what happens next."

"The next move is up to them." McGuire shrugged. "Your job is to sit tight and wait to see if they call you in again. Just remember, you are not to talk to anyone from law enforcement, including the Sheriff's Department and the County Solicitor's Office. Call me if anyone from those offices tries to talk to you or if you have any questions." He started to walk toward the parking lot, half turned, and said over his shoulder, "Oh, and for goodness' sake, avoid the press at all costs."

"The press?" Dolores looked baffled. "I never even thought of the newspapers or local television. I mean, our wedding was in the society news and Willis has been mentioned here and there for some business deal or charity work, but I can't imagine being in the news for . . . this."

I linked my arm through hers and tried to sound as positive as I could while we strolled to the car. "Don't worry about the press. Mr. McGuire is clearly pleased with how today's interview went. Perhaps this is the end of it."

I didn't believe a word that came out of my own mouth, but I thought it was imperative to keep Dolores feeling optimistic. "Now, why don't we get into the Escalade and see what Lucinda has prepared for us to snack on while we head off to keep your appointment with Marcus Holmes?"

The law office waiting room looked like a library. The walls were covered with floor-to-ceiling oak bookshelves filled with dark-covered hardback books. Brown leather chairs and love seats were arranged neatly around a Persian rug. The only office fixtures were a corner desk and computer and Mr. Holmes's fifty-something assistant. Her nameplate specified she was Elizabeth Duett, Executive Secretary, but she could easily have been a librarian.

In keeping with the room's decor, Dolores and I spoke in hushed tones. "Jess, when we are finished with this meeting, I hope I am done with lawyers for a good long while."

"Oh, I doubt that will be the case. You and Mr. Holmes will likely have a long relationship if Willis's business activities were as complex as that storage room indicates, not to mention what we talked about in the car."

Dolores raised a quizzical eyebrow, then realized what I meant. "Oh. Yes. I guess Mr. Holmes will be able to tell us exactly how many more business types like Mr. Carbonetti I'll have to contend with. Willis really got around. I'd never even heard of Carbonetti or his company."

"Dolores, I think that is exactly the point. There are thousands of companies that aren't well-known to the general public."

The secretary's phone gave a short ring. She answered, and after a few seconds said, "Yes, sir."

Elizabeth rose from her chair and said, "Mrs. Nickens, Mr. Holmes will see you now."

When we both stood up, she looked uncertain. "Are you bringing your friend to meet with Mr. Holmes?"

"Definitely," Dolores said. "I want Mrs. Fletcher with me."

Marcus Holmes had perfected the rumpled look you would expect of a backwoods country lawyer, which made me think he was probably sharp as a tack.

After Dolores introduced me to him, Holmes led us to some forest green jacquard chairs arranged in a semicircle around a glass-topped coffee table.

"It's a pleasure to meet you, Mrs. Fletcher. I seem to recall that I've been told that Mrs. Nickens has an old and dear friend who is the very popular mystery writer J. B. Fletcher. Would I be right in assumin' . . . ?" He let the end of his sentence hang in midair.

I smiled politely at his obvious attempt at flattery. "Guilty as charged, I must admit."

"I'm afraid I don't have much time for readin', but I assure you my wife tells me your books are highly entertaining." Then he looked at Elizabeth, who was still standing in the doorway. "Did you offer these fine ladies some refreshment?" He turned back to us. "Coffee? Sweet tea?"

When we both declined, Elizabeth closed the door and disappeared behind it.

Mr. Holmes tugged on the edge of his necktie. "Well then, I guess it is straight to business. But first off, Mrs. Nickens, I need to tell you how sorry I am at the loss of your dear husband and my good friend, Willis Nickens."

Dolores murmured her thanks and said, "This has been an excruciating ordeal made worse by the fact that, so far as I know, Willis's business interests are spread far and wide with no one taking care of them. I am really here for you to give me a crash course so I know what I have to take care of immediately and what can wait. I do recall signing a barrage of papers after our wedding, but I am not exactly sure which entities most of them covered."

"I see. I really do understand your concern. My own position in this matter is truly quite awkward. Let me see how I can say this." He rubbed his hands together in rapid motion, which reminded me of Pontius Pilate on a fateful day two thousand years ago.

It was clear there was a problem, but since Holmes was Willis's attorney and had organized all the post-wedding paper signing, I was not sure what he could possibly be hemming and hawing about.

He cleared his throat. "There is no other way to say this, Mrs. Nickens. As long as Sheriff Halvorson considers you a person of interest regarding your husband's unfortunate death, I am not comfortable sharing any of his business information with you."

"Now just a minute, Mr. Holmes." I was outraged. "You and I both know that as soon as they were married Willis Nickens signed over to Dolores partial ownership of at least some of his business interests and perhaps even full ownership of others." That was a wild, but not unlikely, guess. "She is entitled to information regarding those companies."

Holmes ran a finger around his shirt collar. Clearly he was a man who made pronouncements and expected them to be accepted.

"I wanted to sit down with you, Mrs. Nickens, so that we could have this conversation in person. I am sure that your tribulations with the sheriff's office will be cleared up any day now. As soon as that happens you and I can review every piece of information I have regarding Willis's businesses and his estate."

"You can't be serious." I was about to start another rampage when Dolores spoke, quite calmly.

"As you wish. But rest assured, when that moment comes, and it will, my first act will be to replace you as attorney for all the Nickens holdings." Dolores stood. "Good day, Mr. Holmes."

I jumped to my feet and followed her out of his office, even as Holmes was spluttering, "Now hold on there, just a minute. No need to . . ."

And the rest of what he was saying was lost in the sound of Dolores's slamming his office door.

Chapter Twenty-six

Dolores held her tongue until we got out of the building elevator. Then she looked at me and giggled. "Did you see the look on his face? The old fool. It never occurred to him that he isn't in charge. He's the lawyer. He forgot that Willis and I are the clients."

"Kudos to you. He was completely stunned. I bet Mr. Holmes was hollering for Elizabeth to bring him some headache tablets before we pressed the elevator button."

It was such a relief to me that Dolores had taken command of the situation forcefully. I was far less worried about how she would manage on her own than I was a day or so ago.

Elton was standing at the car, door open, helping hand extended. "Root beer floats will be at the ready, but Lucinda said that y'all will have to dig into her chicken and rib dinner beforehand."

Dolores said, "That sounds perfect to me."

Elton switched on the ignition and said, "Miss Jessica, you will never want to leave South Carolina once you've tasted Lucinda's chicken and ribs."

Dolores was positively bubbly. "Jess, Elton is right. You are in for a real Southern treat. Not a cook alive can make barbecue chicken and ribs like Lucinda. And I am going to bet we are having baked beans and potato salad for the sides. Get ready. We are going to need elastic waistbands for this dinner."

When Elton tapped his clicker to open the gate to Manning Hall, I asked Dolores if she had any idea how many clickers existed and exactly who had them.

"Goodness no. There may be dozens. Having a gate with a clicker was one of Willis's sillier affectations. He loved to remind guests that his estate was gated and they would need to be admitted.

"When I have the time I am going to have a top-notch company come in and organize a security plan for the entire property: Manning Hall, Marjory's cottage, the garages, the gardening shed, even the stables. Once that's done we'll say bye-bye to the clickers."

"Stables?" I was surprised I'd never noticed them. "How could I have missed them when I was out jogging?"

"They are easy to miss. You know that stand of cypress trees behind the house?"

"The ones heavily covered with the Spanish moss? I've avoided the area because there doesn't seem to be a path where I could walk or jog safely."

Dolores nodded her head. "Exactly the problem.

There is a path but it is hopelessly overgrown. Willis planned on having the entire area cleaned out and landscaped when he restored the stables to house Abby's horses."

"Abby's horses? I didn't realize the child had horses."

"She doesn't, but Willis was planning on buying horses and supplying riding lessons in another year or so. Abby's mother was a first-class rider, medals and all. I think Willis wanted to build reminders of Emily so that Abby would always feel her presence. Horseback riding would be one way."

Learning about the softer side of Willis Nickens continued to surprise me.

Elton parked at the top of the driveway, and he was coming to open our doors when the front door of the house flew open and Abby bounced across the veranda and down the steps.

"Mr. Elton! Mr. Elton! Wait until you see." She was waving an oversized piece of drawing paper.

Elton took two quick steps, opened the passenger door next to Dolores, and then flung his arms up in the air. "What have you got there? Something special?"

"I drew this. Look. It's the solar system. And this is Earth, where we live. The moon is this little ball, and it goes around Earth in an . . . an orbit, almost like a circle."

"Wow. You are an excellent artist," Elton said.

"Thank you, but that's not all. Look over here. That is Mars. Remember the story you told me about the Martians and the moon men? We live here, on Earth, the Martians live on Mars, and the moon men live on the moon. And I know where they all are!" Abby did a little happy dance.

Elton laughed. "So now we know you are smart enough and talented enough to be an artist or a story-teller or an astronaut."

Dolores got out of the car. "Abby, can I see, too?"

"Granny Dolores, today was the best day of school in my whole life. I knew lots of things about Mars and the moon. And when Mrs. Creighton asked me how I knew so much, I said because Mr. Elton told me adventure stories. And Mrs. Creighton said adventure stories are a great way to learn."

Dolores said, "We are lucky to have Elton here. He has been a huge support to all of us in so many ways."

Elton was beaming with pleasure. "I'm happy to be of help, ma'am."

And in that moment, as I looked at Abby and Dolores, both so happy to have Elton around, I thought he could easily become the solution to still another problem that was bothering Dolores. I'd have to re-member to discuss it with her when I had the chance.

Clancy came out of the house. "There you are, prin-cess. I thought you were doing your homework in the dining room."

Abby's face dropped. "Bah, homework. I have to do extra homework because I missed some days at school. That doesn't seem fair. I mean, if you don't go to school on a day, why should you have to do home-work for that day? It's either a school day or it's not."

While I could see there was a certain logic to her thought process, it was clear that neither her father nor her grandmother was buying it. Elton and I were wise enough to stay out of the conversation.

We were a noisy bunch as we finally made our way across the veranda and into the foyer. Elton was last, carrying the cooler. As he turned down the hallway that led to the kitchen, Marla Mae came rushing past him.

"Miss Dolores, there you are." She looked flustered and pointedly gave Clancy a wide berth. "Could I have a private word?"

Clancy said to Abby, "No more stalling. Kiss Granny Dolores good-bye, and we'll see her at dinner."

Abby rolled her eyes, gave us a theatrical grimace, and dragged her feet all the way to the dining room door. Only when Clancy had closed the door behind them did Marla Mae speak. "You have a telephone call, ma'am. I suggest you take it in your office." She whispered, "It's Mr. Jonah Harrold, from the funeral parlor. I told him you'd be a minute or two. He said for you to take your time."

Dolores fished a key from her purse. "Come with me, Jess. This could be the moment I've been waiting for. Willis might finally be free of all these sheriffs and coroners."

She hurried to the office. I followed along, thinking that if the Coroner's Office had released Willis's body, that meant they would finally release an official cause of death. I could only hope that wouldn't mean a new, more forceful round of questions for Dolores.

Dolores picked up the phone and said, "Mr. Harrold, how kind of you to wait for me. I was just getting out of the car when you called."

She listened for a moment and then said, "I appreciate that."

When Mr. Harrold began speaking again, Dolores gave me a big smile and a snappy thumbs-up. She put her hand over the mouthpiece. "Mr. Harrold has been given permission to pick up Willis from the Coroner's Office tomorrow."

"That's wonderful." I returned her thumbs-up.

The call lasted a few minutes longer. When she'd hung up Dolores said, "Mr. Harrold will work out scheduling with Pastor Forde. Once I approve the time frame, we can begin announcing the times and locations of the wake and the funeral service to all the interested parties. I think I should put notices in the newspapers as well, don't you? I don't want an invitation-only service. Better to leave the door wide open, as my mama used to say. I want Willis to have a nice send-off with a big crowd of people. Don't you agree?"

I nodded politely, but in reality I couldn't imagine copious numbers of people wanting to participate in services honoring Willis Nickens. "Dolores, do you want to talk to Clancy about any of this? Or are there any other family members you might consult?"

"Abby and I are the only family Willis has. As for Clancy, he couldn't make a decision to save his soul. Anyway, six months from now I don't want him asking for favors and reminding me what a help he was."

I had to admit I hadn't quite thought of it that way. But I had thought of something else and decided to bring my idea to Dolores's attention.

"Dolores, have you noticed how well Elton and Abby get on?" I asked.

Dolores said, "I have always been fascinated by how comfortable Abby is with adults in general. I suppose that comes from being an only child. But I do agree she has bonded with Elton more quickly than most."

"What if"—I searched for the right words—"and this is only a suggestion, mind you, but what if Elton could be available to drive Clancy and Abby on an as-needed basis?"

Dolores gave me an odd look. "As needed? As needed for what?"

I decided to be blunt. "You are worried about Clancy driving under the influence, and rightly so. Suppose you set up some sort of agreement with the car company, similar to the one I have now. Clancy would have the company on call, and whenever he was going someplace where alcohol might be an issue he would agree to use the car service—"

"Why would he . . . ?" Dolores began to interrupt.

I held up my hand and said, "Just hear me out. It really wouldn't matter which driver the car company sent to drive Clancy; however, anytime Abby would be with him or have to go somewhere and her father was in no position to drive, well, then the company should be sure to send Elton if at all possible."

Dolores was digesting it all, and she didn't look convinced. "Jess, you know what I really want is for Clancy to join a twelve-step program, and I don't think tomorrow would be too soon for him to attend his first meeting. Still, I am not sure how I could get him to make that commitment. Just because I know all about his DUI record doesn't mean he would willingly do as I ask. And the same thing applies to your car service suggestion."

She stopped for a few seconds, as if to organize her thoughts, then said, "I'm not saying your idea is a bad one. It's only that I'm not sure it would work. Give me some reasons why you think Clancy would go along with it."

I was ready with several. "First off, I know it's not a twelve-step program, but it would keep both Clancy and Abby safe until such time as Clancy comes to grips with his alcohol addiction. Clancy may not worry about his own safety, but he would surely want to keep Abby safe.

"Second, you would promise that you would not be using Elton and the car company to check up on Clancy's whereabouts and activities.

"Third, we know Clancy goes to court on another drunk driving charge in a few weeks. He stands a very good chance of losing his driver's license, at least in the short term. Then how would he get around?"

I could see that Dolores was starting to follow my way of thinking, and I was sure I could clinch the deal with reason number four. "Lastly, each and every month you will pay Clancy's car service bill, no questions asked."

Dolores sat quietly mulling over my suggestion. After a while she said, "That might be a workable plan. Give me a day or so to think it over. Right now I have other things . . . I have to pick out an outfit for

Willis to wear. Mr. Harrold would like me to drop it off sometime tomorrow afternoon. His navy blue wool suit has always been my favorite. I admit it's a little heavy for the season, but Willis looked so handsome when he wore it."

"Of course. I understand. I just wanted to pass along the thought while it was still fresh in my mind," I said.

"Speaking of fresh, shall we go to the kitchen and find out what time our dinner will be ready? I would love to take a short nap so I have plenty of appetite and plenty of energy for our barbecue and root beer float party."

That sounded perfect to me. I was hoping there would be enough time before dinner for me to run an errand.

Chapter Twenty-seven

Lucinda assured us that she'd be busy at the stove for another few hours, so when Dolores opted for a nap, I found Elton in the library and asked him to take me to Jessamine House.

"And I promise we will be back long before Lucinda and Marla Mae begin serving the chicken and ribs."

Elton said, "That is good news, ma'am. A body always wants to be first in line for Lucinda's chicken and ribs, because there's unlikely to be any leftovers for latecomers."

It wasn't until we pulled into the driveway of Jessamine House that I realized I had no actual plan. The best I could hope for was a few minutes alone with Tom Blomquist. As for Candy, after our last conversation it wouldn't surprise me if she hid at the very sound of my voice.

"I thought I recognized the Escalade—that metallic blue is hard to miss." Tom Blomquist was coming from the gardens, carrying pruning shears. "A guest got her skirt caught on the prickly stems of one of the brier rose bushes, so I thought I'd do some trimming before that becomes a routine problem and people are sending me clothing repair bills."

"Candy took me into the garden on my last visit. Your brier roses are lovely," I said.

"Well, Candy's out and about, taking care of a few errands. Can I offer you a cup of tea? I do recall mint juleps aren't your first choice." Tom was jovial but it seemed forced, as if I'd interrupted his plans for the afternoon.

I decided to get straight to the point. "Actually, I came to see you."

His smile became less certain. "Well, I am flattered. Now tell me what I can do for you. Or does Dolores need my help with something?"

"Actually, I am here on Dolores's behalf. Can you tell me whatever you know about a company called Available Options and its owner, Randall Carbonetti?"

A frown slithered across his face, and then he was all smiles once again. "Ah, Randall's a local boy, inherited the company from his father. Wouldn't surprise me if there was a grandfather somewhere in the business as well. The company has a sterling reputation among the old families round here. Been helping them out of financial scrapes for decades."

"Yes, that's what Mr. Carbonetti told me."

That caught him by surprise, and not in a good way. I noticed a thin sheen of perspiration forming on his upper lip. "I didn't realize that you know Randall. I suppose Dolores does as well?"

"Actually, I spoke to him as a follow-up to paperwork we found in Willis's file cabinets. How would you describe Available Options? How does the company function?"

Tom's discomfort was growing. "Ah, I guess you could say it is a private loan company, with the loans based on collateral."

"And how long does Available Options hold the loans?" I knew I had passed the point of polite inquiry, but Tom answered.

"I guess that would depend on the terms of the loan. Jessica, may I ask what your interest is? Are you planning to do business with Randall? Is Dolores in need of funds?"

I shook my head. "No, it's nothing like that. This is somewhat awkward. I wanted to ask about your loan, the loan Dolores now owns."

"My loan? From Dolores? I don't know what you are talking about. I have no such loan." He seemed absolutely convinced.

I realized what the mix-up must be. "But you do have a loan with Available Options."

"If I do, that's private and none of your concern. Now if you'll excuse me . . ." He started to walk away.

"Randall Carbonetti sold the loan to Willis Nickens," I said, and that stopped him on a dime.

"What? That's not possible. I would know." Tom was totally flustered. "You must be mistaken."

"I'm afraid not." I took the letter from my purse and pointed to his name. "See, there's your name, right in the middle of this list of loans Mr. Carbonetti was transferring to Willis Nickens for a staggering sum of money."

"I . . . I don't understand."

Even when I'd explained the process Tom remained confused. "Why would Randall sell my loan to Willis?"

"Not only your loan. According to Mr. Carbonetti it is a common business practice. He sells existing loans to investors so that he can accumulate ready cash to extend more loans. And when the loan is due you pay Available Options, and then they pay the investor with the proceeds of your repayment and a percentage of the accrued interest. The company keeps the rest of the interest—that's their profit."

"Ah, I admit I do have a working relationship with Available Options, but I had no idea of the rest of it— investors and all that. Do you think that's why Willis dangled us? Because he knew we were already in debt?"

"I have no idea. I can't be sure of what was going on in Willis's brain. But you must have known that another loan on top of your existing loan with Mr. Carbonetti would put Jessamine House in great jeopardy. I assume you used Jessamine House as your primary collateral."

"Jessica, when you say it like that, it does sound exceedingly foolish, but Jessamine House is all we have, and compared to the modern hotels . . . While our guests desire the beauty and elegance of a quaint atmosphere, they demand air-conditioning, en suite baths, and even elevators."

"But when you and Candy discussed it, one of you

had to realize the potential problems such hefty loans could cause."

"Candy doesn't know anything about the loan from Available Options. She thought I used some non-existent savings to do the last upgrade. It would devastate her to learn that we are in that kind of debt. Now, please leave me to deal with it as best I can, and for heaven's sake don't mention any of this to Candy."

When I got back into the car Elton said, "Well, that was really a short and sweet kind of visit."

I could agree that my visit with Tom Blomquist was a short one, but it was certainly nowhere near sweet. I knew I'd caught Tom by surprise when I brought up his loan with Available Options, and he seemed genuinely shocked when I told him Willis had bought the loan. To my mind that meant until this moment he had had every reason to believe that, with Willis out of the way, Dolores might be willing to provide capital for a rehabilitation project of Jessamine House. Had he been desperate enough to kill Willis to make that happen? I wasn't sure. He didn't seem bold enough to take such a risk.

And although Tom and Candy appeared to care for each other genuinely, it was a wonder that their marriage had endured when both of them kept such dire secrets to themselves.

When we got back to Manning Hall the house smelled like barbecue, and we heard lots of chatter coming from both the kitchen and the dining room. I went to my room and changed into jeans and a comfortable cotton knit shirt. I checked my cell phone one more time, but there were no calls or texts. I knew

Harry McGraw would do his absolute best for me but I was becoming more anxious. Once Willis's body was released by the coroner it was likely the sheriff would step up his investigation, and I was afraid Dolores would wind up in the hot seat.

I'd nearly reached the bottom of the stairs when Abby came racing out of the dining room, with Dolores behind her.

"Miss Jessica, you are just in time. Marla Mae says everyone should wash up because dinner will be set out in a very few minutes. And there's potato salad. Miss Lucinda makes the best potato salad." And she ran past me up the stairs.

Dinner was outstanding. A delicious fresh beet and asparagus salad preceded the chicken and ribs smothered in tangy barbecue sauce. Dolores had accurately predicted the side dishes of baked beans and potato salad. And just when I thought I couldn't eat another bite, Lucinda and Marla Mae carried in two trays filled with root beer floats in tall ice cream parlor glasses.

And for the first time since I arrived, it appeared as though everyone was stress free. Norman told a very funny story about how he and his college roommate had wangled an invitation to a sorority picnic and decided to make a potato salad to impress their hostesses.

"We followed the recipe perfectly. Yellow mustard, sweet pickles, hard-boiled eggs, mayonnaise, and what all else. The base, of course, was three pounds of russet potatoes, which we chopped diligently and then mixed with everything else." Norman looked around the dining table to be sure he had everyone's undivided attention.

"Then, brash boys that we were, we insisted—insisted, mind you—that each and every young lady at our table taste our wonderful creation. We thought it was a surefire way to gather phone numbers."

When Norman paused, Clancy jumped in with the obligatory question. "And did it work?"

"Sadly, no. It might have, but we had managed to skip one very crucial step. We didn't boil the potatoes. They were hard as rocks."

Amid the roar of adult laughter, Abby said, quite seriously, "I don't think Miss Lucinda would ever make a mistake like that."

Dolores gave her a pat on the head. "I'm quite sure she wouldn't, but Mr. Norman isn't quite the same caliber of cook."

We lingered over coffee, and when Norman asked Marla Mae to bring in a bottle of brandy, Dolores excused herself to read to Abby and I took the opportunity to retire to my room for the night.

The first thing I did was text Harry McGraw a Call me message, and when I hadn't heard from him within a few minutes I put on my pajamas and settled into the comfy blue wing chair with the latest Detective Inspector Vera Stanhope novel by Ann Cleeves. The story was engrossing, but as the clock ticked past midnight even Vera's adventures on the Northumberland coastline couldn't keep my eyelids from drooping.

The ping on the phone startled me. I shook off the

drowsies, grabbed my cell, and read the text that popped up from Harry. U still up? Give me a call. I couldn't hit the speed dial button fast enough.

"How's it shaking, Jessica?"

"Harry, I am so glad to hear from you. Dolores has a lawyer, and he seems pleased with how her case is going, but I am getting more nervous each day. When we first spoke I said I needed a suspect pool of more than just a person or two to take the spotlight off Dolores. But, hard as I've tried, none of the evidence I've gathered so far is strong enough for me to convince the sheriff to look at someone, anyone, other than Dolores. Please tell me you have something I can use."

"Well, my IRS contact said that Willis Nickens is the original Mr. Clean. His personal taxes, all of his business taxes—and the guy's got businesses too numerous to count—everything is squeaky clean. He's been audited a couple of times, so we know he passed the fine-tooth-comb test. All my 'connected' friends say the same thing—tough as nails but never crosses the line."

"I don't understand. Why do you think that helps Dolores?"

"Well, maybe it doesn't help her directly, but it does point out that whoever the killer is, he, or she, is close to home. The odds are that the victim knew his killer in a personal setting, because he didn't have a business life filled with shady backroom deals and questionable characters."

I picked up Harry's idea and added my own view. "And he was killed on his own property, with a houseful of guests, which is hardly the kind of atmosphere conducive to what my students used to call 'stranger danger,' is it?"

Harry chuckled. "Hardly, but on the flip side, that spurs the local law to take a real close look at the wife. If the motive is more likely to be personal, who is more personal than a spouse?"

I got a sinking feeling in my chest. "So what you are saying is that my friend Dolores is in deeper trouble than she knows."

"Not saying that at all. Although she might be. But don't you get discouraged. After all, if the killer is someone the vic knew, then chances are that by now you know him—or her—too. Anyway, I have a couple more chits outstanding, and maybe tomorrow or the next day I'll have something better for you."

I put my phone on the charger and crawled into bed. If Harry didn't come up with something to clear Dolores within the next twenty-four hours, I was going to have to figure out a way to do so myself.

Chapter Twenty-eight

The first thing I did when I awoke was to check my cell phone, but apart from a text my editor had sent requesting an appointment to talk about my next book, there was nothing of interest. All I could do was wait for Harry to dig a little deeper while I snooped a bit more on my own. Maybe we would get lucky.

I did my stretches and put on my jogging clothes. After I stopped in the kitchen to let Lucinda and Marla Mae know that I wouldn't be gone long, I went out the back door. The morning fog was dense but seemed to be lifting, so I walked to the rear of the house to take a closer look at the thick stand of moss-covered cypress trees that Dolores had mentioned yesterday. The Spanish moss and the heavy fog mixed so tightly together that I half expected the Headless Horseman to come clomping through the trees with a fiery pumpkin in his hand. Or did that happen only in Sleepy Hollow?

I walked along the edge of the tidy boundary between the trees and the neatly manicured lawn, but no matter how I tried I couldn't see so much as a suggestion of the path that once led to the stables. I turned in to the sitting garden and began to walk more briskly. At the koi pond, I came to a dead stop.

In that instant I realized I'd forgotten to tell Dolores that the koi were coming home today. "Oh dear," I said to myself.

I was disconcerted when a voice behind me said, "It is a sad sight, isn't it? Without the fish?"

Norman Crayfield had a cigar in one hand and his cell phone in the other. "I'm sorry. I didn't mean to startle you. I often come out here in the early morning to make calls to Europe. I just finished a call to a company we do business with in London. Of course the hardest part of these calls now is passing along the news that Willis is . . . gone. I take comfort in the fact that I can at least spare Dolores that unpleasantness."

That struck me as odd. All these days after Willis's murder, why was Norman still telephoning the information to business associates in such a piecemeal fashion? A large company should be more organized. I said, "I would think the news of the death of someone of Willis Nickens's stature would have spread through the business community like wildfire."

"You're right, of course. Here in South Carolina and in a number of other states people knew within hours of Willis's demise. Outside that small sphere . . .

Well, to be perfectly honest, Willis and I ran our businesses like a mom-and-pop candy store in so many ways—you know, homey, down-to-earth. And I'm sure Dolores will want to continue the same way." His eyes narrowed as he looked at me for confirmation.

"Oh, I have absolutely no head for business." I was not about to give him hope. "I'd be the last person on the planet whom Dolores would confide in about her future plans for Willis's business ventures. She'd be much more likely to tell Vivian LaPort, who was a year ahead of us at Harrison and majored in economics. Of course, I lost touch with Vivian decades ago. I wonder if Dolores has her number."

As I prattled along I watched Norman deflate before my very eyes. He was beginning to realize that if there was an easy conduit through which to maneuver Dolores to trust him with her business interests, I wasn't it. He'd have to search for another access point.

After a quick shower, I changed into my gray pantsuit and a green and pink striped blouse. Once again I opted for flats, as I expected it to be a long and busy day, possibly quite hard on my feet.

Before I went down to breakfast, I sent a text to Harry. Will be with D most of the day. Text if you have any info and I will call ASAP. I knew I was pressuring him, but I couldn't shake the dream that woke me around two a.m. Dolores was standing at Willis's graveside with a detective's raincoat haphazardly thrown over her hands because they were neatly cuffed together. I chalked the image up to some old gumshoe movie I'd seen on Turner Classic Movies but couldn't quite remember which one. I tried to shake off the image. I was not about to let that happen to Dolores.

Clancy and Abby were in the dining room. Abby's cheerful "Good morning, Miss Jessica" erased any gloom and foreboding that might otherwise spoil my breakfast.

I poured a cup of coffee and put a slice of sourdough bread in the toaster. While I was waiting for it to pop, Clancy began hurrying Abby along, scolding that she would be late for school if they didn't leave in the next two minutes. Dolores met them in the doorway and gave Abby a grandmotherly good-morning kiss. Her greeting to Clancy was remarkably cheerful.

When she turned toward the buffet table I raised the coffeepot, more as a question than as a greeting, and she said, "Thank you, Jess. I am going to need all the caffeine I can handle today."

I put two cups of coffee on the table, then went back for my toast and put some scrambled eggs on a plate. "Dolores, what will you have for breakfast? There's plenty to choose from. Come take a look."

I spread a thin layer of butter on my toast while Dolores fixed a plate of sausage and scrambled eggs for herself. We each took a small plate of blueberries and orange slices and sat down at the table.

Dolores looked around, and then half whispered, "Norman is among the missing once again. I am starting to be curious about where he goes and what he does all day."

"I did see him outside when I went to exercise. He said he was making intercontinental business calls."

I took a sip of coffee. "I was under the impression that he wanted me to encourage you to allow him to remain in charge."

Dolores's long sigh echoed a mixture of sorrow and frustration. "Willis was so busy treating me like an empty-headed princess that I have no idea where the business lines are drawn between my interests and Norman's. Of course, that old fool Marcus Holmes could untie all the knots on that ball of string, if only he wasn't a coward. I can't wait to fire him."

"Now, there's the spunky Dolores I know." I was feeling more confident in her by the moment. "This is going to be a difficult day. Then you will have to get through the wake and funeral. Once those events are behind you, it will be time to sort out how your life will be without Willis."

"Jess, I know you speak from your own experience, but no one accused you of murdering Frank." Dolores's hand flew to her mouth. "Oh dear, I hope that didn't sound as harsh to you as it did to me."

"No, no, it's fine." I patted her hand. "You are in an unusual position, of course. What I meant was that even while you and Mr. McGuire are contending with your, ah, difficulties with the sheriff, you still have to work to get your life back on track."

"Without Willis? Oh . . . I don't know if I can."

"Dolores, you have already started. Look at the adaptations you have begun. You've decided to do whatever it takes to keep Abby in your life. You are planning on being an active participant in the family businesses. Most important, you are keeping people who are loyal and compassionate like Marla Mae and

Lucinda as part of your life, while dismissing anyone who isn't supportive. Marcus Holmes comes to mind."

"And I am lucky enough to have a lifelong friend like you," Dolores said. "Now, my first challenge of the day is to put together a dashing outfit for Willis to wear. One thing we don't have to worry about is his hair. He got a haircut a little more than a week ago. He would hate to look scraggly."

As she pushed back her chair and stood, so did I, ready to help.

Dolores nodded her thanks. "I always thought that our having separate rooms was silly, but since . . . he's gone . . . that has made it easier to pretend Willis is in his room and that I will see him after the late news, or at breakfast. Now it's time for me to face the empty room."

Willis Nickens's bedroom was as dark and gloomy as I'd imagined it would be. A tallboy chest with deep drawers and the four-poster bed with thick stanchions were made from heavy mahogany. A tan leather recliner next to a beige reading lamp on a small table filled one corner. Dark brown drapes flecked with gold thread completely covered the windows. The connecting door to the dressing room stood partially open, allowing a thin shaft of light from inside to cut across the middle of the bedroom.

Dolores said, "Thank goodness Willis forgot to turn his dressing room light off. Otherwise we'd be stumbling in the dark." She pulled the drapery cords and the bright South Carolina sunshine flooded the room.

Dolores reached over and gave the bedspread a tug

with one hand as she smoothed it out with the other. "With a perfectly decent recliner in here and a chair in the dressing room, Willis consistently rumpled the bed linens when he bounced down on the bed to change his shoes or make a quick phone call. As I am sure you've already noticed, a bed made up by Marla Mae could pass the test of any drill sergeant."

Dolores stepped into the dressing room. It seemed to be larger than the bedroom, but with the myriad shelves, closets, drawers, and huge racks of suits, jackets, and slacks, it was crowded. I decided to stay in the doorway so that Dolores could move around freely.

"It has to be a suit, of course. Where is my favorite navy blue? . . . Oh, here." She pulled a dark blue double-breasted suit off a rack and hung it on a wall hook. "What do you think, Jess? Now that I look at it, the fabric is so obviously winter. I wouldn't want Willis to look awkward. Still, navy is the color, am I right?"

I agreed that it was. As she slid hangers along the rack, I was amazed at how many navy or near–navy blue suits hung there. There appeared to be close to a dozen.

Dolores narrowed the search to a double-breasted navy cotton-wool mix and a single-breasted linen suit, perhaps one shade lighter than navy. She hung them side by side on wall hooks and stood looking critically at first one, then the other.

"I think the single-breasted linen is a winner. Double-breasted suits are passé in my book, although I never could get Willis to part with the ones he had." She put the cotton-wool mix back on the rack, opened one of the built-in drawers in the far wall of the dressing room, and pulled out a tailored white shirt. She gave it the once-over. "Long collar, button cuffs. Looks fairly new. This will do. Now we'll need a tie."

She twisted a brass knob on the wall and a door next to the shirt drawer popped open. Four metal tie stands—two top, two bottom—held at least a hundred ties.

Dolores said, "I'm thinking subdued stripes," and in a few minutes she'd narrowed her choices to three. She held each one against the shirtfront and then draped it over the suit jacket.

After due consideration, she held up a silk tie with slim gray, blue, and white stripes. "We have a winner."

Dolores opened still another drawer and pulled out a pair of dark socks. Then she began to look through the shoe racks that lined the floor. After what turned out to be a futile search, she picked up a pair of black oxfords.

"I can't find the patent leather dress shoes I want him to wear. I'll have to settle for second best. No one will see his feet anyway." She handed me the shoes. "Could you put these on the floor by the bed? I'll bring his clothes and we can make sure we have all we need."

As I stepped up to the bed, my foot hit something. I looked, and it was the side of a shoe. I bent down and found a pair of black patent leather shoes half-hidden by the edge of the bedspread, right where Willis had sat and left it wrinkled.

Dolores came into the bedroom with an armful of clothes. While she was laying everything on the bed,

I held up the patent leather shoes. "By any chance are these the dress shoes you couldn't find?"

"Yes. Willis loved wearing those. When he was a boy his parents used to dance at night to the radio. Songs by Tammy Wynette and Buck Owens, country music. His father wasn't a churchgoing man, and when Willis's mama used to ask how he planned on getting into heaven, Daddy would grab her in his arms, swing her around, and say he was going to dance his way right past Saint Peter. Willis said these patent leather shoes made him feel like he could dance his way into heaven, too."

Dolores smiled at the memory, then went back into the dressing room and came out with a garment bag.

As I watched her pack everything carefully, I remembered when Frank died and I had to do these same chores. The worst of times began when the chores were done and the emptiness crowded around. Dolores would face that very soon. And through it all she would have to contend with Sheriff Halvorson.

Chapter Twenty-nine

Elton placed the garment bag and the shoe carrier in the rear of the Escalade with great reverence. Dolores and I took our usual seats, and I noticed Elton had his dark gray jacket folded neatly on the front seat.

We were quiet during the car ride, which I guess befitted the solemnity of the occasion. Elton eased the Escalade into the mortuary parking lot and stopped near the main entrance. He put on his jacket and then came around to open our doors. As he helped Dolores from the car, he offered to carry the garment and shoe bags inside for her.

A dark-haired young woman dressed in an unadorned black suit and white blouse with a Peter Pan collar greeted us. "I am Carolyn Harrold. Welcome to the Harrold Brothers Funeral Home." She looked from me to Dolores and back again. "Mrs. Nickens?"

"I'm Dolores Nickens. These are my friends Jessica Fletcher and Elton Anderson. They have been invaluable to me during this terrible time. I'm grateful to have them with me."

I stole a glance at Elton and was surprised to see a lone tear sliding out from under his eyeglasses, even as he said a polite hello.

Carolyn led us to the same conference table where Dolores and I had met with Mr. Harrold on our last visit. "Please make yourselves comfortable. Uncle Jonah will be right with you."

Then as if noticing for the first time that Elton was carrying bags that certainly contained the deceased's final outfit, she said, "Mr. Anderson, may I take those?"

Elton looked at Dolores, who nodded and said, "Thank you, Ms. Harrold. Then Elton can comfortably join us at the table."

Elton handed off the bags and instantly moved to the table to pull out a chair first for Dolores, then for me. He sat down and we all waited in silence until Jonah Harrold joined us. He offered his condolences politely, and then gently began explaining the process and the schedule that he and Pastor Forde had put together.

Dolores asked a question or two and suggested very minor changes. She also added a rendition of "On Eagle's Wings" during the service, and requested that it be sung by a soprano.

Mr. Harrold took careful notes and promised that once the adjustments were confirmed with Pastor

Forde he would e-mail the final program to Dolores, later in the day.

As we stood to leave Mr. Harrold said, "I am truly sorry for the delay, Mrs. Nickens, but with this kind of death we are at the mercy of the coroner and the sheriff. I suppose you, of all people, understand that."

Dolores's expression might have been unfathomable to him, but I could see she took his words as a reminder of her status as both widow and person of interest. Her face crumpled and she began to cry. I pulled some tissues from a box on the table and handed them to her. She said a soft good-bye to Jonah Harrold and walked quickly from the room.

Dolores was still crying quietly when Elton pulled out of Harrold Brothers' driveway and turned toward home. "I knew it would be hard, Jess, but I never imagined it would be this hard. Tell me now. Is it going to be worse during the actual wake and funeral?"

Such a difficult question. How could I answer?

"Dolores, grief ebbs and flows. One minute you feel as though it's manageable, and the next minute you are overwhelmed, immobilized. With the passage of time the grief becomes more manageable, but in the first few weeks and months your grief can become unwieldy at the oddest moments. It is so difficult to predict."

"Who could think I would kill Willis? That sheriff should see me now. He should feel my grief, my loneliness."

I leaned over and put my arms around her. "You are stronger than you realize. I promise you will get through this."

"And can you promise that the vile murderer who took Willis from me will be caught and punished?"

I hesitated. "I can't be sure, of course, but a few things have been bothering me. I can't quite make the puzzle pieces fit, but it is possible that we will find out who killed Willis before too long."

"Is your private detective friend still helping you?"

"Harry? Yes. Yes, he is. In fact, he may hold the final key," I said with more confidence than I felt. "And I expect to hear from him soon."

When we passed through the gate at Manning Hall and began winding along the driveway, I stretched my neck and peered over Dolores's head. When we reached the koi pond I asked Elton to stop.

"Dolores, take a look. Your friends are home," I said, hoping that what she saw would cheer her. That was a gamble I thought worth taking.

"Wh-what?" Dolores followed my gaze. "Jess, my koi! They're back. How did you know?"

"Deputy Remington told me yesterday that they would be coming home today. With all that was going on, I forgot to tell you. This morning was so emotional—gathering Willis's clothes, going to the funeral parlor—that, well, it slipped my mind. I thought once we got settled in the house I would tell you to expect the koi, but they are already here."

"Jess, Willis died here, at this pond he had built especially for me. I think I'd like to stay here for a minute or so. You and Elton go on up to the house. I will walk up when I am ready." Dolores got out of the car.

Elton jumped out of the car and ran up to the sitting garden. He came back with a white wicker chair with flowered cushions, set it next to Dolores, and got back into the car.

"Elton, that was very thoughtful," I said.

"I figure Miss Dolores should be comfortable if she's gonna stay even five minutes." Then he asked, "Should I drive?"

"Yes," I said. "Dolores needs this time alone with her koi and her memories."

Just as Elton finished parking the car, my cell phone pinged. Harry! He wrote, Hit the mother lode.

I replied, Will call in ten.

I asked Elton to let Lucinda and Marla Mae know that Dolores was at the koi pond and that I would be in my room making some telephone calls.

"Sure 'nuff. Be happy to. I'll be in the library if you need me to take you anywhere later on today."

I knew I did have someplace to go, and I had an important question to ask, so I said, "Grab yourself a nice snack while you are in the kitchen, because we are definitely heading over to the Sheriff's Department in a short while. Oh, and don't say anything to Dolores. I don't want to get her hopes up."

As soon as I closed the door to my room, I hit the speed dial for Harry on my phone and he answered midring.

"My message got your attention, huh? I kind of figured it would." Usually unruffled no matter what the situation, Harry sounded jubilant, and that told me he was sure he'd cracked into information that would draw the sheriff's attention away from Dolores and point a finger squarely at someone else.

"Harry, my curiosity level is lighting up at around a thousand megawatts. What have you got?"

"Money, Jess, that's what I got. Lots and lots of money, which is the reason that someone decided Willis Nickens had to go, and that someone sure wasn't your friend Dolores."

"Then who, Harry? Who are you talking about?"

"I'll get to that, but first I have to tell you that I now owe dinner to the nicest lady at the South Carolina tourism board, should I ever get down that way—but you know how I hate to leave Boston. Even for work, I try to never travel south of New York."

"Harry!" I knew I sounded sharper than I'd intended, but it brought him around.

"Okay, Jess, okay, I'm just playing with you. Here's the skinny . . ."

I listened carefully, scribbling a word or two on a piece of the fancy stationery from the desk drawer. "Harry, say that again. Okay, got it."

I asked a couple of questions, and then Harry had one for me. "So, how does my info square with what you've been digging up?"

"It squares flawlessly. I just need to confirm one thing, and then, hopefully, Dolores will be . . ."

"Off the hook." Harry finished my sentence.

"Yes, Harry, thanks to you, Dolores will be off the hook."

On my way downstairs I met Marla Mae coming up, carrying a tray. "Miss Dolores is going to have a snack in her room and then take a rest. She said she would be down for dinner."

That fit my plan perfectly. I told her Elton and I would be out for a while but would return before dinner. At least I hoped we would.

Elton pulled into the parking lot of the Sheriff's Department and asked again, "Are you sure you don't want me to come inside with you?"

"Thank you, but I am very sure. I think I will do better on my own. People may speak to one person in confidence, but a second person too easily becomes a witness."

"Be sure you have my number in your cell." He held up his phone. "I have mine right here and can be there in a flash if you need me."

"Elton, you are behaving more and more like a mother hen," I said with a smile.

I was glad to see Deputy Remington at her usual spot behind the counter. That would save my having to explain who I was. Of course I would still have to explain what I wanted.

The deputy looked up and gave me a cheery smile. "Mrs. Fletcher, you are becoming quite a regular. I should give you an application to join the department. Then you could be here full-time."

I gave her what I hoped was my warmest smile. "I am afraid I don't have nearly the proper qualifications to be a deputy, much as I admire all of you who fill that role."

She returned my smile and asked, "How can I help you today?"

"First off, I want to thank you. The koi are back in their pond, and when I last saw Mrs. Nickens she was sitting by the pond enjoying their antics. Such a relief for her to have one normal thing at a time like this."

"Well, I'm glad I could help. Now, if there is nothing else . . ." She held up a pile of folders as an indication that she was anxious to get back to work.

"Actually, I am also looking for Deputy Lascomb. Is he in by any chance?"

Remington glanced at her computer screen. "Sorry, ma'am. Lascomb is on patrol. He won't be back until the end of shift, and that's hours from now."

I sighed. "Oh, that is a disappointment. I was hoping to get all my thank-yous done in one trip." A small white lie, but I hoped it sounded sincere. "I guess there is no point in waiting . . ."

"No, ma'am. If you want to leave a message, I can see that Lascomb gets it."

"That's just not the same, though, is it? Thank-yous should be said in person." I tried to look hopeful. "Perhaps if I knew where he was on patrol, I could find him."

"Mrs. Fletcher, really, you know I can't . . ." Remington looked as if she was hoping I would disappear, and when I didn't she said, "Okay, but you came across him totally by chance. You never even saw me today."

"Cross my heart."

She hit a couple of computer keys and said, "You're in luck. He responded to a car accident on Shop Road, in the state Department of Motor Vehicles office parking lot. That's quite a place to have a car accident, isn't it? Anyway, looks like a fender bender, no injuries, but he should be filling out paperwork on-site for another twenty minutes or so."

I thanked her profusely and ran out the door.

Elton knew exactly where the Department of Motor Vehicles was located. As soon as we'd pulled into the parking lot I saw the turret lights of a Sheriff's Department car at the left side of the building. Now all I needed was a few words from the normally taciturn Deputy Lascomb.

Chapter Thirty

Elton parked two rows away and I walked to the accident scene, careful to stay out of the deputy's line of vision. There were very few onlookers but I managed to stand behind two of them, a middle-aged man and woman, until they decided watching the accident site was even more boring than renewing the woman's driver's license—or at least that's what I got from a snippet of their conversation. When they walked away I moved behind a tree.

Within a few minutes the deputy appeared to be finishing his duties. He handed papers to the drivers of the involved cars and held back what little traffic there was until they each drove safely away.

When Deputy Lascomb headed for his cruiser, I stepped out from behind the tree and called his name.

He was laughing when he turned toward me. "There you are, Miz Fletcher. For a while I thought we were

playing a game of 'now you see me, now you don't.' I
would have been disappointed if you went about your
business without saying hello. Are you here to register a car? Get a South Carolina driver's license?"

"I must confess, as a resident of Maine, I don't even
know where the Maine Department of Motor Vehicles
office is, so my answer to both those questions is no."

His eyes became a shade more guarded, even as he
took one more try. "Are you lost?"

"Good heavens, no. My driver"—I waved vaguely
in the exact opposite direction from where Elton was
waiting for me—"had to pick up some papers for his
supervisor. I was so tired of being cooped up in Manning Hall that I decided to come along."

He crossed his arms and remained silent, a posture
of his that I'd seen before.

"And then I had the good fortune to see you and
thought I would watch you in action."

"How'd I do?" he asked, and I wasn't sure he was
joking.

"Just as you've been in all of our interactions, you
were courteous and professional with those drivers,
particularly the woman who seemed so upset."

His shoulders relaxed. "That is very kind of you to
say, ma'am. Now, I'd best be getting back to patrol."

"Well, I do have one question."

"I've told you before, Miz Fletcher—questions and
answers are above my pay grade."

I nodded. "You have mentioned that but this question has nothing to do with Willis Nickens's murder."

The guarded look vanished from his eyes. "I get it.

You are wondering about the softball game. We won six to three. I hit two doubles."

I was effusive in my congratulations, and slipped my actual question in at the very end.

"You're incorrigible, Miz Fletcher, and extremely persistent. Still, I get your point. It has nothing to do with the actual murder, so I guess there's no harm in answering."

And he told me exactly what I wanted to know. We spoke for a few more minutes, until he got a call on his radio. He thrust his business card at me and raced off to respond.

My brain was so busy bouncing ideas around that I barely noticed when Elton drove us through the gate to Manning Hall. When he parked the car by the veranda, he said, "Are you okay, ma'am? Not like you to be so quiet on the ride home."

"Elton, I am perfectly fine. I do have a lot on my mind. By any chance are you able to stay past the dinner hour tonight in case I need you, or do you have a class?"

"I'll be here, no problem. You can find me in the library as usual. 'Course, this'll give me a chance to see what is on Lucinda's menu. I'm already wondering about dessert."

Elton went directly to the library while I followed the sound of voices to the kitchen. As I passed Willis's office I noticed the door was open but Dolores was nowhere in sight, making me doubly glad that the folders that held the most interest for me were snugly hidden in my room.

I entered the kitchen in time to hear Dolores say, "That's terrific. You saved me a phone call. We'll see you for dessert.

"Ah, Jess, there you are. Marjory happened to call to see how I'm doing, and when she mentioned that Tom and Candy were having dinner at her house I invited them all to come here for dessert."

"How nice. Oh, and Elton will be staying later than usual. I may need him for a chore or two."

Lucinda said, "We have a pecan pie, a chess pie, and benne wafers. I suppose I should whip up a cobbler, since we still have those blueberries. That'll give them plenty of choices."

"Thank you, Lucinda. That will put everyone in a good mood before I put them to work." Dolores picked up a sheaf of papers from the table. "Mr. Harrold sent the wake and funeral arrangements we agreed upon. I can give Marjory, Tom, and Candy copies right away, and they can begin making lists of all the friends we'll want to make sure know that they are welcome to come and pay their respects to Willis. I wouldn't want anyone to miss the notice in the newspapers, which Mr. Harrold assures me was sent out this afternoon."

Abby came running into the kitchen, skidded to a stop, and greeted everyone politely. Then she said, "Granny Dolores, guess what happened today. Because it is such a beautiful day, with all that blue sky and sunshine, Mrs. Creighton said, 'I declare today a no-homework day.' We are supposed to play outside instead."

Dolores dropped her papers back on the table and gave Abby a hug. "And what did your father say?"

"He said to ask if you would take me to the hummingbird feeder. He's in the living room talking to Mr. Norman."

"That's a great idea. We can see if we need to make more nectar." As she opened the back door, Dolores said, "Jess, would you please shut the door to the office? I think I left it open."

I was relieved that she didn't invite me to go along. I had one or two things to do. I went to my room to gather what I needed and made one quick phone call. Then I stopped in the library, asked Elton to leave the library door open, and gave him instructions as to what I needed done.

I threw my shoulders back and walked into the living room, closing the door behind me.

"Jessica, you've had a busy day." Norman eyed the folders in my hand. "I heard you went with Dolores to the funeral home to finalize the arrangements. You are a loyal friend."

Clancy said, "I would have gone along but I didn't realize that was scheduled for today. Can I offer you a drink? Wine? Something stronger?"

"No, thank you. I just want to ask Norman about something that Dolores and I came across in Willis's office. Something we don't quite understand."

Norman said cordially, "I've told Dolores repeatedly, I stand ready to help in any way I can."

"I am so glad you feel that way. We found a folder labled 'Norman's Screwups' and I am afraid the notes, all in Willis's handwriting, indicate numerous instances of financial mismanagement on your part."

"Jessica, you barely knew Willis but Clancy can tell

you, even when Willis Nickens made a mistake, it was never *his* mistake. It was always someone else's." He walked over and put an arm around Clancy's shoulders. "C'mon, Clancy, tell her I'm right."

"Willis was a perfectionist and did have a temper." I noticed Clancy chose his words very carefully.

"And did Willis ever make a mistake? Never." Norman raised his voice. Flecks of spittle began to accumulate on his mustache. "Ha! He made mistakes all the time, and then attached them to me. It was his mismanagement that hurt both of us financially, and that's the truth."

"And yet somehow the proceeds of those 'mistakes' wound up in a tax-sheltered personal trust that you opened some years ago on the island of Nevis." I looked him straight in the eye.

"What are you talking about?" Norman puffed out his chest and tried to look indignant. "To maximize my retirement funds I may have some offshore accounts, but they contain only my personal savings. No company funds whatsoever."

I shook my head. "I'm sorry, Norman, but that's just not true. My friend Harry McGraw, who is a private investigator, was able to discover that over the years, each time one of these business 'mistakes' occurred, you made a similar-sized deposit in your offshore trust account. If Harry was able to discover it, then I suppose Willis found out about your secret account and confronted you about the money it held. So he had to go."

"That's absurd. Positively absurd. Willis and I were friends and business partners for more than thirty years. You are making this all up to try to get your friend Dolores out of the sheriff's line of vision. She's nothing but a schemer who married Willis and then killed him for the fortune that should rightfully go to Clancy and his sweet daughter." Norman looked to Clancy for support.

Clancy, however, stepped away from Norman's side and said, "Keep me out of this. What Jessica is saying does make some sense."

"Sense?" Norman stormed. "You mean nonsense. All she has is a coincidence of withdrawals and deposits."

"That's not quite all," I said. "Do you remember when you and Clancy were giving me tidbits for Willis's obituary and eulogy?"

Norman looked at me with knitted eyebrows. "Yeah, so?"

"You wanted me to be sure to mention that Willis was a dapper dresser. You said you were sure that Willis was 'up in heaven complaining to the angels that he looks ridiculous wearing a tuxedo with his ratty old brown suede slippers.'"

"So?" Norman's sneer was getting aggressive.

"I was wondering when you saw Willis wearing his suit with his suede slippers rather than his patent leather shoes."

Norman shrugged. "That's a serious question? You are asking me about footwear? I guess it was the night he died. After dinner, before bed, I suppose. I can't honestly remember."

"Well, it must have been very close to when he died, because the medical examiner said Willis died around midnight. It was well past eleven thirty when I saw him in the office with Clancy. He still had his dress shoes on. Do you recall that, Clancy?"

Clancy answered, "He certainly did. He had his feet on the desk and kept crossing and recrossing his ankles. Those shoes were practically in my face. Sorry, Norman, but that's the truth."

"And yet, I found the shoes at Willis's bedside, where he had set them down after he took them off for the night. I suppose then you, Norman, came knocking at his bedroom door to invite him out to the garden for a cigar, pretending it was some sort of peace mission. He slid into his slippers and went outside with you.

"I'm not sure if you planned to kill him or if, during your conversation, one thing led to another. But when I found his body he was wearing the slippers. Today Deputy Lascomb assured me that I was the only person from the house who saw Willis's body in the pond. In fact, he said he was surprised that when the sheriff went up to the house he didn't bring Dolores back to the koi pond with him. So it's clear, at least to me, that only the murderer would have seen Willis wearing the slippers."

Norman pushed past me to the door. "I've had quite enough of this parlor game. I'm going out to find more congenial company. Don't wait up."

He yanked the door open. Sheriff Halvorson and Deputy Lascomb were standing in the foyer. Norman froze when the sheriff said, "Care to come with us, sir? We have a few questions we'd like to ask you."

As Deputy Lascomb took Norman's arm he gave me a broad wink, and I flashed him a thumbs-up.

Behind me I heard Clancy mutter, "I need a drink."

I walked over to Elton, who was standing in the library doorway. "Thank you."

"My pleasure, ma'am. Easiest job I ever had. Look out the window, open the front door when the sheriff's car pulls up, and point to the door of the room you were in. Sort of like knowing ahead of time which door to open in that story 'The Lady, or the Tiger?'"

I linked my arm through his. "Shall we round up the household and tell them the good news?"

Chapter Thirty-one

More than a week had gone by since Willis Nickens's funeral. Dolores was behind the wheel of her snazzy red Porsche. I was in the passenger seat and my luggage was tucked in the backseat.

Dolores said, "I honestly don't know how I would have gotten through any of this without you, Jessica. I can't thank you enough."

"I'm glad I was here to help. Don't forget I did have my picture taken with the famous Busted Plug. That's certainly something to show off."

"Oh my, that seems so long ago," Dolores said. "But look at the progress I've made. Your suggestion of calling the business department of the college with an eye toward hiring some help to organize all of Willis's business files was brilliant. Two of the applicants are so knowledgeable I may hire them both. It will take a while but eventually I will have the files at the ready for my new lawyer. Francis McGuire recommends her highly, and we have an appointment tomorrow. Marcus Holmes will soon be history."

"Judging by the immense floral arrangement he sent to the house after the funeral, I suspect he is starting to believe he is on his way out," I said.

"I instructed my new lawyer, Ms. Salazar, to contact Marcus immediately to let him know she would be taking over and to arrange for an orderly transfer of any necessary documents. I suspect you're right. She contacted him and he ordered the flowers. As if roses and orchids would sway me after the way he treated me. Ha."

Dolores switched topics. "More important, I had a heart-to-heart with Clancy last night. He thinks it is essential for Abby to have me in her life. We are really all each other has left. We discussed the idea of using Success City Cars when Clancy plans to, shall we say, socialize. He seemed thankful I wasn't trying to get him to quit drinking altogether."

I was relieved the conversation had gone so well, and I told her so.

Dolores added, "Marla Mae told me that Elton is graduating from Midlands in less than a year. If everything works out, I just might invest in helping him to start his own car service."

"I think that is an excellent idea," I said. "And when I come back he can drive us around to see all the sights."

"Then you will come back? That's a definite?"

"Of course it's a definite. I thought I would have to come back to be a witness at Norman's trial, but since he confessed, well, that means I will be able to return strictly for fun."

"Jess, I never liked Norman, but I still can't believe he would kill Willis for a few dollars."

"Dolores, it wasn't a few dollars. It was several million dollars."

"He'd been siphoning off money for years. It began when Willis was distracted when Emily was sick and then died. Norman had the nerve to say that when I came into Willis's life, I diverted his attention from the business, so Norman upped his game. Imagine him blaming me."

"He wasn't really blaming you. He was excusing his own contemptible behavior."

"I guess you're right. Anyway, that money will be put to good use. Dribs and drabs of the money Norman swindled from Willis are already coming back to me. As the money comes in, I'll use it to pay down the Blomquists' Available Options debt."

That took me by suprise. "To help them hold on to Jessamine House you're whittling down a loan they actually owe to you. Now that is a mark of a true friend."

Dolores sighed. "I hate to admit it, but Willis toyed with the Blomquists as if their livelihood, their very survival, was a game. I'm determined to straighten things out."

"And what about Marjory Ribault?" I brought up what I considered to be a thorny issue. "The papers we found in Willis's files indicate you are the alternate trustee for the revocable trust that includes her cottage and her income. How do you plan to handle that?"

"That's an easy one. While I can't give her Manning Hall, I do intend to tell her that for our purposes the word 'revocable' is meaningless. She can remain in the cottage forever and have complete access to the grounds and gardens, including the kitchen garden."

"Ah, so Lucinda told you about the vegetables."

"She told me, yes." Dolores laughed. "And she was surprised when I said I already knew."

"How did you learn the big secret? I know you didn't come across Marjory pilfering carrots while you were out for a run," I teased.

"Not likely. But my bedroom window frequently offers a bird's-eye view of Marjory roaming through the pines from the cottage to the kitchen garden and back again."

I laughed along with her. "Aren't you the sly one?"

Dolores expertly maneuvered through the downtown Columbia traffic and made one final left turn, into the train station parking lot. Dolores and I hugged goodbye and a courtly porter escorted me to my roomette.

I waved out the window to Dolores and watched her walk back toward the parking lot. I knew from experience that it would take time, but I was sure she'd be able to manage forging a new life for herself.

My cell phone rang. Seth Hazlitt.

"Yes, Seth, I am on the train, and after a brief stop in New York City to see Grady and his family, I'll be on my way home. You can tell Doris Ann that if she sets the library furniture committee meeting for any day next week, I will be there to save the budget."

"Don't forget to make certain the chairs the committee buys are well padded," Seth said, continuing his unending lobbying for extra-comfortable chairs.

"I'm sure you'll remind me a dozen times before the meeting. I've heard quite enough about library furniture. Now, please tell me the latest news from Cabot Cove."

And as the train began to make its way north, Seth said, "Ayuh, I'm not as up on things as the girls at Loretta's Beauty Parlor, but I did hear . . ."

Read on for an excerpt from
the next *Murder, She Wrote* mystery by
Jessica Fletcher and Terrie Farley Moran,

DEBONAIR IN DEATH

Coming in November 2021 from
Berkley Prime Crime

Chapter One

Jessica, I really think you should let me fluff up the top." My favorite hairdresser, Loretta Spiegel, used her fingers and the handle of a roundheaded brush to push my ash blond hair about an inch higher than I normally wear it. Then she turned the easy-to-rotate salon chair I was sitting in from right to left and back again, so I could view it from all angles in the mirror in front of me.

"No, thank you, Loretta. I am happy with my hair the way it is." Then I added, "At least for the time being," to soften the blow.

Loretta and I had some version of this same conversation nearly every time I came in for a trim. She kept trying to make small changes to my hairstyle, which I was sure would eventually lead to major changes. My current short hair, layered with just enough waves to have an agreeable, feminine look, suited me perfectly. I found it easy to manage, which is a boon to keeping my life stress-free because I spend a lot of time traveling—what with book tours, research trips and my favorite jaunts: visits to family and friends. Although I constantly resisted every suggestion Loretta made, that never stopped her from making them.

Loretta pulled one of the long, pointed stainless-steel hair clips off a cardboard placard standing upright on her countertop and snapped it open to section off the side of my hair she was ready to cut. "If you say so, Jessica, but I wish you'd let me make a small change here and there. I think it would give you a more modern look."

My longtime friend and neighbor, Ideal Molloy, had recently vacated the chair I was sitting in. Now she was tucked under a pink-domed hair dryer a few feet behind us, wrapped in a kimono-style smock. Her dark hair was covered with rows of plastic curlers held in place by a bouffant hair net. Ideal raised her voice as if not sure we could hear her over the whirring of the dryer. "More modern. That's exactly right, Loretta. Thank you."

Coreen Wilson, the salon's manicurist, has worked as Loretta's assistant since she was a student in high school. At the moment she was standing in front of Ideal, holding open a plastic nail polish display case filled with inch-high bottles of lacquer in every color of the rainbow, along with a few odd shades I couldn't identify. Coreen ran one hand through her own honey blond curls while she waited patiently for Ideal to look over the entire selection and then choose her usual deep-red polish. She'd said it so many times, even I knew the name—Dark Cherry. So when Ideal veered off, we were all taken by surprise.

"Loretta, that's exactly what I want. A more modern look for my fingernails. Maybe this time I'll even do my toes. Should I go with royal blue or stripes? Or something bolder? Every time I thumb through a magazine, I feel frumpy when I look at the models. To tell you the truth, I am sick of red, red, red all the time."

Loretta caught my eye in the mirror and gave me a quick wink. I answered with a smile. Neither of us said a word to Ideal, who turned back to examining the box filled with polishes. My money was still on Dark Cherry.

"Coreen, you're the one who would know; how are the young girls coloring their nails? Not the teeny boppers, I mean the college girls, or even the mid-twenties crowd."

I watched their reflections in the mirror. Coreen was as hesitant as Ideal was insistent. Coreen was barely in her twenties and probably thought of Ideal as motherly, if not grandmotherly. I'm sure she was having a tough time visualizing Ideal as a trendsetter. I could see she was having difficulty hiding her grin while she tried to come up with a suggestion that would mollify Ideal and, hopefully, not look ridiculous on a woman of a certain age.

I could almost see the lightbulb flash over Coreen's head when she thought of something that might do the trick. "Here's what I think, Miss Ideal. Since your hands look so pretty with the deep-red polish you get

every week, you might want to keep the same color
but jazz it up by adding sparkles on the tip of one nail.
I can tell you for sure that look is extremely popular
with, ah, girls my age."

Coreen held up two bottles from the nail polish
case. Rays of sunlight beamed through the front window and bounced off glittery silver sparkles in one
bottle and shimmering gold sparkles in the other.
"Take a look, Miss Ideal, you can pick."

Ideal pondered for a moment and then agreed.
"Coreen, that sounds like a good start. If I like it we
can go bolder next week. First, I have to decide which
finger I want to sparkle and shine." Ideal held out her
hands, examining them critically. "How about my left
ring finger? I've been divorced for so many years even
the tan line from my wedding ring is long faded. Metallic sparkles will perk it up. Jessica, what do you
think? Silver or gold? Which would you do?"

As someone who likes my nails to be neat and unobtrusive, I wouldn't opt for either one. While I was
trying to think of a diplomatic answer, the front door
opened and drew everyone's attention to our local Re-
altor, Eve Simpson, who began complaining before
the door shut behind her.

"Wouldn't you know it? That would be my luck. I
was on my way here for my weekly hair appointment—
I'm not late, am I, Loretta?—and I stopped at the post
office to mail some brochures about the Barkley house
to a few of my out-of-town prospects. You know the
house I mean, that gorgeous two-story with the wraparound porch near the cliff top. The one with a stunning view of the water. I'm positive it's going to go

super fast and for top dollar, too. Anyway, Debbie promised me the brochures would be on their way to Boston in this afternoon's mail. Then, when I turned to leave, who do you think was walking in as I was walking out?"

We all knew that when she was midstory Eve's questions were nearly always rhetorical, so we silently waited for her to continue, and, in less than two seconds, she did.

"I've been dying to run into him casually, to have the opportunity to strike up a more private conversation, if you get my point. But not today. And certainly not when I look like this."

Eve stopped to take a breath and looked around the room, wide-eyed as though she was expecting wails of sympathy from every corner. But since we actually had no idea what she was talking about, we patiently waited for her to continue. When she crossed her arms and began tapping her toe, Loretta took the hint.

"Who did you meet, Eve? Who is this Adonis who has you so bothered?"

"Who do you think? Who have I been trying to wangle a few private moments with for months now? The handsome, distinguished, and so very cultured Nelson Penzell. You all know him. He owns La Peinture, down on the dockside. Naturally we all must admire a man who uses the French language to name his shop. I did hear that he was a college professor at one time. He probably taught art history or romance languages. He is *très* continental."

She pulled the black cloche hat off her head and dropped it on a chair alongside her purse. "And here

I am, *les cheveux en désordre*. Couldn't I have met him later today, after Loretta has worked her magic and I look totally stunning? Of course not. He held the post office door for me and smiled rather warmly. And he ensured that the door was less than fully open so I was able to brush his arm ever so lightly as I walked through—you know, a signal of interest. But I'm sure it was all for naught. How could he possibly realize how attractive I am? There I was with my hair a complete mess and wearing that silly hat that barely hid my untidy hair."

She may have believed she looked awful but I thought Eve looked absolutely perfect, as she always did. She was wearing a fitted light gray jacket with notch lapels over an emerald mock turtleneck and tapered black slacks, which complemented her trim figure. Her expertly applied makeup added subtle color to her finely chiseled features. And other than a strand of hair that moved slightly out of place when she pulled off her hat, her light brown hair didn't look to me like Loretta needed to do a thing.

"Eve, take it from me: You shouldn't waste your time on that Nelson Prenzell. He may be good-looking, but from what I've heard, he's a real playboy. The love 'em and leave 'em kind." Ideal's conversations generally centered around the up-to-the-minute recipes she'd discovered on the Food Network or her frustration trying to complete her latest craft project, so I was surprised to hear her pass along cutting-edge romantic gossip.

But Eve simply waved her off. "Nelson Penzell is a cultured gentleman, and we are extremely lucky to have him as a part of our community. Why, as soon as he bought a partnership in that slovenly tourist trap Angus Michaud unimaginatively named the This and That Shop, Nelson turned it into a quality establishment. Within weeks he upgraded it to an art emporium I am proud to recommend to my new homeowners as they begin decorating their Cabot Cove houses. Angus still has some of his touristy junk for sale, but I guess Nelson felt that couldn't be helped."

Ideal, who generally retreated as soon as anyone disagreed with her, stuck to her guns. "You may see him as a classy businessman and you may be right, but when it comes to his personal life, well, according to the ladies in my ceramic's class, he is . . ."

Eve wasn't having any of it. "Oh them! Ideal, who would pay attention to anything those old biddies have to say?"

I suspect Coreen was trying to make peace when she interrupted. "I do Mr. Penzell's manicure every week and, well, he's always on time and a good tipper." She trailed off when she saw the look on Eve's face.

Eve's jaw dropped, her eyes popped, and her tone rose to manic. "Coreen, what are you saying? Are you telling me I've been in danger of having Nelson Penzell walk in here to get his nails done when I am sitting under the dryer looking exactly the way Ideal does? Good grief, why didn't anyone warn me before now?"

Ideal pushed the dryer away from her hair and stood up, hands on her hips, ready to do battle. "Eve Simpson, exactly what is wrong with the way I look?"

Loretta leaned in and whispered, "Jessica, I'll be right back."

She quickly moved into the middle of the room and held her hands up as if she was surrendering, when in reality, she was taking charge. "Ladies, we're all friends here. Can we please stop the bickering? Coreen, why don't you put out a plate of those donuts I picked up at Charlene Sassi's bakery this morning? Ideal, Eve, can I offer you a cup of coffee?"

Ideal was instantly diverted. She licked her lips and asked, "Are any of the donuts chocolate crème?"

In contrast, Eve ran her hands over her waistline and said, "Only coffee for me. Black, thank you."

While pouring coffee into oversized pink mugs decorated with pictures of blow dryers, scissors, and curlers, Loretta said, "Eve, I can promise you will never run into Mr. Penzell here."

Eve's tension began to dissolve. "Thank you, Loretta, I knew I could count on you to handle the scheduling with discretion so I don't have any, er, embarrassing encounters when I am not at my best."

Loretta laughed. "Eve, I don't have to do a thing. When he first moved to Cabot Cove, Mr. Penzell dropped by and asked if he could arrange for a weekly manicure at his home. When he saw that I wasn't keen on his request, he offered his shop as the site and threw in a ten percent 'travel bonus.' Coreen and I talked it over and we agreed to accommodate him."

But Eve was taking no chances. "What about when he gets his haircut? Don't tell me he goes to the barbershop. Why, every man in this town comes out of there with a flattop straight out of the nineteen fifties."

"Not a problem. He still travels to his stylist in Portland. From the look of him I would say he makes the trip at least once a month."

Loretta came back to my chair, picked up her scissors, and mumbled so only I could hear, "Crisis averted."

Ideal nibbled on a chocolate crème donut she held carefully between her thumb and index finger to avoid smudging her nail polish. She watched as Eve settled into a chair and opened the latest copy of *Vogue*.

"Eve, you have such great taste." Ideal began with flattery as though their mini altercation hadn't happened less than five minutes ago; then she got to the point. "What color looks better with red? Would you say silver or gold?"

"Every year I decorate my office Christmas tree with silver twinkle lights and red ornaments, if that is any help," Eve answered, then quickly buried her head in the magazine to show she was still miffed.

Happy to have the decision made for her, Ideal stretched her left hand toward Coreen and said, "Silver."

The front door opened again and a young woman dressed in jeans and a bright green Celtics sweatshirt hesitated in the doorway, then walked to the desk and looked around uncertainly. Her bright blue eyes met mine, and she gave a tentative smile, which widened when I smiled back.

Loretta said, "Give me a minute, Jess," then asked, "Can I help you?" as she walked to the counter.

"Yes, ah, hi." She curled an unruly lock of ginger hair around her finger. "As you can see, I'm in need of a trim. I was wondering if you'd have an appointment open later today or perhaps tomorrow."

Loretta glanced at the appointment book that lay open on the desk. "We are a little busy right now, but how about after lunch, say two o'clock? Name?"

"Erica. Erica Davenport."

"I'm Loretta, and I will be doing your cut. If you'd like a manicure while you're here . . ."

Erica shook her head. "I'm embarrassed to admit I bite my nails. I keep promising myself that I'll quit, but so far no luck. My dream is to have perfectly manicured nails, but I haven't gotten the discipline yet."

"You're in the right place. While I am cutting your hair, our manicurist can give you a few tips on how to conquer the nail-biting habit. Free of charge."

Erica laughed. "As long as it doesn't involve that evil-tasting stuff my mother used to slather on my nails when I was junior high, I am grateful for any advice."

"Great." Loretta handed her an appointment card. "We'll see you at two."

Erica nearly turned toward the door and then stopped. "One more thing . . . Could you tell me where I might find a shop called La Peinture. I know it's somewhere in town."

Eve's head snapped up, and her copy of *Vogue* slid onto the floor.

Loretta answered, "Sure, honey. You know where the wharf is? Where all the boats are moored?"

Erica nodded.

"Right along the dockside there are a number of stores, Mara's Luncheonette being the most popular.

A few doors down from Mara's you will find La Peinture. You can't miss it. There is a huge painting of a
storm-tossed trawler in one window and some toy-
sized boat models and touristy knickknacks in the
other," Loretta said.

"Thank you. I'll be back this afternoon." And Erica
practically flew out the door.

"Well!" Eve bent to pick her fallen magazine. "What
could she possibly want at La Peinture? She doesn't
look the type to be able to afford high-end artwork."

"Maybe she's a friend of Angus Michaud or, more
likely, Nelson Penzell. Maybe they are dating." Ideal's
innocent tone was belied by her devilish chuckle.

"Don't be ridiculous. She's a mere child," Eve insisted. "A man of Nelson's taste would clearly prefer
a more mature, experienced woman."

Fortunately for us all, a timer bell dinged and Loretta told Coreen it was time to take the curlers out of
Ideal's hair.

Saved by the bell, I thought.

Chapter Two

The next morning I awoke to one of my favorite perks of living on the Maine coast in late September—a flawless autumn day.

I belted my robe over my pajamas, opened the back door, and stepped outside. For as far as the eye could see, the sky was bright blue, interrupted here and there with soft, billowy clouds puffed like down pillows. I took a deep breath. The air was pleasantly cool and clear. I thought I detected a tinge of firewood, which made me wonder if my neighbor, Maeve O'Bannon, was making hearth bread. The modern kitchen in her nearly two-hundred-year-old house still had an ancient fireplace with iron rods that crisscrossed the firebox and acted as a brace for a flat iron pan suspended from thick chains. The setup allowed her to "bake" bread over burning pine logs. Maeve told me more than once that when she was a child her grandmother taught her how to cook over an open flame and helped her memorize the recipes she still uses all these decades later.

The thought made my stomach growl, reminding me that I was meeting Seth Hazlitt, my close friend and our town's most popular doctor, at Mara's Luncheonette down on the dockside for breakfast. I hurried upstairs, showered, and jumped into a pair of jeans. I tied the sleeves of my blue pullover around my neck on top of a plaid man-tailored shirt. If a chill hit the air, I was ready.

It was a perfect morning for a bicycle ride as I pedaled along the streets of Cabot Cove. Fall foliage was almost upon us. Leaves were beginning to turn, with wide swaths of gold peeking through the green in the old beech trees I passed, while the tall oak trees displayed splashes of crimson and orange. On every block a friend or neighbor called out "good morning," and I waved a greeting as I rode by.

As always, I couldn't suppress a smile when the harbor came into view. Most of the sturdy fishing boats and the narrow lobster boats, which the locals call peapods, had already gone far out into the Atlantic Ocean. By this time of morning the crews were hard at work. Even so, there were dozens of pleasure boats dotting the harbor. I could see tiny pontoons, skiffs, and midsized power boats securely tied to the dock cleats. Several of the extra-large slips reserved for yachts were empty, but I did notice one, at least a sixty footer, which had the name BREW'S BABY stenciled on the bow.

All along the wharf there were people carrying out the daily chores that came with boating and fishing—

cleaning, loading, unloading. Two men I recognized as shipwrights from the boatyard were gesturing animatedly as they inspected the hull of a sailboat. The man they were talking to didn't look at all happy. I supposed he was the owner and the needed repairs were going to cost a pretty penny.

I propped my two-wheeler in the bicycle rack at the north end of the dockside and walked past three or four storefronts. When I reached La Peinture, remembering Eve's frenzy yesterday at Loretta's Beauty Parlor, I automatically glanced through the window, but the shop looked deserted.

I opened the door of Mara's Luncheonette and was immediately caught up in the familiar sights, sounds, and smells. The round stools that lined the long counter were filled with shopkeepers and recreational fishermen who were gossiping and joking like old friends. On the far side of the counter thin coils of smoke rose from the grill, accompanied by the sizzle of bacon and sausage. Both smelled delicious. Mara gave me a wide smile and held up the coffeepot. I nodded yes and she pointed to Seth, who was sitting at a table in the middle of the room with his back to me. I could see that he was tapping his fingers on the Formica tabletop, a sign that he considered me to be late. I came up behind him, slid into the chair to his left, careful not to catch my sleeve on a tear in the vinyl seat back, and said, "Good morning, Seth. Isn't it a magnificent day?"

"Ayuh, we don't get many days like this, but when we do, 'magnificent' is the word. Woman, you're late. I have patients who'll be lining up in my office in less than an hour, and I planned on a leisurely breakfast. Completely unrushed." His blue eyes peered over the top of his horn-rimmed glasses, waiting for my reaction.

I knew better than to let his teasing rattle me. "Well then, I hope you ordered your breakfast."

"Sure did. Ordered mine and yours as well. Two short stacks of Mara's blueberry pancakes, along with real maple syrup. I never understand why anyone orders that sugar-free stuff. What is the point?"

"Now, Seth, as a doctor, you know very well there are some people who can't have syrup; can't have sugar."

He harrumphed. "Well then, those people likely shouldn't be eating blueberry pancakes. My guess is they should be the folks who order two poached eggs and decaffeinated coffee."

Maya came along with the coffeepot to fill my cup and refill Seth's. "Two short stacks of blueberry pancakes coming right up. Is that okay with you, Jessica? Doc Hazlitt ordered for you both a few minutes ago."

"Exactly what I am longing for, a taste of your championship blueberry pancakes," I replied.

Mara's blueberry pancakes won prizes in county fairs all over the state of Maine, and lately she had branched out into Vermont and New Hampshire, taking home ribbons and trophies from both states. During the height of the Maine blueberry season, which coincides closely with tourist season, we locals would have to get up extra early if we didn't want to wait on line for a table at Mara's. Fortunately, both seasons were dwindling to an end and life was getting back to normal here in Cabot Cove. Of course, the "leaf peepers," as we called the tourists who come to see our amazingly colorful fall foliage, would begin arriving soon.

Mara came back and set down two plates. We could see the steam rising from pancakes dotted with succulent blueberries. She pulled a bottle of maple syrup from her apron pocket and deposited it on the table about an inch from Seth's hand. "Here you go, Doc. Delivered yesterday. You can have the honor of opening the bottle."

"Thank you, Mara. Jessica, would you look at these pancakes." Seth dabbed a pat of butter on the top of his stack and then drowned everything in the fresh maple syrup that Mara regularly ordered from a farmer up near Bangor. "Nice and hot, and that's the way I like 'em."

Mara and I exchanged a smile. Seth said the same thing every time he ordered blueberry pancakes, which was practically any morning we had breakfast at Mara's.

Just over my shoulder a mobile phone rang; then I heard someone mutter, "What now?"

I glanced and saw Angus Michaud, co-owner of La Peinture, sitting at the counter. He was dressed in his usual jeans and a sturdy but ancient pair of Timberlands. He was one of the very few of Mara's customers who tucked a napkin in the collar of whatever he was wearing under his navy blue windbreaker.

"Can't a man have breakfast in peace?" he snapped into the phone.

I could only hope he wasn't talking to a customer.

"What is? When? Today? Can't you ever take care of anything?" He listened for a minute, said, "Oh, all right," then shoved the phone in his pocket.

He swiveled his seat and scanned the counter, tables, and booths as he called, "Mara? Mara?"

She came out from the kitchen, her arms loaded

down with plates of pancakes and said, "In a minute, Angus."

True to her word, she was back in a jiffy. "What do you need?"

"What I need is a new business partner, but I will settle for you wrapping up the rest of my breakfast to go. And, do me a favor, add a couple more sausages, they were extra tasty this morning."

Mara took two sausages off the griddle, wrapped them in foil, and put them in a hinged cardboard food container.

Watching her transfer the remains of his breakfast from plate to container, Angus said, "I'll tell you one thing, Mara. You were smart to open this place on your own. Business partners are like a five-hundred-pound weight around your neck. No getting out from under."

He grabbed his breakfast leftovers and charged toward the door, bumping against Seth's chair as he went.

Seth stared after him with raised eyebrows, and then turned back to me. "Well, I'll be . . . Here I thought the partnership of Michaud and Penzell was doing so well, for all they gave the This and That store a silly French name."

I nodded, "I thought so, too, but we can't be sure that it was Angus's partner on the phone."

"Jessica, didn't you hear Angus congratulating Mara for keeping her business solo? Sounds to me like he is sorry he didn't do the same. I thought they had worked out an arrangement: Nelson Penzell handles the expensive items, and Angus remains in charge of the more affordable, touristy fare."

"Good morning, Seth, Jessica." Ryan Hecht stood resting both hands on the vacant chair opposite mine. Tall and clean-shaven with closely cropped dark hair, Ryan wore a conservative three-piece pinstriped suit, and looked every inch what I'd always known him to be—an extremely trustworthy accountant. He nodded toward the door that Angus had slammed shut. "Seems obvious Angus and Nelson aren't managing their separation of duties as well as they'd hoped."

Mara stopped by our table with a coffeepot. I quickly put my hand over my less-than-half-full cup, but Seth gratefully took a refill.

While she poured, Mara said, "All I can say is that Angus and Nelson fight like an old married couple. Pick, pick, pick—and always about money. Nelson tries to keep his private business private, but, well, Angus . . . This episode was one of the many examples of his inability to control his voice or his temper."

"Shame that," Ryan's wife, Julie, a business-savvy fundraiser who worked with many of the nonprofit endeavors I supported, chimed in. "We had planned to stop in La Peinture after breakfast. My sister, Marcy, and I recently moved our father into a nursing home."

"Oh, I am sorry that's become necessary," I said. My sincerest wish was that my nephew Grady and his wife, Donna, would never have to make that decision for me.

Ryan tried to put his arm around Julie, but I noticed she moved slightly away from what I thought was a comforting gesture. I guessed she was still feeling too guilty to accept any solace for what she had been forced to do.

Julie went on to explain. "Dad couldn't manage by

himself anymore. At first we had a part-time care-taker, but then it became evident that he needed help brushing his teeth and cutting his meat . . . and he had a number of falls. It was only a matter of time until he hurt himself seriously. Marcy and I both have de-manding jobs, and she lives all the way down in New Hampshire, right outside of Manchester. We really had no choice."

"The one thing Dad really misses is the sea." Julie's chocolate-colored eyes moistened and she quickly blinked before tears could form. "Ryan had the idea that we should buy him a true-to-life seascape. If we hang it in his bedroom, he can visit the waterfront whenever he likes."

I nodded. "That's a wonderful plan." I wanted to encourage Julie's confidence that she was doing as much as she could to make her father comfortable in his new surroundings.

"It's a plan we are going to have to put on hold for a day or two," Ryan said. "After listening to Angus carrying on, well, this probably isn't the best time for us to pop into the This and That shop for a painting."

"Ryan, really? The store name changed months ago. It's La Peinture, which is French for 'the painting.' It shouldn't be that hard to remember," Julie scolded.

Ryan let out a sheepish chuckle. "It's not hard to remember. It strikes me as an awfully phony mast-head for a store that sells model boats and jigsaw puz-zles of purple lupine flowers dotting the fields and byways of Maine. Almost as phony as that Nelson Penzell fella Angus brought on as partner."

Julie gave him a light tap on the arm. "Hush. We

can't have anyone overhear a prominent accountant making fun of a local business owner. That could hurt your business more than his."

"Julie's got a right pertinent point there, Ryan," Seth said in the tone he uses when he's half serious, half teasing. I was one person who knew that tone well.

Julie offered Seth a grateful smile. "Thank you. Well, we have to run along, but I hope I will see you both tomorrow at the committee meeting for the renovation of the children's wing at Cabot Cove Hospital."

I said, "Absolutely. We wouldn't miss it. I am anxious to see what Dr. Zhou and the hospital administrators have in mind."

After they left, Seth took a long sip of coffee and then said, "I see you got a haircut. So tell me, what is the latest news from gossip central?"

Seth was right on that score. Loretta's was second only to Mara's when it came to spreading the latest facts or fantasies through the Cabot Cove grapevine. Our local newspaper, the *Cabot Cove Gazette,* had a difficult time keeping up.

"Pretty much same old, same old, although if you run into Ideal Malloy be sure and compliment her on her left ring finger."

Seth looked startled. "Don't tell me she's run off and gotten engaged or married or some such foolishness."

I laughed. "Nothing that drastic. She added a touch of sparkle to her manicure and is quite pleased with herself. Oh, and a young girl came in to make an appointment. Maybe up from Boston. As I recall she was wearing a Celtics sweatshirt. Got everyone's curiosity riled."

"I'm not surprised. Doesn't take much to get those gals a-wondering. Pretty redhead, about five feet six and one hundred twenty-five pounds or so. That would do it." Seth gave me a Cheshire cat grin.

"You know who she is!" I leaned closer, ready for him to spill the beans.

"If you must know, her name is Erica . . ."

"I know that. She had to give it to Loretta when she made her appointment. Now tell me how you know her."

"Lavinia Wahl tripped a couple of weeks back while docking her sailboat. Broke her leg in two places. I kept telling her she was too old to handle a thirty-foot sailboat on her own, but you women don't listen." Seth waggled a disciplinary finger in the air at all the patients who ignore his warnings.

It was as though he was trying to irk me. "I *know* all about Lavinia's leg. Tell me about Erica."

"Nothing to tell. She's Lavinia's grandniece on her sister Laverne's side, and she's come north to help out. Lavinia is so awkward using crutches, I had to confine her to a wheelchair before she fell and broke another bone or two."

"Well that will be a big disappointment to the girls at Loretta's. No big mystery after all." I sighed.

But I had spoken too soon.

Ready to find
your next great read?

Let us help.

Visit prh.com/nextread

Penguin
Random
House